The Barbary

The Barbary Run

by

FRANK ECCLES

Michael O'Mara Books Limited

This paperback edition published in Great Britain in 1995 by
Michael O'Mara Books Limited
9 Lion Yard
Tremadoc Road
London SW4 7NQ

First published by Longman Group Limited, London

A CIP catalogue record for this book is available from the British Library.

ISBN 1-85479-742-5

1 3 5 7 9 10 8 6 4 2

Printed and bound by Cox & Wyman, Reading

I

CAPTAIN LAWSON looked down from the side of H.M.S. *Comus* as the small boat with its damaged mast and sagging sails drifted alongside. Of the three people in it, only the woman was conscious and she appeared to be in the last stages of exhaustion. She was wearing a yellow dress and she still had enough of her wits about her to hold the top of it together but she could do nothing to conceal her legs. Part of the skirt had been torn off.

'Is there any sickness among you?' the first lieutenant shouted.

Clearly the woman had not understood the question.

'Are any of you diseased?'

She shook her head slowly and sank back against the gunwales.

'Have them brought aboard, Mr Jones,' Captain Lawson ordered. 'It was her dress we saw at the masthead, not the Yellow Jack. The boat's full o' holes and both men are bandaged, I see. Suggests an action rather than the plague, don't you think?'

The first lieutenant signalled to the men at the hoists and rubbed doubtfully at his fat cheeks as the litter was lowered over the side. The boat had hoisted a yellow flag and that meant plague, according to the signal book. If he'd had his way, Doctor Baxter would have been sent out to examine them. One could not take chances off the Barbary Coast.

They sent the woman on deck first. Captain Lawson looked her keenly over for any sign of the dreaded purple patches that had been known to carry off three-quarters of a ship's company in the Mediterranean Fleet. There were none as far as could be seen. Suddenly he became aware that she was watching him : listless grey eyes, strangely out of place against the sunburned face.

Chandler, the frigate's youngest lieutenant, removed his jacket and draped it across her exposed legs. She thanked him with a flicker of a smile and closed her eyes.

'Take her to the sick bay, Mr Chandler.'

'We've eight men in there, sir.'

'So we have,' the captain replied.

He paused indecisively. The small area on the starboard bow, screened off from the rest of the maindeck, would hardly be a suitable place to send a young woman even if there were no sick occupying it. Where else was there? If he were to turn Jones out of his cabin to make room for her, a whole chain of movements would be started as each lieutenant ousted his junior. Since the frigate had its full complement of officers and men there was only one place where she could be accommodated without upsetting a dozen people.

'Put her in my day cabin for now,' he grumbled. 'And tell the surgeon that I'll have him in irons if he's not on his feet and sober by the end of this watch.'

One of the men had been swung on deck. He wore a blue frocked coat favoured by merchant captains. Around his head was a blood-soaked strip of yellow material that must have come from the woman's dress, and his trouser leg was seeping blood on to the litter. He was old and the greyness of his face suggested that death was not far away.

'This is Captain Mallory, sir,' Jones said. 'He's the master of the *Princess Mary*. One of the fastest ships in the Mediterranean : first class passengers, mail and the more valuable cargoes. Does a lot of carrying for the government, too.'

The man's eyes fluttered open at the mention of his name. They wandered vaguely about until they settled on Captain Lawson when they filled with urgency. He tried to raise his head and his lips moved soundlessly.

'He's trying to say something, sir !'

2

Lawson bent to listen but the man had already lost consciousness. He turned to the second officer, a dapper Scotsman with a waxed military moustache.

'Get him out of the sun and give him plenty of watered wine, if he can take it, Mr Jamieson. Report to me when he comes to his senses.'

'The last one's dead, sir,' Jones said gloomily. 'Do you want the body on board?'

'I don't want it but you know damn well I've got to have it,' Lawson replied testily.

He turned away and began to pace the weather side of the frigate. The body was a nuisance but they would have to give it a Christian burial or someone would be sure to cause trouble. In any case the men would expect it and Lawson was human enough to want to create a good impression during this first week of his command.

The ship had been hove-to with her fore top gallants braced on the opposite tack to the balancing canvas on the mizzen-mast. As the open boat, with the body inside, was plucked from the sea, the captain raised his speaking trumpet.

'Ready to get under way,' he shouted.

The two lines of men on each side of the frigate seized upon the ropes leading to the top gallant yards and took the strain. The belaying pins were pulled clear and the freed lashings fell to the deck.

'All ready, sir,' the boatswain reported.

'Let her go then.'

'Give way starboard. Port side heave. Put your backs into it now, lads.'

The men on the port side came aft at a run, taking with them the long cable that reached up through the maze of rigging to the end of the great wooden spar that formed the fore top gallant yard. The heavy timber pivoted around the mast and the canvas cracked into a smooth curve as the breeze filled it. Slowly the bows of the frigate fell away, dipped and settled on a starboard tack. Mainsails dropped into place and were

3

sheeted home. The deck tilted and the confused swirling of the water under the frigate's stern gave way to a straight track of bubbles.

'Course two points south o' east, sir,' the quartermaster called when the compass card had steadied.

'Thank you, Mr Postill. Keep her there.'

At that moment the ship's bell rang : four double beats marking the end of the watch. As the sound died away, a small stout man with red face and bleary eyes climbed to the quarter-deck from the main deck below and blinked owlishly in the bright sunshine. Suddenly he saw the captain glowering in his direction. He started visibly, pulled at his coat and walked with drunken dignity towards him.

'I understand you wish to speak to me, sir.'

'I shall have a lot to say to you later,' Lawson said threaten-ingly. 'Meanwhile get over to my cabin and see to the young woman. Then I shall expect you in the sick bay. And mark my words, Doctor Baxter, if you touch the bottle again today, I'll make you wish you had never come to sea.'

He glared after the doctor's retreating figure then walked over to examine the boat they had brought aboard. It was most certainly not from the *Princess Mary*. Its timbers gleamed with fish scales and the name painted on the stern was in Arabic. He shrugged philosophically. Either Captain Mallory or the young woman would explain it shortly.

Jamieson, the second lieutenant, reported to the captain an hour later. His eyes gleamed excitedly.

'You'll be interested in what Captain Mallory has tae say, sir.'

'Perhaps you'll be good enough to tell me, Mr Jamieson,' Lawson replied dryly.

'Lost his ship tae pirates a week ago,' Jamieson said cheer-fully. 'Claims they were led by this fellow we're looking for— Yussaiff Ahmed !'

Lawson strode towards the sick bay. Of all the pirates operat-ing in the Mediterranean, Yussaiff Ahmed was the most

4

wanted. His successes against British ships alone had cost Lloyds a quarter of a million pounds and his latest exploit was likely to double that figure when the final assessments were made.

'Oh!—There's another thing,' Jamieson said, as he tagged along behind. 'The lady in your cabin is the wife of Robert Dullant.'

'Our Robert Dullant?' Lawson asked incredulously.

'Yes, sir.'

'Damn it all, man! Why didn't someone recognise her? Surely you'd make a point of remembering a rear admiral's wife?'

'I'm sure we would, sir, had we seen her before. She didna come out with him. Took the overland route, of all things, and spent the last month in the Neapolitan Court with friends. She was on her way to join her husband at Gibraltar when the *Princess Mary* was taken.'

What woman in her right senses would travel across Europe with Napoleon's ex-soldiers turned bandit on every high road in France and Italy? Lawson thought as he made his way to the sick bay. Come to that, what husband worthy of the name, would let her?

The sick bay was nothing more than a screened off area, well forward on the starboard side of the maindeck. Four open gun ports let air and light into it, and the beds, canvas on wooden frames, were well spaced. It was the pleasantest part of the frigate that could be occupied by the lower ranks but it was a very temporary affair. When the ship cleared for action the screens would be stacked away with the beds to make room for the guns, and the sick would be lashed to hammocks and swung down to the stink of oil lamps and bilge on the orlop deck.

Captain Mallory occupied a bed remote from the others. His face had lost some of its greyness but he still looked a very sick man. Lawson removed his hat, introduced himself and sat down on a stool at the head of the bed. A pair of surprisingly blue eyes looked up at him appraisingly.

'What ship am I on?' he demanded.

'H.M.S. *Comus*, forty-four gun frigate,' Lawson replied with a smile.

The old man nodded and closed his eyes.

'I am told that you know the whereabouts of Yussaiff Ahmed,' Lawson prompted after an interval. 'If you can let me have his last known position, the details of your capture can wait until you have recovered your strength.'

The blue eyes opened suddenly and glared fiercely.

'It will not wait, Captain,' he replied with vigour. 'If the Lord saw fit to bring you to these waters today, He did it for a purpose. We'll not thwart Him by waiting.'

A Whitby Bible thumper, Lawson thought, recognising the accent of his native town with pleasure. Aloud he said, 'How can you be certain it was Yussaiff Ahmed?'

'I met him. Lived in his house for a week. And I'll tell you something else that'll surprise you, Captain. He's English!'

'English!'

'True as I'm a-lying here. Educated upper class, I shouldn't wonder, an' he's been a Navy man; that's for sure. Everything about him is Navy; his mannerisms; some of the words he uses; even the way he gives orders; as if he were talking to dogs. —No offence meant, Captain. He sticks out among that pack of heathens like a John o' Company ship in the midst of a fleet of Newcastle coal boats.'

He lay back, panting with exhaustion but his eyes still gleamed fire. Lawson pulled the covers about his shoulders.

'He let us escape,' Mallory said thoughtfully. 'Directed us to a boat. It was small but seaworthy and he'd provisioned it; enough for a week or more. We'd have got clear away if the watch at the mouth of the bay hadn't spotted us.'

Lawson nodded, remembering the bullet holes and the smashed water cask in the boat they had hoisted from the sea.

'Said he'd done it for me,' the old man mused, 'because my manner of speaking reminded him of an old shipmate. It were a lie I fancy. There was something betwixt him and the young

6

woman. If they hadn't known each other before, then I know nowt about folk.

'The young woman? Do you mean the one that's with us now—the admiral's wife?

'Aye.'

He began to cough; a slow wheezing cough that went on and on. Lawson raised his shoulders and gradually he got over it but he had exhausted himself.

'My coat.——Look in the pocket.'

His clothes had been placed in a hanging locker. Lawson found the jacket and removed several papers. A quick look through satisfied him that here would be all the information he needed. They were pages torn from the *Princess Mary*'s log, covered with neatly drawn charts and notes.

On the starboard side of H.M.S. *Comus*, between two guns on the main deck, a wide plank had been raised to rest one end on the bulwarks. After reading Mallory's report on the *Princess Mary*'s capture, Captain Lawson had been so busy plotting a new course and setting extra sail that he had completely forgotten the dead man until after dark, so, in accordance with standard Naval practice, the burial had had to wait until sunrise. Now a few seamen stood with bowed heads around a body stitched into old canvas and weighted with scrap. The captain looked down upon them from the height of the quarterdeck and opened the ship's Bible. His voice carried easily over the distance.

'—We therefore commit this body to the deep—'

He paused and scowled over the book.

'Lift the bloody thing,' the boatswain hissed audibly.

The two seamen at the head heaved the board to the height of their shoulders. The flag covering it rippled as the grey shape slid into the sea. Lawson continued.

'—to be turned into corruption, looking for the resurrection of the body when the sea shall give up her dead—'

He droned on to the end of the service, handed the book to Evans, thrust on his hat and turned his mind to the problems of the day.

'That was a very moving service, Captain.'

Lawson swung around. Admiral Dullant's wife was less than four yards away. Had she heard the bo'sun? May the devil take him for the irreverent heathen that he is.

'Good morning, ma'am.'

As he bowed he noted her dress. That was Chandler's boat cloak for sure but what was the white skirt beneath it? He stared at it too long.

'It is a table covering, Captain,' she said with an air of defiance. 'Your duties occupied you so fully that I was obliged to seek help from your servant. I should have missed the funeral else.'

Lawson acknowledged the rebuke with a slight inclination of the head. He had not found time to visit her and the few words he had heard from Captain Mallory had left him with some doubts about Cecilia Dullant.

'My regrets, ma'am. Had I known that you were well enough to leave your bed, I should have arranged for Evans to turn out a few bolts of indifferent silk that I have in my chest.'

As he spoke he cursed himself mentally. He was apeing the manners of the flagship poppinjays. Indifferent silk! They were the best that could be had and if his sister had no use for them, they would fetch a tidy penny in Yorkshire.

'Deck, sir,' came the thin call from the masthead. 'There's a hulk, dead ahead, lying close to shore.'

Lawson nodded to Barty, the senior midshipman, who was already poised at the foot of the mizzen mast shrouds. The youth sprang onto the bulwarks and climbed rapidly aloft. Cecilia Dullant watched him in silence until he swung himself over the edge of the platform high above.

'Is something interesting happening, Captain?'

Lawson had been noting the delicate curve of her cheek and her finely shaped nose and mouth and his observation left him

8

in no doubt that she would be beautiful when her skin had lost its angry shade of red. He recalled himself with a jerk.

'I believe the hulk they have sighted might well be the one that you came across last week : the one guarding the entrance to Yussaiff Ahmed's hide-out.'

2

IT took them all day to approach the hulk, despite the studding sails and scraps of impatient canvas set by the first lieutenant to catch the failing south-westerly airs. Now it was on the starboard beam, glowing red in the setting sun and a mile to windward. Lieutenant Jones turned a gloomy face to the midshipman of the watch.

'My compliments to the captain. Ask him if we may tack to bring us within gunshot.'

'It's as I said,' he complained to Lieutenant Jamieson. 'If we had steered two points closer to the wind at noon, we should have passed within half a cable's length. Now we'll have to beat to windward and they'll no doubt shoot us to bits before we can use our broadside.'

'Maybe he does na' want tae attack,' Jamieson replied. 'There's more ways o' killing a pig than cutting its throat. Our captain is no fool, I can tell you. That's why my Lords of Admiralty sent him out here.'

'Friends in high places,' Jones said scornfully.

'Not him. He's naught but his own reputation to help him. Come up the hard way and I doubt if his occasional Yorkshire-isms would go down well with the fine folks at court. He's in the Mediterranean to get results and if he does na stop the activities of this fellow, Yussaiff Ahmed, a few more heads will fall besides his. It's no every day that a pirate captures an Indiaman. John o' Company is out for blood, and blood they'll have, depend upon it.—Whisst the man himself.'

Lawson walked on the quarterdeck well aware that every man's eyes were upon him. It gave him no sense of elation. Six years of command had subdued the burning feeling of inferiority that had driven and plagued him in his youth. Now he was as good as any of them : captain of a frigate at thirty-nine, and neither his lowly birth nor his accent could prevent him from becoming an admiral, if he kept out of trouble and lived long enough. His large solid frame contrasted favourably with that of the plump first lieutenant who handed him the telescope.

The captain twined his arm through the shrouds and began to examine the mastless hulk as it rocked at anchor, close to a channel through the cliff. It was a three decker, probably French, judging by its lines, and forty gun ports were presented to the open sea. One of these swung idly on its hinges. His glass crept along its side revealing shot holes and splintered bulwarks. It looked as though it had been abandoned; the perfect bait for an unwary coasting vessel. The slight list to seaward might possibly have warned an experienced captain of her present role. They would need to use more ballast on the landward side to balance the battery of guns. He lowered the telescope and rubbed his eyes.

'Shall we stand in closer, sir?' Jones asked.

Lawson ignored him. There had been a movement on the forward part of the hulk. He focused his glass again and examined it in detail. Jones raised his eyes in despair and shrugged his shoulders for the benefit of the watching quarterdeck.

Something was different, Lawson thought, yet the wreck seemed the same as before. Suddenly he had it. It had been the lack of movement that had attracted his attention. The gun port which had been reflecting the light from the water as it swung, was now still. Some hand inside the hulk had secured it.

'They're waiting for us, Mr Jones, and I'd say at a guess that there are as many pairs of eyes watching us, as an Arab mongrel has fleas. We can't take the chance of approaching her in daylight.'

'Your orders, sir.'

'Continue on your present course.'

'But would it not be better to——?'

'You have your orders!'

It was the expression on the captain's face rather than the curtness of his voice that halted Jones in mid-sentence. Hard eyes blazed into his face beneath fierce brows and the yellow scar running down the left cheek seemed to become one with the tightly compressed mouth. Then the tension went out of him. The great shoulders relaxed; the fists unclenched and something resembling the flicker of a smile softened the forbidding grimness.

'You'll be well advised, Mr Jones, to keep your ideas to yourself until I ask for them,' he said quietly. 'I don't know what sort of an arrangement you had wi' your previous captain. You'll obey orders without question, while I am in command.'

Jones ran a finger nervously under his collar and glanced anxiously over his shoulder. He had been badly frightened and worse. He had been deflated before the subordinates he tried so hard to impress.

Lawson began to pace the starboard side of the quarter-deck, his eyes fixed on the shore. Groups of seamen watched him covertly and in silence while Jones fussed about the binnacle and wrote busily on the order slate. At length Lawson halted and called the first lieutenant over to him.

'Hold your course until one hour after sunset. Note every landmark that is likely to be visible after dark. I want to be in a position to attack just before dawn. If you have any suggestions to offer, I shall be pleased to hear them tonight. You shall have the credit for——'

He broke off suddenly. Mrs Dullant was leaving the cabin under the poop deck.

'Go back inside, ma'am,' he ordered sharply.

She halted in the doorway, her eyes gleaming angrily. He gave her no time to think of a suitable reply. Before she realised what was happening, he had bundled her back through the door and closed it behind them. She was trembling with fury.

'I asked you to keep off the open deck until we have left this hulk behind.'

'And supposing I don't choose to?'

His lips tightened.

'Then I shall instruct the marine sentry, at the door of your cabin, to keep you here.'

'This is outrageous.'

'It's common sense, ma'am. If they see you on board they'll know we're on to them. They'd mount a double watch tonight and turn out boats to guard against surprises. It would make all the difference between success and failure. Your evening stroll on deck could lose us a dozen lives or more.'

The tenseness went out of her face and her shoulders drooped.

'I'm sorry, Captain. It was thoughtless of me.'

Lawson's face cracked into a smile.

'Thank you, ma'am. Now if you will excuse my presence for a few minutes, I have some things to do here.'

He unlocked a large, metal-bound box and removed an official package. He already knew the contents but he spread the papers on the chart table and began to study them. They were dated 13 March 1816 and he had underlined the important passage.

'—You are instructed to seek out the aforementioned pirate, Yussaiff Ahmed, destroy or capture the ship he commands and bring him, and such of his men as survive the action, to justice.'

Carefully he read through the rest of the papers referring to the exploits of Yussaiff Ahmed. Nowhere could he find any suspicion that the man was not as his name suggested; a typical Barbary Coast corsair yet, in the light of the information given by Captain Mallory, a pattern did emerge which indicated that this particular pirate was familiar with naval procedure and he might even have knowledge of fleet movements.

'Would you agree with Captain Mallory's opinion that Yussaiff Ahmed had probably served in the British Navy, ma'am?' he asked suddenly.

She started in such a manner that Lawson's mind immediately returned to Mallory's second opinion, the one that had been worrying him all day. Had she really known Yussaiff

13

Ahmed before he had turned pirate? The idea seemed absurd.

'I should say that many odd fish have served at one time or another.'

'But you will confirm that he is an English gentleman?'

'He—behaved like one.'

'But I am told that you and Captain Mallory lived in his house for a week. You would have wondered about him; tried to place his accent.'

'Not all accents are as easy to place as yours, Captain. If you have finished with your papers, perhaps you will be kind enough— I feel very tired and should like to go to bed.'

Lawson glowered and gathered up the dispatches.

'I wish you good night, ma'am,' he said stiffly.

In the cramped space of his sleeping cabin Lawson pulled at his neckcloth savagely and tossed it on the cot. Evans, the negro servant he had inherited with the ship, tactfully switched off his permanent grin and helped him out of the heavy tunic coat.

'Bring my razor.'

Evans' jaw dropped in astonishment.

'You want to be shaved, sir?'

'Why else would I want it?' Lawson grumbled.

'Yes, sir. Right away, sir.'

He backed nervously out of the cabin. Lawson took the sword and scabbard from the cabin wall, drew the blade with a flourish, fell into the on guard position and began to practise a few of the foot movements and thrusts taught him by a fashionable fencing master the last time he had been in London. The exercise ended when he cracked his head on one of the low beams.

'Damn the woman,' he muttered to himself as he flopped into the chair. 'She makes me feel dirty.'

Evans whisked a bib around Lawson's neck and began to lather his chin vigorously. The negro looked worried.

'You—you been shaved once today, sir?'

'Now I am being shaved again,' Lawson said equably.

The servant's teeth gleamed into a relieved smile.

14

'Yes, sir. You is being shaved again.' He chuckled deep and throatily. The joke was not on him this time. Here was a gentleman who shaved twice in one day; the second time when he was due to go out into the night on a quarterdeck. This would make good gossip in the forecastle. Maybe he was thinking of spending part of the watch with the lady.

'Will there be anything else, sir?' he asked when he had finished. 'Shall I lay out your best coat?'

'You can lay out my pistols. Then you can get to bed. I shall not need you for a few hours.'

When Evans had gone, the captain took up the two pistols and handled them lovingly. They were perfectly balanced and had rifled barrels; an expensive present from the Graf von Oldenburg in return for a service he had given during the spring of 1809.

He took the charge from the leather case, broke open the end and trickled the black powder into the barrel. Then he screwed up the empty packet and rammed it after the powder. The oversized bullet had to be driven home with the tiny mallet provided, so that its soft lead surface would be squeezed into the grooves of the rifling. This would impart a spin to give twice the range and accuracy of the smooth-bore pistol. When both weapons were loaded he pressed the percussion caps into the touch holes and carefully lowered the hammers to rest on top of them. It was a ritual; not without meaning. His life might depend upon their reliability before morning.

On deck the watch had changed. The third officer, Mr Chandler, hurried forward as Lawson appeared. His face was just visible in the darkness.

'Course east north east as handed over, sir,' he reported. 'Wind south west and we're under topsails.'

'Thank you, Mr Chandler. Call the watch and put the ship about. We are going back along the course we followed this evening.'

Lawson turned to the dark North African coastline, apparently taking no notice of the activity about him. Yet he could

15

sense the close proximity of the men lining the starboard braces and felt at one with them in their anticipation of the order to heave. If the officer of the watch misjudged the position of the ship's bows in relation to the wind, the ship might be taken aback with all the tiresome business of getting her under way again. Ten minutes' light work would become half an hour of back breaking toil with tempers flaring and the boatswain using his cane indiscriminately. An officer would soon find himself with disciplinary problems if he made many such mistakes.

'Helm a starboard!'

The ship spun easily upon her heel and came up into the wind. The canvas slatted noisily and the heavy yards cracked back against the masts.

'Starboard braces! Give way port!' Chandler shouted.

The lines of men took the ropes backwards at a run and the yards, each one shaped from a sizeable pine tree, pivoted on their supporting chains around the three massive masts. The frigate heeled to the wind and surged forward on its new tack. Lawson made his way across to the port side and resumed his watch on the coastline.

For two hours he remained in the same position, completely indifferent to the stinging spray. At last he shouted for the midshipman of the watch.

A youth came at the run from the shelter of the bulwarks and jerked to a halt in front of him. He was clearly no more than fifteen years old but the squareness of his shoulders and slimness of hips promised a fine athletic body when he reached manhood. He had travelled from England with the captain and it was evident to the ship's company that there was a close bond between them.

Lawson's weather-hardened face relaxed into a smile.

'Ah, Mr Saunders,' he said pleasantly, 'how do the prospects of your first action appeal to you?'

'I am looking forward to it, sir.'

Lawson nodded approvingly and mopped at the salt water on his face.

'Your father would give a lot to be here, I do believe. When it is all over you will have to write a full report for him. Go below now to Mr Jones. Give him my compliments and ask him if he will be good enough to join me on deck.'

Lawson stared pensively after the midshipman. Twenty years ago there had been another Midshipman Saunders with a flair for mathematics and for getting into scrapes. He had carried Lawson with him in both activities. Then it had been Lieutenant Saunders, with a dozen successful actions to his credit, gaily leading Lawson under the guns at Toulon to scoop out three fat coasters. He had married Lawson's sister on the prize-money. Now it was poor blind Saunders, Captain R.N., living on half pay at Whitby.

'Why the devil did he send the boy to sea?' Lawson muttered.

'Did you speak, sir?'

Lawson collected himself with a jerk. It would not do for his subordinate to get the idea that he had a mumbling fool for a captain.

'What speed are we making, Mr Chandler?'

'About seven knots, sir; taken half an hour ago. The wind doesn't seem to have altered much.'

'Have them take it again.'

As orders were being given for the log to be dropped astern, the first lieutenant appeared on deck.

'Now then, Mr Jones, according to my calculations we should be coming up to the bay in about one hour's time. Do you think you can find it?'

'Easily enough, sir. There's a stretch of white cliff to the eastward at about three miles. It'll make an excellent landmark.—Might I make a suggestion, sir?'

'What is it?'

'I wondered if we might try the Nelson plan for the Battle of the Nile, sir. Run between the hulk and the shore. They would have no guns there. We could pound her until she strikes and deal with whatever is lurking in the bay with our shoreward broadside.'

'I see that you are familiar with naval history, Mr Jones.'

'My favourite reading, sir,' he replied virtuously. 'One learns much from the past and an imaginative man can often apply his knowledge to the present and avoid the mistakes of the old captains.'

Lawson grunted sceptically.

'If we sail to landward of this hulk there might be another mistake for the Naval Chroniclers to record. The fleet had up-to-date charts of the Nile Delta. We know nowt o' this bit of coast. There could be rocks waiting to tear the bottom out of us. What other ideas have you?'

Jones pulled at his fat cheeks thoughtfully.

'We might try a boarding party, sir. These Arabs won't keep much of a watch. We could run alongside, grapple her and be aboard before they could get out of their hammocks; assuming they enjoy such luxury,' he added with a laugh.

Lawson was not amused.

'We seem to have forgotten that this hulk is guarding the entrance to Yussaiff Ahmed's base. All they have to do is hold us off for fifteen minutes or so and every man ashore that can swing a scimitar will be on our decks. No it won't do. I'm going to attack with the main armament. If they don't strike their colours we shall sink them and to hell with the prize money.

There was an awkward silence. Lawson walked across to the weather rail. Jones followed.

'The wind's off the land, Mr Jones.'

'Yes, sir?'

'So it'll turn the hulk around for us.—I've no doubt you're right when you say that all her guns will be facing seaward. They'd have had the devil of a job ballasting her to keep her decks as level as they are but there's plenty of rock close at hand and enough labour ashore to carry it on board and secure it.— It needs no more than an enterprising boat party. They'll creep up on her and cut her windward cable. Then as she swings we must be ready to take advantage; a couple of broadsides from the starboard battery and we'll knock the arse out of her.'

'I should be honoured to take command of the boat party, sir.'

A movement on their left indicated that little of their conversation had been missed by the officer of the watch. Chandler too would like to be in command. In days of peace and slow promotion every aspiring officer sought to have his name brought favourably before the powers at the Admiralty. The man in charge of the cutting adrift party would surely be mentioned in the captain's report even if the others were forgotten. Jones' suggestion that they should board, had not impressed the captain.

'This is a job for a junior officer.' He turned to the dark shape by the binnacle. 'Mr Chandler, you will detail a boat party. See that their faces are blackened and provide yourself with something that will cut through an anchor cable. Arm each man with a cutlass and carry half a dozen loaded muskets in the boat.'

'Aye aye, sir,' Chandler replied cheerfully. 'Ten men and a midshipman?'

'A midshipman?'

'If it's convenient, sir.'

'Which midshipman?'

'Mr Saunders here would do very nicely, sir.'

'Too young. Get someone with more experience.'

'Too y——? Aye aye, sir.'

Anyone old enough to rate a midshipman's berth should be able to serve as second in command of the ship's launch but Chandler had more sense than to voice his opinion. His surprised silence was more effective.

'Oh very well! Take him with you.'

It would not do for the boy to suspect that his uncle was sheltering him. He would naturally resent it and in any case he had to learn his job and take his chance with the rest.

'Mr Jones will give you your orders. If anything unforeseen happens, get back to the ship as quickly as you can.'

19

3

'THOSE are the cliffs I spoke of, sir. We've three miles to go.'

'Very good, Mr Jones. We'll leave the coast for a spell now. I don't want to pass them too closely. Change course four points to starboard.'

The stars swung in an anti-clockwise arc as the frigate turned her sharp bows away from the land. Sails were trimmed to accommodate the new angle of a breeze that had increased a little since sunset, and the foam under her forefoot hissed anew.

'Clear for action. No drums; no more noise than is absolutely necessary.'

'Aye aye, sir. I'll see that they keep it quiet.'

Lawson glanced quickly at his second in command. There had been something odd about the way he had replied. His voice had had an exultant ring. Was he enjoying some secret joke? He shrugged the thought aside. The prospects of action affect men in many ways.

There was no moon and the sea had given way to a gentle swell. Both conditions were ideal for the task in hand. Chandler's party were steadying the boat dangling over the side and staring silently at the reflected light of the stars on the glassy surface of the water. Time for thought and the opportunity for prayer. Some of them might not see another dawn.

Chandler's tall silhouette was easily recognised amid the dark shapes of his group. Lawson paused in the shadows to listen to the orders he was giving. He had a lot to learn about his officers. What he heard gave him no cause for anxiety.

'You'd better get into the boat, Mr Chandler,' he said, revealing himself. 'We'll lower you as soon as we heave-to. Head due south until you reach the coast. You'll have the best part of two miles to row. Then you'll follow the shore to the east. When you come across the hulk, how will you find the cable?'

'It'll be to windward, sir; probably reaching the sea at half the hulk's length,' he answered without hesitation.

Lawson nodded approvingly.

'They might have two windward anchors so you'll have to look around. On no account will you cut the leeward cable. We want her to swing on it.'

He suddenly saw Jim Saunders clutching a sheathed cutlass which seemed ridiculously large in his hands.

'You'll remember that half a ship's length is well within the reach of musket shot. Do the job quickly and get out of the way. You can run to us as soon as the action starts. It should be dawn by then, so you'll have enough light to find us. I'll trail a cable and marker. If you can't get aboard us, hook on to the cable. We'll tow you until it's convenient to pick you up. Is that clear?'

'Aye aye, sir.'

'Good luck!'

He turned abruptly away and walked back to the quarter-deck, his mind brooding over Jim. It had not seemed so long ago since he had taught him to catch crabs among the rocks at Whitby. He had worried about the boy cutting his feet then. Now he was sending him out; perhaps to have his head blown off.

'Damn the Navy,' he muttered.

'I share your sentiments entirely, Captain Lawson,' an icy voice said within a foot of his ear. 'Damn any service that sends a dozen men into a lady's sleeping chamber to turn her out of her bed at three o'clock in the morning.'

'I beg your pardon, ma'am?'

'Your gun crews, Captain.'

Suddenly Lawson realised what had happened. The ship was clearing for action. They would have removed the stern window from the day cabin and dragged the two twenty-five pounders into position. Her bed had been alongside the window.

'My sincerest apologies, ma'am. I had forgotten completely that you were on board.'

'Indeed!'

That one word was even icier than her opening sentence but Lawson missed it. His mind was already dwelling on the perfidious Jones who obviously had remembered the lady. That was what he had been gloating about.

'Now that you have been reminded that I am on board, what do you suggest I should do?'

'I'll have you escorted to the orlop deck, ma'am. It will not be pleasant but you'll be safer there.'

'Isn't the orlop deck down on the waterline?'

'Yes, ma'am. You would be protected from any musket-balls and reasonably safe from flying splinters, should they manage to bring their guns into action.'

'But I should be the first to drown.'

'There's no likelihood of that ma'am. Should any balls enter us below the waterline, we have the carpenter and his mates with nothing else to do but plug the holes,' Lawson replied patiently.

'Very interesting.—I shall remain on this deck.'

'You will go below.'

'Do you intend to force me?'

Her chin tilted defiantly. Lawson sighed.

'No ma'am. You may please yourself but I should have thought that the fear of disfigurement would have overcome your concern about getting wet. It would be a tragedy if your beauty were permanently destroyed.'

'What do you mean?'

Lawson traced the line of his scar with his finger.

'This was a splinter, ma'am. Only nine inches long so I was told, but it split my face open. One thirty-two pounder shot striking the bulwark here'—he struck the heavy timber with his hand—'could send a hundred such splinters flying across the quarterdeck. I'm sorry to appear so dramatic but I wish to make sure that you fully understand why I want you on the orlop deck.'

Her eyes lowered. Lawson watched her face intently. All the arrogance had left it. She looked up suddenly and smiled.

'Forgive me for being foolish, Captain. I shall do as you suggest.'

'All cleared for action, sir,' Jones reported some three minutes after Mrs Dullant had gone below.

Lawson scowled at him. There would be time later to wipe that smug self satisfaction off his face. Now there was work to do.

'We'll heave-to while the boat gets away.'

The ship swung around into the wind, and the boat, which might otherwise have been swamped by the wash of her passage, dropped cleanly away into the night. The operation had begun.

Lawson paced the deck as the frigate gathered way again. His problem was to time his attack so that he would reach the hulk just after the mooring had been cut. If they delayed, the pirate would maybe warp himself back into position. He turned to the quartermaster at the wheel.

'Mr Postill!'

'Sir?'

'The wind will be over on our starboard beam after we've gone about. What speed do you estimate we shall make with our present spread of canvas?'

The elderly quartermaster left the wheel to his mates and walked to the weather side. There he stood with his nose raised, as though smelling the wind. Then he turned and craned back his head to examine the sails towering away into the darkness.

'Better'n five knots, sir; but not six.'

'Thank you.'

It was time for the frigate to do its part. Lawson had reckoned that the boat crew would need forty minutes to creep up to the cable and cut it. He shouted the order to go about. The canvas flapped once in the darkness above as the bows crossed the

23

wind. Then they were on a starboard tack and heading for the land.

On the gun deck, dark shapes crouched in readiness. The heavy pieces had been hauled into position with their muzzles projecting through the open gun ports. Fuses smouldered in the buckets within reach of each gunlayer's hand, ready to be puffed into red glows and thrust into the linstocks should the flintlock action fail to fire the powder. The boys worked in between the guns, sprinkling sand on to the red planking so that the bare feet of the gunners would not slip as they heaved at the tackles.

In the chains two men stationed with a weighted line would take soundings as soon as the order was given. The coastline suggested that there was plenty of water, even close to the shore, but Lawson was not prepared to take chances. If they were to run aground it would be the end of them.

'Gunfire off the port bow!'

Captain Lawson was just in time to see two more flashes in quick succession. The dull boom of the first shot, followed by the rumble of the second and third reached them. Obviously the boat had been seen.

A picture of shattered timbers and bobbing heads filled Lawson's mind : his own experience at Copenhagen. This time it was young Jim Saunders. Grimly he began to calculate the distance. Three seconds between the flashes and the explosions. —Dear Mary and Jim, It is my painful duty to inform you—. Three seconds, and the sound of the guns would travel at eleven hundred feet per second—Your dear son died shortly before dawn—Eleven hundred yards at the most, and they were doing five an a half knots.

'Keep your eyes open, Mr Barty. We should see them any minute.'

Every man on deck was peering forward, searching for the hulk against the dim edge of dawn. The captain walked over to his first lieutenant.

'You have men posted who will keep the channel under

observation, to report the armed dhows, should they come out of the bay, Mr Jones?'

'Yes, sir.'

'There it is, sir,' Barty hissed.

Lawson followed his pointing finger and found the dark shadow of the hulk. It had certainly swung around from the shore and, provided Chandler had not made the unlikely mistake of cutting the leeward cable, all their guns would be pointing away from the frigate. The attackers had a tremendous advantage. With the pitch black western horizon behind them, they would not be seen on board the hulk until it was too late for them to do anything about it.

'Warn Mr Jamieson on the starboard gundeck. Lively now! We're almost upon them.'

He turned to Postill at the helm; quietly efficient, keen eyes fixed steadily ahead, fingers sensitively feeling the movement of the vessel through the spokes of the wheel.

'Can you see her, Mr Postill?'

'Yes, sir.'

'We are going to run close alongside her. If events deprive you of an officer, you will stand out to sea as soon as our guns can no longer bear. On no account will you pass to leeward of the target.'

'Aye aye, sir.'

'You understand why?'

'You expect her to have all her guns concentrated there, sir.'

Lawson looked at him sharply. Had there been a slight emphasis on 'you'?

'Is that not your opinion? Speak up man,' he added kindly, 'I should welcome your views.'

'Well, sir,' Postill replied hesitantly. 'If I were commanding yonder hulk, I do believe I should have a gun or two facing the land. They'd be loaded wi' grapeshot just in case any o' my friends ashore got over-ambitious. Treacherous part of the world, sir, is the Barbary Coast.'

Lawson nodded approval.

25

'You may well be right, Mr Postill. Nothing to be done about it though. We are upon them.'

The length of the target lay across their path less than eighty yards away. Now someone was screaming the alarm on board the hulk.

'Bring her round now.'

As the quartermaster expertly spun the wheel, the ship turned her bows seaward. Her starboard side now lay parallel with the pirate at point blank range. There was a rattle of musket fire from across the water, suddenly cut off by the deafening roar of the starboard broadside.

Jones clutched at a mizzen-mast stay as the deck heaved from the shock of the guns.

'That'll give them something to think about, sir,' he shouted excitedly. 'Shouldn't wonder if she don't heel over.'

The captain nodded absently. His mind was below on the gun deck. They should have sponged out now. Fresh charges would be coming forward. Already the better gun crews would be ramming them into place. Now the shot. It was a race against time. Each gun should get three away. The best would manage four before they passed beyond the line of vision. They could drop anchor to hold the frigate in position but it was important that they should be able to manoeuvre in case the dhows came out of the bay. The gunners would have to make the most of their opportunities.

The first gun fired and was followed immediately by another. Then began a ragged bombardment which continued until the battered hulk passed beyond the maximum angle at which the aftermost guns could be brought to bear. The attack had been a complete success.

Lawson watched the wreck going astern and listing badly. With luck another broadside on the return tack would send it to the bottom and it was important that they should see it sink. The pirates must not be given the opportunity to get the guns off her.

'Bring her about, Mr Jones.'

26

It was becoming lighter. Already the eastern horizon was glowing red. Soon the sun would be up. Then, if the dhows dared to show themselves, H.M.S. *Comus* would keep them busy.

A seaman, breathless and excited, ran onto the quarterdeck. He was one of those who had been taking soundings.

'Yes! What is it?' Lawson demanded.

'We just ran our boat down, sir.'

'Our boat?'

'Yes, sir. When we went about. She was half full o' water and sluggish, sir. They couldn't get out of the way. One of the boat crew managed to get onto our sounding line. I left Johnson and a couple of others to heave him aboard while I came to report. —I hope I did right, sir,' he added anxiously.

'Yes, lad, you did right,' Lawson said kindly. 'Tell this man to see me as soon as you get him aboard.'

'God, let it be Jim,' he prayed silently.

They were now fairly about but it had taken long enough, Lawson thought, and they had lost a lot of leeway. Now they would have to sail as close to the wind as they could and progress would be slow. Already the area around the hulk was lightening and there could be no doubt that the frigate would be clearly visible. Lawson raised his telescope quickly. A boat had put out from the hulk. The white spots of its threshing oars revealed its progress.

'Are we going to look for the men from our boat, sir?' Jones asked.

Lawson glared at him.

'What do you think those buggers are up to, Mr Jones?'

Jones laughed.

'Heading for the shelter of the shore, sir. Judging by the rate of the strokes, they should be making record time.'

'You're a bloody fool!' Lawson hissed exasperatedly. 'You've got the idea into your head that these people are a pack of savages. They've already demonstrated that they can keep a watch as well as the British Navy. How long will it take you to realise that they are seamen as well?'

'I'm afraid I don't understand, sir,' Jones said coldly.

Lawson forced himself to speak calmly.

'That boat will have a ship's anchor lashed to it. The hulk will be paying out a cable and as soon as the boat reaches a suitable angle they'll cut loose the anchor. Then the hulk will be able to manoeuvre into whatever position they fancy wi' no more than a few turns on the capstan. If we waste time looking for our men in the water, we'll find ourselves facing a battery of guns. Be good enough to ask the crew of the bow chaser to try sink the boat.'

Jones hurried white faced from the quarterdeck leaving the captain to scowl silently over the intervening water.

The dull sheen of sail, crested with red from the rising sun, appeared from behind the hulk. The first of the dhows had finally got under way and was leaving the lair to join in the battle. Lawson watched the new development with expressionless face. According to Captain Mallory there might be another four or five to deal with before the day was out.

A flash from the bows, followed by a roar and the acrid smell of powder, as the smoke whipped back over the deck from the gun's mouth, announced that Jones had passed on his order. The captain watched disinterestedly for the fall of the shot. There was not much chance of hitting a small boat with one gun. In any case the result might be the same because the anchor would probably bite even if the boat were sunk. Now it no longer mattered. The hulk was once more in the line of fire.

This time it was the turn of the port side guns. They had evidently been ordered to fire as they bore. Three blasted away as the bows of the frigate crept past the end of the bulk. The other guns followed suit; every shot smashing through the rounded stern at the waterline. Suddenly it crumbled. The pressure of the sea had become too much for the weakened timbers. The floating fortress was stricken.

As Postill had forecast, they had received a few shots in

return. Two bodies lay on the deck by the foremast and several men were being carried below. Lawson wondered vaguely who they would be whilst he calculated the distance separating them from the approaching dhow and a newly arrived companion which was just clearing the channel leading from the bay.

He had lost interest in the hulk. It had already made its death lurch. Soon her guns would break from their tackles under the strain as the deck heeled away from them. Then it would be the end.

'Cease firing,' he shouted.

Immediately a piercing whistle was heard, followed by a silence, comparative silence, broken only by the preparations for the next round.

Somebody had been standing at his side for some time. He turned, expecting to see Jones. Instead he found a very wet third lieutenant and behind him, equally wet, Midshipman Saunders. Chandler grinned at his obvious surprise.

'We're back on board, sir. We lost the boat and the muskets but all men are accounted for.'

'Never mind about your losses, Mr Chandler. I am delighted that you are all safe. Your battery has done very well in your absence, but there's more to come so perhaps you'd better take over. Not you, Mr Saunders,' he added as the midshipman turned away with Chandler. 'I want you to place yourself at the service of Mrs Dullant. You'll find her on the orlop deck.'

Now that Jim was back on board and safe on the orlop deck, Lawson felt cheered as he viewed the approaching dhows. Then the shock of his own long gun set his pulses racing. He became a fighting machine, eagerly poised over the quarterdeck rail, his eyes taking in everything, his body accurately gauging the movement of the ship, his cheek registering the force and direction of the wind and his ears taking in the orders that were being given on all sides. His mind, conditioned by a lifetime of war, was working furiously, sifting the information, working out his manoeuvres and thinking of alternatives in case they should go wrong.

'Bring her round two points to port.'

The second dhow had gone to windward of the leading craft. There was no sense in engaging both at once. The slight change of course would bring them nicely to leeward of the first dhow. They could rake her with the starboard guns, then cut across her stern and give his port gunners a chance at the other whilst he was going about. The two pirates had made a mistake in leaving the shelter of the bay where the frigate would not have such freedom of movement.

'She's going about, sir,' Jones warned.

The pirate was not going to allow *Comus* the initiative. She was going over onto a port tack revealing a line of guns. Almost immediately the side of the dhow became obscured by puffs of white smoke. Before the smoke dispersed, the shot arrived.

Lawson felt the passage of a shot but he was too concerned with what had happened on the foredeck to comment on it. The broadside had left them without a single ship's boat. They had been lashed together alongside the mast. Now their planking was strewn in all directions.

'The devil take them,' he said savagely. 'If our starboard guns don't blast them to hell, I shall want to know the reason why, Mr Jones.'

Jones did not answer. He was sitting on the deck staring in horror at two jagged white bones surrounded by pulsating red flesh. His right arm had been severed just above the wrist.

'See to him,' Lawson ordered abruptly. Then he turned away and scowled at the rapidly approaching dhow.

The dhow had two ten pounders mounted aft. As the frigate began to cross her stern, both fired in quick succession. The sound of the shot striking home was lost in the thundering reply from the frigate's guns.

'Hard a starboard.'

The frigate swung around; her speed rapidly increasing as she felt the benefit of the wind on her beam.

The dhow was in trouble. Her rudder had been almost completely shot away and she was turning helplessly into the wind. Soon she would be taken aback. *Comus* moved in for the kill.

In two minutes it was all over. The starboard guns of the frigate greatly outnumbered those on the dhow and they were far more efficiently served. The single mast of the enemy toppled and she began to settle deeply in the water. Lawson set his course for the other.

It had decided to run for it. Already, with a freshening wind on her beam, she was almost a mile away. Lawson looked aloft to the tiny figures on the yards awaiting his orders. She would stand more canvas, he decided. As he raised the speaking trumpet to shout his orders, his subconscious mind suddenly thrust a question forward.

'Why did they leave the bay?' he asked himself.

He looked at Jones, now unconscious and being strapped to a litter for his journey down to the orlop deck. He was doing exactly as his subordinate had done. He was underestimating the enemy. They had not come out to engage him. They were too small for that. Their purpose had been to lead him away. There was perhaps something remaining in the protection of the bay that they did not want him to see. Mallory's ship, of course. Maybe they were still unloading her, but in any case, if what he had heard about the *Princess Mary* were true, she would be worth a dozen dhows to Yussaiff Ahmed. She was reputed to be the fastest vessel in the Mediterranean.

No one knew the possible results of discontinuing an action better than Captain Lawson. As a midshipman he had witnessed the hanging of his own captain for the same offence. It had made a deep impression upon him; particularly the injustice of it. If there were nothing in the bay, maybe they would say that he had abandoned the pursuit because he had been afraid to close the enemy.

On this tack the dhow was probably faster than the heavier frigate. She would keep just out of range until night-fall. Then she would disappear. Meanwhile whoever was in the bay would be strengthening their defences against his return.

'Bring her around,' he ordered abruptly. 'Set your course for the entrance to the bay.'

'Aye aye, sir,' Postill replied. If he had any doubt about his captain's motives he intended to keep it to himself. His face showed no surprise.

Lawson glanced astern and saw the cable with its marker bobbing in their wake.

'Mr Chandler!' he shouted.

The lieutenant hurried aft from his position at the guns.

'I gather that you found the cable we trailed for you most useful after we ran you down?'

'Yes, sir,' Chandler replied cheerfully. 'We had little difficulty in getting on to it.'

'Then why the devil didn't you have it hauled inboard when it had served its purpose?'

4

A FEW spars and a solitary barrel bobbing in the greasy swell were all that remained of the hulk but the men who had manned its guns would have had plenty of time to make the shore. Jamieson's glass swept the rocky entrance to the bay.

'Nae sign o' life, sir. Not even a gull. Yet the rocks are covered wi' their droppings, so we can take it that the place will be teeming wi' men.'

'Armed with muskets, Mr Jamieson?'

'And nae doot a gun or two,' Jamieson replied cheerfully, 'but I'm thinkin' we'll be more than a match for them. Both batteries are loaded with canister. If they show themselves we'll make 'em sorry they turned their hands to piracy.'

Lawson smiled at the infectious humour of his acting second in command. Certainly he seemed to have more about him than the unfortunate Jones, but his confidence might be the result of a habitual optimism rather than sound reasoning.

'Do you think it likely that they will attempt to defend the channel?'

Jamieson shot him a shrewd glance.

'They'd have tae have something well worth while in the way o' guns or it would be suicide. But it is a fact that men are there waiting and I can see no suitable positions for gun emplacements so maybe they've got something else up their sleeves.— Mayhap they expect us tae go aground.'

Lawson nodded his agreement.

'That's what it will be, Mr Jamieson. I'll stake five pounds we'll touch bottom as we pass through the entrance. Those shoulders of rock were surely continuous at one time and I've

33

no doubt that there'll be a ridge under the water directly in line with them. Have the mains'ls and tops'ls clewed up. We'll creep in under topgallants.'

'By the line, four,' came the chant from the chains.

Lawson turned to the midshipman of the watch.

'Get forward and keep your eye on things, Mr Barty.'

As the midshipman hurried to join the men in the chains, Lawson examined his preparations. Aloft every yard had its complement of marines and seamen armed with muskets. Sharp shooters were there too, with rifled muskets. These men would be invaluable at five hundred yards but the ship relied on its carronades for the bloody close quarter work. They were mounted on the quarterdeck and forecastle; squat, large bore pieces. When charged with half a pound of powder and a bag of musket balls, they could clear the decks of boarders far quicker than a company of marines.

'By the line three !' the leadsman shouted urgently.

The captain stood perfectly still, facing the bows. He knew that all the men on the quarterdeck were watching him closely. It was important that he should show no sign of anxiety.

'By the line two and a half,' Barty's voice called.

Their bows were almost under the shadow of the rock. Lawson tensed himself for the shock then suddenly remembered those on the yards.

'Hold tight aloft. Get a grip on something,' he roared.

The frigate shuddered violently and checked her pace. A scream from the mainmast drew his attention in time to see a marine falling through the maze of ropes to the deck. Immediately the ridges on both sides of the channel came to life with a tremendous rattle of musketry.

The noise had no effect on Postill. His hands alone were on the wheel. He was coaxing his charge along; his eyes darting from the top gallants and back to the bows; his head slightly on one side as though he was listening to the scraping of the keel on the ridge. They were working their way painfully over the obstruction, helped by the swell and a freak wind that was curving around the basin shaped side of the bay and filling the canvas on the foremast.

Lawson watched the quartermaster in fascination. If they could gain a few more yards, the wind would fill the canvas on the mainmast and they would have all the drive they needed to get clear.

A deafening roar a few yards away drew Lawson's attention back to the other part of the struggle. A nearby carronade had just blasted a group of three men who had been carrying a barrel. They were thrown back across the rock as if a giant hand had struck them. The barrel rolled down the slope and wedged itself against a jagged tongue of rock at the water's edge. Immediately the pirates on that side of the ship took cover.

He looked curiously at the barrel. Smoke was creeping from one end. It was a mine. They had intended to float it over the twenty yards of water separating the frigate from the land.

The blast from the explosion was deflected from those on the quarterdeck but the falling debris, stones and fragments of the barrel, fell about them like hail.

'What are you doing here, Mr Saunders?' Lawson demanded sternly as the midshipman hurried by. 'Your orders were to remain with Mrs Dullant.'

'She said she didn't want me, sir. She's helping with the wounded.'

'Helping with— What the devil is the surgeon thinking about?'

'More mines, sir,' a seaman shouted.

The warning drove Cecilia Dullant's odd behaviour out of Lawson's mind. Three barrels bobbed towards them, pushed by the wind from the bayward side of the projecting ridge. They were within forty yards and getting closer.

'Tell Mr Chandler that I want the whole of his fire directed at the barrels. If one of them gets alongside we'll have a hole big enough for a coach and horses to drive through.'

Saunders ran from the quarterdeck and Lawson forced his

attention from the dancing mines to consider the effect of increasing sail. They were probably half over the underwater ridge. Every lift from the swell helped them to advance a few yards. Extra canvas would cause them to heel slightly and so reduce draught but it would also increase their speed and there might be further obstructions waiting to tear out their bottom. In any case the barrels would have done their work before the sails could be shaken out.

With a mighty blast, the barrel farthest away blew up. It had not been caused by a hit. The guns were only now directing their fire towards them.

'Faulty fuse,' Lawson said to nobody in particular.

The fuse would consist of black powder inside a coiled leather hose liberally coated with pitch. The fire had jumped from one loop to another and set the charge off prematurely.

A wall of water from the explosion rushed towards them. He noted it with satisfaction. It would help lift the frigate over the obstruction. Then he thought of the effect on the two mines which were in the path of the wave. They would be pushed nearer. A hail of shot demonstrated the truth of this by striking the water beyond them. The gunners had fired just as the wave had borne them forward.

The men on the shore to starboard were now openly showing themselves. They had the advantage of shooting without being shot at. A musket ball thudded into the rail at the captain's hand but all his attention was on the approaching mines.

The water boiled round the barrels. Now there was only one left but it was almost upon them. All the shot was striking the water beyond.

'If ever we get out of this, I'll give them gunnery practice from morn 'till night,' Lawson fretted. Then he realised what the trouble was. The barrel was too close. They could not depress the guns enough.

'What the hell are you doing?' he shouted suddenly.

Jim Saunders was poised on the bulwarks.

'Jim! Get back on deck!'

36

A groan escaped his lips. The boy had leapt into the water.

All pretence of imperturbability was now thrown to the winds. He rushed along the starboard side. Jim had reached the barrel and was kicking out as hard as he could to work it astern. Musket-balls began to strike the water around him.

'Blast you!' he roared at his men. 'What the hell are you gawping at? Direct your fire at the shore. Drive the scum under cover.'

Fascinated, his eyes jerked back to the barrel. At any moment it could explode and a life which meant more to him than any other would be ended. There was nothing he could do to help. Aften twenty-five years at sea he was unable to swim a stroke and he could hardly order a seaman over the side to his death. Slowly he followed the barrel astern.

'Leave it now!'

He flung a coil of rope expertly. Saunders caught at it but continued to push at the mine.

'I said, leave it,' Lawson roared. 'I order you to leave it.'

The boy gave the barrel a final push and struck out for the frigate with his free hand whilst Lawson and a seaman hauled furiously. Between them they plucked him from the water like a hooked fish and hoisted him to the edge of the bulwarks. From there many hands clawed him inboard.

The mine exploded. In his relief at seeing Jim safely on board the captain had not given it another thought. Now, as the decks reeled from the wall of water passing under their stern, he was recalled to his duty. Hurriedly he returned to the quarterdeck and looked about him.

They were free of the obstruction and the frigate was gaining speed. A wide expanse of water stretched to starboard but the view of the bay on the other side was blocked by a sheer rock face as high as the masts.

'By the line, six,' came the reassuring shout from the chains.

'Keep her as she is, Mr Postill. We'll find all the water we need close to the rock.'

The firing ceased and the quiet passage along the channel

37

seemed unreal after the noise of the skirmish. Lawson gradually relaxed. One action was behind him and he had no doubt that another was just around the corner of the long rock face, but for the moment there was peace and he could enjoy the beauty of a ship in motion. There was the soothing creak of the blocks and the hum of the breeze through the fine tracery of cordage above. If he could shut his eyes on the men sitting tensely at the guns, he could imagine they were taking a pleasure cruise around Whitby Bay.

A long-drawn-out scream from below jerked him back to reality. One of the men at the nearest carronade crossed himself nervously. The others looked grim. Doctor Baxter was operating. Suddenly Lawson remembered that the admiral's wife was down there. He called Saunders over.

'My compliments to the lady and ask her if she will kindly join me on deck.'

He began to wonder about Lieutenant Jones. Probably the surgeon would already have seared the stub of his arm and he would now be lying half stupefied with pain and laudanum. His chances of living would be about even. If he were lucky, the burnt flesh would not putrefy and he would get better. Then he could look forward to the rest of his life on half pay. The Navy would not be likely to call upon a crippled lieutenant while eighty out of every hundred naval officers were without employment.

'Damn the peace,' he grumbled.

Like many another officer, he half hoped that Napoleon would escape from St Helena, just as he had from Elba. War could be a sickening experience but it was all he had ever known, except the shortlived peace following the Treaty of Amiens, when as an unemployed lieutenant he had tramped the streets of London, half starved and almost out of his mind with the inactivity and uselessness of his life. That had been hell.

'Yes, Mr Saunders?'

'She said, please forgive her, but she is too busy to come on deck, sir.'

38

'What the devil is she doing down there?'

'She's reading to some of the wounded, sir.'

'Reading!'

'From the Bible, sir. The men appear to welcome it.'

Lawson shook his head in wonder. Religious practice, as far as he was concerned, consisted of the compulsory Sunday morning divisions over which, he, as Captain, must preside: a very brief affair, followed by the reading of Naval Law. It was common knowledge that those at the back spent the time dicing.

The men in the bows had become excited. Something interesting had evidently been seen around the rock face. Now they were looking expectantly towards the quarterdeck but none of them had the initiative to report whatever had interested them. Lawson shrugged and waited philosophically whilst the frigate crept forward.

The wall of rock had reduced itself to a line of jagged teeth, revealing through the gaps a straggle of white adobe dwellings along the eastern margin of the bay. Now they could see the village; a cluster of squalid hovels and a few larger stone buildings at the water's edge. None of these things had excited the men. All their attention was riveted on the three vessels, moored side by side, hard against the quay.

'There's a penny or two in prize-money yonder,' Jamieson said with satisfaction. 'And the insurance company will pay plenty tae get the *Princess Mary* back.'

'Which is the *Princess Mary*?'

'The one alongside the quay, sir. She's a rare beauty. Mind you, the two that are lashed to her are not to be sniffed at, as far as can be judged from this distance.'

Lawson examined them carefully through his telescope. Not one of them was ready to put to sea and, more important under the circumstances, only the outermost ship was in a position to use its broadside. His glance swept beyond the ships. There was no sign of life anywhere in the village. The local inhabitants had either retreated inland or they were waiting quietly.

Lawson had no doubt that there would be many eyes watching and many guns primed and ready.'

'Mr Chandler!' he called. 'Put me a ball through the nearest hovel. Let's see what they are up to.'

'I'll supervise, sir,' Jamieson said with a grin. 'We don't want tae scratch the paintwork on any of the ships.'

The sound of the shot echoed and re-echoed across the bay. One house, a crude white stone building with wooden roof, trembled and showed a jagged hole. Then all was still. The shore was as empty as before.

'A bit of target practice now,' Lawson called. 'A shot at each building. One gun at a time.'

He was not going to risk having all the guns of the port side battery reloading at the same time. At any moment the outermost ship might thrust its guns out and blast its heavy shot at them. If the frigate's gun crews knew their work, the first gun would be sponged out and recharged before the fifth had fired.

Lawson raised his telescope and watched the destruction; his mind automatically registering the interval between each gunfire. Jamieson, with grim humour, was maintaining the regulation five seconds required for a salute and every shot was finding its target. The bombardment brought no reaction from the shore.

'Cease firing,' Lawson shouted after the twentieth shot had crashed home.

The frigate crept silently across the waters of the bay. All those on the upperdecks looked expectantly towards the captain.

'Cavalry, sir!'

Lawson smiled at the description as he examined the motley collection of horses and riders approaching the village at a gallop. This was the most disreputable cavalry he had ever seen. Nevertheless they were armed. A musket swung at the shoulder of each rider. For a moment he was tempted to put a shot over their heads to warn them into good behaviour. They were waving their arms vigorously now, suggesting that they expected to be fired upon.

'It seems that they want tae parley, sir,' Jamieson said in some astonishment.

'So it does,' Lawson replied.

He was feeling somewhat at a loss at this turn of events. A good broadside from the nearest ship would have been more in keeping with the situation. This group looked like a deputation, and deputations meant politics. Lawson would have preferred the broadside.

'I think they want tae come aboard, sir.'

A dozen had halted at the edge of the water. It was clear from their gesticulations that they wished for closer contact. Lawson focused his glass on the three in the centre of the group. They were obviously superior to the others. None of them was waving but they were certainly leaders. The middle one, an enormous man, who sat his white horse as though he were a part of it, seemed the most important.

'Signal them to come aboard, Mr Barty.'

'Using Naval signals, sir?' the midshipman asked in astonishment.

'Unless you can contrive some other manner of putting the request to them, Mr Barty, it would appear to be the only way,' Lawson replied caustically.

'Aye aye, sir.'

The bunting fluttered up to the masthead while Lawson scowled gloomily over the water. He did not expect them to read the signals either but perhaps they would understand what he wished them to do. The only alternative was to send someone paddling ashore on a grating. Apart from the indignity of such a procedure, it would show them that they had destroyed his boats.

The signal caused a stir amongst the party on the shore. They were pointing at the flags and talking amongst themselves. Lawson grunted with satisfaction as the one he had identified as the leader waved some of them away to the village. They were going to find a boat.

'Drop a stern anchor, Mr Jamieson.'

For some time he had been noting the growing anxiety of the quartermaster as the ship had moved closer to the shore. They now had a good angle between themselves and the dangerous ship. They could anchor in safety. Should an emergency arise they could haul on the anchor cable and stand out in the middle of the bay again. He waited until the acting first lieutenant had given his orders.

'Now you can have all hands piped to dinner and when that is over, order the starboard watch to stand down.'

They had been at battle stations for nine hours. It was important that some should have a rest. If they were to stay in the bay for the night they would need a very alert ship's company.

As the boatswain's whistle shrilled its welcome message around the ship, Evans appeared on deck, carrying a small table and a basket.

'Is yo' hungry, sir?'

Lawson wondered vaguely how long his servant had been waiting to bring his dinner. He had everything prepared. As though by magic, food began to appear from the basket to be tastefully arranged on the gleaming white tablecloth.

'Cold chicken, sir. No fire today,' he grinned.

The captain smiled at him. Certainly there was no fire. All would have been doused when they had cleared for action. He hoped that the cooks in the galley had had the foresight to boil the salt beef the night before, just as Evans had cooked the chicken. If not they would be having a poor meal. Mentally he made a note to look into the messing arrangements at the first opportunity.

'Mr Postill!' he called on a sudden impulse, 'be so good as to join me at dinner.'

He caught the sideways look that Jamieson directed at Chandler but he made no comment. So they had not seen a warrant officer sit down with a captain before. He shrugged and beckoned Postill to the table.

Evans produced another chair and the old man sat down,

42

if it could be called sitting. He was as near to a position of attention as was possible on a high-backed chair.

'Boat putting out from the shore, sir,' Chandler reported some ten minutes later.

'Thank you,' Lawson replied. 'Let me know when it is alongside.'

He had finished his share of the chicken and vegetables and was mopping at his lips with a napkin when the boat reached them.

'I can strongly recommend the cheese, Mr Postill, but I regret I must leave you to it. Please continue with your dinner.'

The boat bumping alongside was dangerously overloaded. Eleven men were jammed into it and there was seating for only six. Two of these were occupied by the fat man whom Lawson had identified as the leader.

'We'll have the three in the stern on board,' Lawson told the warrant officer at the entry port. These were the ones he had identified as the leaders. They were richly dressed with bejewelled fingers and headdresses.

'Three,' said the boatswain, holding up three fingers.

Half of them stood up and the boat rocked violently.

'Threaten to drop a ball through their planking if they don't sit down.'

The boatswain took an eighteen pounder from the rack and poised it over their heads. They sat down hurriedly. Lawson nodded in satisfaction.

'Now tell them three again.'

The boatswain repeated the performance with his fingers and the man in the stern stood up. One of them pointed to a shifty little fellow with a straggly beard.

'All right. Four it is,' he conceded.

Probably straggly beard was an interpreter, he thought. He could see no other reason for their wanting the most disreputable member of their party aboard.

As they climbed aboard he was able to assess them individually. The big man carried himself with the dignity of a local sheik but he was certainly not Yussaiff Ahmed. He was too fat and bore all the marks of easy living. His two companions were probably his sons. The dirty little man left his role in no doubt.

'We come from the great prince,' he said before he had his feet on the deck. 'Our prince want to know why you shoot at his village.'

'I too come from a great prince,' Lawson replied. 'My prince is angry because you have stolen his ship.' He pointed to the *Princess Mary*. 'Where is Yussaiff Ahmed?'

The sheik spoke at length. Lawson watched his face and waited for a translation.

'He say that Yussaiff Ahmed is very bad man. Bring plenty trouble to this village. He say you must go and take your prince's ship.'

'Compensation,' Jamieson whispered. 'It would be a pity if we left the other two beauties.'

Lawson frowned at him. Naturally they were all keenly interested in the prospects of prize money but the responsibility for any action taken by the ship was the captain's, and it would be Lawson's head that would fall if anything illegal took place.

'Go aboard the *Princess Mary*, Mr Jamieson, and check her inventory; cargo and equipment. Captain Mallory will no doubt tell you where you will find her lading lists. If we discover that anything is missing we can talk further about compensations. Send a couple of men to disembark this lot on the beach. Then you can make use of the boat.'

He turned back to the sheik and explained, through the interpreter, what he intended to do. The man bowed in acknowledgement.

5

As Lawson had expected, the *Princess Mary* had been picked clean. Now they were waiting for the sheik to make good his promise to have the stolen cargo returned before morning. Meanwhile the men were resting.

Cecilia Dullant lay stretched on a hammock under the awning abaft the wheel and Lawson had taken the canvas chair to keep her company but the warm afternoon sun after a sleepless night soon proved too much for them. Lawson had been asleep over an hour when a midshipman shook him gently by the shoulder.

'What is it?' he growled.

'The village is filling up with men, sir.'

'Very well.'

'More are coming in from the surrounding countryside, sir.'

Lawson opened both eyes and glowered.

'Mr Barty,' he said acidly, 'the navy, in its wisdom, decreed that warrant officers and the likes of you, may be entrusted with the watch whenever a king's ship is lying at anchor. The reasons will be obvious. Firstly to allow the officers to rest and secondly to provide an opportunity for senior midshipmen to get used to responsibility. Your duty is to ensure the safety of the ship.'

'But these men are armed, sir.'

'Did you see any field pieces?'

'No, sir.'

'Are they manning the ships that are lying at the quayside?'

'No, sir.'

'You can't see an armada of small boats anywhere?'

'No, sir.'

'None of these armed men are swimming out to us?'

'Er—no, sir.'

'Then leave me in peace.'

'Aye aye, sir. But——'

'Bugger off!'

The midshipman retreated hurriedly and Lawson settled back in his chair. Suddenly he noticed that the lady was watching him.

'I beg your pardon, ma'am. I had—that is, I thought you were asleep.'

'No, Captain, you had forgotten once again that I am on board. I must be a singularly uninteresting person.'

She was smiling, Lawson noted with relief; a pleasant, girlish smile, revealing white, even teeth. He grinned ruefully and nodded.

'Forgive me, ma'am. I had been asleep.'

'And you are not concerned about your midshipman's report? Do you think it unlikely that they will attack?'

'They'll have a go at us before morning, ma'am. That's for sure. I am equally certain that they'll wait until after sundown, so we might as well get all the rest we can.'

'What do you propose to do with me this time?'

'Well, ma'am, unless they use artillery, and I think it unlikely, you might just as well spend a comfortable night in my cot—that is the cot you are using in my cabin,' he amended hurriedly.

She laughed delightedly. Lawson's face lightened in a brief smile. For some time he had been aware of the outline of her body, clearly silhouetted against the bright wall of light at the end of the canopy. The humidity of the late afternoon had caused the makeshift dress to cling, revealing a far more shapely figure than he had suspected. He rose to his feet.

'Are you going to leave me again?' she asked with mock reproof.

'I must write up the log before I give my orders, ma'am.'

'Then perhaps you will join me at dinner.'

'I should be delighted, ma'am.'

In the temporary privacy of his day cabin he wrote busily for an hour recording the actions of the past twenty-four hours. It was possible that he would be dead before morning. Their passage into the bay and Jim Saunders' gallantry must be noted. He knew little of Lieutenant Jamieson, who would assume command in the event of the captain being killed, but he was well aware that many an officer had been known to forget the contributions of their juniors, thereby adding to their own credit. When he had completed the record he carefully wrote down the orders he was about to issue, then ordered the Marine sentry outside the door to summon the officers and certain warrant officers to join him. They gathered around the table and waited expectantly.

'Before morning we shall be attacked by that rabble on the shore.'

There was a stir of interest but no comment was made. He had their undivided attention.

'In thirty minutes we shall work our way closer to their ships,' he went on. 'By the time we have completed the manoeuvre it will be dark. Then we will rig nets to make it difficult for boarders, and row guard. The one boat we have will have to suffice. All guns will be loaded with grape or case shot but they will have ball ready, to be used in the unlikely event of any of the ships moving away from their moorings. I should be pleased, Mr Jamieson, if you will order the master at arms to issue pikes, muskets and cutlasses.'

He addressed himself to the carpenter, who was pursing his lips thoughtfully in the background.

'Mr Clark, you will instruct your mates to fill half a dozen barrels with oil rags and see that they are placed at intervals around the ship. When the alarm is given, you will set fire to the rags and drop the barrels overside. That should give the gunners a bit of light. Half a fathom of chain nailed to the bottom of each barrel will ensure that they hit the water the right way up. Any questions?'

Chandler cleared his throat. Lawson shot him a quick glance.

'Don't you think it likely, sir, that the ships at the quay will work around under cover of darkness to give their guns a chance?'

'I think,' Lawson said, laying the emphasis on the 'I', 'that they have few guns left, or we should have received a warm welcome when we first poked our bows into the bay. My belief is that most of the guns that were aboard these ships are lying with the hulk at the bottom of the sea.'

'With all respect, sir,' Jamieson said, 'how can you be sure that they are going tae attack tonight?'

'They must. We've caught them red-handed with a pirated ship. Their only chance of escaping full retribution would be to return all the cargo. The local sheik is unable to do that because he has no more than his share. Yussaiff Ahmed will have taken the bulk of it. I am empowered to level the village, seize the ships and hang any man I can catch. They know it, and so they have no alternative but to try to board us under cover of darkness. When they do, we'll teach them a lesson that will show every sheik the dangers involved in harbouring pirates, and no quibbling lawyers will be able to question our motives.'

He waited expectantly for more questions.

'Very well, gentlemen, if you have nothing more to say, you may go about your duties.'

As they began to move out, the captain recalled the idea he had to keep young Saunders off the deck. There could be hand to hand fighting. The picture of the boy and the enormous cutlass was still fresh in his mind. He could stand no chance against a man skilled in the art of close fighting.

'Mr Barty, you will be in command aloft. Take Mr Saunders and man the top gallants, fore and main. You will need two top-men each. Have them ready to loose the gaskets. We may need to get under way in a hurry.'

'Aye aye, sir,' Barty replied without enthusiasm.

Clearly, the senior midshipman considered the task to be

beneath him but he knew better than raise objections. Saunders too looked very disappointed.

Lawson grinned to himself as they walked dejectedly from the cabin. He knew exactly how they felt. Clinging eighty feet above the deck they would see very little of the action. As long as they had the good sense to lash themselves onto the yard, they would be as safe there as down below the waterline.

The dinner was not a success. At the lady's request, Lawson had produced the only members of his ship's company who could be spared from their duties. Saunders and an older midshipman proved to be useless. They shovelled the rare luxury of freshly slaughtered mutton into their mouths, contributed to the conversation in monosyllables and concentrated most of their attention in the sounds of activity outside. Doctor Baxter was feeling an urgent craving for alcohol and a resentment against the captain for keeping a close watch on the wine. Among other things, Lawson was worried about the tension of the anti-boarding nets that Jamieson would be rigging around the ship. It was a relief to all when Midshipman Barty arrived with an urgent request from the second in command for the captain to join them.

When Lawson appeared on deck, the ship was as secure from boarders as the ingenuity of the navy could make it. The anti-boarding nets had been erected. Canvas containers of small shot had been stacked in the racks alongside the guns. A number of empty beef barrels stood at the foot of each mast with oil casks and old rags. Everywhere there was an air of expectancy and tenseness, oddly at contrast with the gentle movement of the ship as she rode easily at her new anchorage.

Chandler and Jamieson were engaged in a whispered conversation; two dark shapes on the landward side of the bows. Lawson joined them; the clump of his feet sounding unnaturally loud.

'There's a deal of activity going on ashore, sir,' Jamieson told him. 'A wee while ago we heard something heavy being dragged along. They were using horses tae pull whatever it was.'

'Guns do you think?'

'Very likely, sir, or mortars. Sounded as if they might be hauling them over rollers.'

The captain stood with hands gripping the foremast shrouds. There he remained in silence, straining his ears. About him, crouched in readiness for any command, were his men. Suddenly he felt the weight of his responsibility and with it came anxiety. As long as the pirates had nothing outrageously new at their disposal, he was ready to deal with them. If they had something as surprising as the mines of the morning, he was not so sure.

'What the devil was that?' he demanded irritably as a sharp twanging sound came to their ears.

'Shipyard noise, sir. Like a heavy plank that's been dropped from a height.'

There was a splash on their left, followed immediately by the movement of many seamen towards the port side.

'Keep still there,' Lawson hissed.

The ship became so silent that the snick of a musket being cocked amidships was clearly audible on the forecastle. Everybody from the captain to the lowliest powder monkey, strained his ears for any sound that might indicate the intentions of those on the shore.

There was a loud twang of timber against timber, followed within three seconds by a splash on their starboard side but this time there was no opportunity for comment. The blinding flash of an explosion, followed immediately by an ear-splitting roar, sent them all to cover.

'They're using some kind of machine tae hurl barrels of gunpowder at us,' Jamieson said. 'A mediaeval catapult perhaps, such as they used tae toss boulders over the walls of castles. Yon cunning de'il has taken a page out of history.'

'No doubt you're right,' Lawson replied. 'Mr Chandler, kindly go aft and have us hauled astern on our anchor cable. Aloft there! Stand by to set t'gallants. Get the men under cover,

Mr Jamieson. There'll be no boarding parties while they're tossing fused barrels of powder at us. I will be at the wheel.'

He hurried along the length of the ship to the quarterdeck where Postill was awaiting orders. Before he reached him, a barrel landed fairly on the forecastle. It bounced on a coil of heavy cable and skidded through a group of men to come to rest against the foremast.

'O'er the side wi' it,' Jamieson roared. 'Look alive, me lads, or it'll blow ye all tae kingdom come.'

He seized at the barrel but those who could have helped, hesitated. Jamieson had made a mistake in adding that last unnecessary sentence. He paid for it with his life.

A searing hot flame engulfed the forward end of the ship, thrusting itself with concussive power along the foredeck, against the base of the foremast and at the port and starboard bulwarks, which crumbled at its touch. On it raced, leaping the well of the main gun deck and on to the quarterdeck. Then all was quiet saving the echoes but the damage was not over. Slowly, with a horrible rending of splitting timber, the foremast toppled, held crazily for a moment, then fell into the sea. The port side shrouds whipped across the deck, tautened into iron rods and held the wreckage alongside.

Chandler and his party, who had been struggling with the anchor cable on the deck below, were thrown sprawling when the frigate had heeled over from the force of the explosion. Before they could scramble to their feet the waters of the bay had foamed through the gun ports and washed them up against the stern bulwarks. There they were trapped underwater in the confined space of the 'tween decks until the stern of the ship lurched out of the sea and hurled the floodwater forward in a five-foot wave along the entire length of the gun deck.

Chandler watched it go; dousing the fires that had been started by the hot breath of explosion. He turned back to his men to find them rubbing their bruises and shaking the water out of their clothes.

'Heave on that capstan,' he snarled. 'Look alive now or you'll have the next bloody barrel amongst you.'

He waited until they were hauling the cable aboard then hurried away to see what had happened on the deck above.

He reached the place where a few minutes earlier had been the wooden steps leading to the upper deck. Only a few shattered beams sticking out of the bulkhead like broken arms remained. He stretched for the highest and pulled himself up.

Wounded and dead lay around the site of the blast. He stumbled over a body and measured his length on the deck. A small hand, wet and sticky, touched his face. He thrust it away and scrambled to his feet. A voice whispered for help.

'Later, laddie.'

He looked around him. There were several small fires burning on the upper deck. By their light he found Jamieson's mangled body and made his way aft to the quarterdeck. Then he realised that he was in command. Captain Lawson lay sprawled in a pool of blood.

'You there!' he shouted to the stunned men manning the carronades. 'One of you see to the captain. The rest of you get for'ard and cut the wreckage away.'

The men rushed to obey his orders. He scrambled over the debris after them and began to slash at the cordage with his sword. Then he saw them coming over the side.

'Boarders!' he roared, his voice cracking into a scream with excitement. 'What the blazes are the guns doing?'

The guns on the starboard side of the gun deck had been underwater when the frigate had heeled over. The flintlock mechanism of the guns refused to spark and the rope fuses had been doused. Whoever was leading the attack had evidently taken this into consideration. None of the boarders approached the port side where they would have been given a warm reception.

'Carronades! Direct your fire along the starboard side.'

Even as he shouted the order, Chandler remembered that he had sent the men away from the carronades to clear the wreckage. Now they were using their axes against the scimitars and pikes of the boarders.

'To me!' screamed Chandler. 'Rally round, *Comus*. Sweep the swine into the sea.'

He lunged at the first pirate. The blade passed through the man's guard and took him full in the chest. Clark, the carpenter, a dozen seamen and a marine won their way to his side. Together they faced thirty or more and they could expect little help from the men on the main gun deck. The boarders had dragged a carronade from the forward battery to cover the well amidships and all the other escape routes had been battened down.

'Close up, lads. Keep them in front of us,' Chandler panted.

He parried a savage blow aimed at his head, then had the satisfaction of seeing the bayonet of the marine slide under the exposed arm of his attacker. A wild hairy face appeared on his right. He cut at it and turned to engage another man on his left before the first had fallen to the deck.

By now the swarming pirates had cut down most of the defenders of the upper deck but the group around Chandler had lost only two. Slowly they gave ground; working their way along the protection of the starboard bulkhead towards the quarterdeck, but there were so many attackers around them, that further resistance seemed useless. It could be only a matter of a minute or two before they were hacked to pieces. The marine went down and knocked Chandler over. Another man fell. The boarders, screaming with excitement, surged forward in a rush that would have overwhelmed the remainder, had not a blast of grape-shot suddenly ripped a path through their massed ranks.

Chandler scrambled from under a writhing body and staggered to his feet. He had few left of his party. He turned desperately to the quarterdeck. The explosion had come from there. The dark shapes around the carronade must be *Comus* men.

'Fall back on the gun,' he shouted.

53

They ran aft through the hanging smoke. A British seaman was thrusting a case of musket balls into the muzzle of the starboard carronade. Sagging against the bulwarks behind him, half supported by Cecilia Dullant, was Captain Lawson, his face covered in blood.

'It's you, sir!' Chandler exclaimed.

'Aye, it's me,' Lawson growled. 'Man the carronade. We'll maybe not save the ship but we'll give a good account of ourselves before it's over.'

'Why not surrender?' Cecilia Dullant pleaded. 'You have done all that any man could do. You are bleeding to death.'

'Lock yourself in the cabin, ma'am.'

'There's one man walking forward on 'is own, sir. 'e's waving a white cloth,' the seaman said excitedly. 'A tall feller 'e is. Looks as if 'e wants ter talk wi' us.'

'Surrender your ship,' the man called in faultless English. 'You cannot save it. I have two hundred men on board. There will be no more bloodshed if you lay down your arms. You have my word on it.'

'Are you English?' Chandler asked in astonishment.

'More so than His Majesty, King George, I do declare.'

'Who are you?' Lawson demanded. 'I've heard your voice before.'

'So you have, Captain, many times. We were midshipmen together. Men now call me Yussaiff Ahmed. You knew me as Peter Heward. I must confess myself disappointed that you don't recognise me.'

'Recognise you,' Lawson snarled. 'If I could see you, I'd be at your throat. That blast of yours burned my eyes. I'm blind, damn you. Damn you—to hell.'

He slipped through the lady's arms and fell to the deck.

6

A NAGGING call of duty brought Lawson out of his fever three days later. He had been rising in a crazy spiral of flashing lights and stabbing pain, with Peter Heward at every level, looking just as he had in his midshipman days but dressed in an outlandish costume of baggy trousers, curled up slippers and a fez. He awoke to find himself in pitch darkness and lay for a few minutes trying to unravel the facts of the last few weeks from the fantasies of his illness. His eyes had been damaged. That much he could remember without difficulty because the pain was still there and by lowering and raising his eyebrows he could feel the dressing about his head. But he had been on the deck of his ship. Now he was in a bed and on shore at that. Obviously he was a prisoner. Even as the realisation came to him he noticed that his arms were restricted. He struggled to free himself but relaxed when he found his bonds to be nothing more than a bed sheet swathed around him. He eased one arm free and was exploring the bandages over his eyes when a long-drawn-out breath, only a few inches away, froze him into rigidity. Someone was sharing his bed.

He listened in disbelief to the quiet breathing that followed, before sliding an investigating leg in the direction of the sleeper. Its progress was arrested by the blankets tucked under him. Cautiously he extended his arm. Whoever it was lay above the coverings and the waist he encountered was surely too soft and slim for a man. His hand crept higher. Now there was no doubt. His sleeping companion was wearing the flimsiest of garments. She sighed and though he withdrew his hand instantly, she was awake.

He felt her slip from the bed. Then her fingers were at his pulse and the back of her hand against his cheek.

'The fever seems to have left you. How are you feeling, Captain?'

'Who are you?'

'Cecilia Dullant.'

He lay in silence considering this piece of information. In bed with the wife of an admiral—! A stab of pain in his head drove the wonder of it from his mind. He groaned involuntarily.

'Drink this.'

She raised his head carefully and held him closely in the curve of her arm. Lawson gulped at the liquid and grimaced.

'God! What's that stuff?'

'Something the doctor left to get rid of the fever.'

'I thought the only medicine known to our surgeon was alcohol.'

'It was not from Doctor Baxter. He is down with the wounded in a warehouse that's in use as a hospital. You are in the care of a medical man especially brought for the purpose by Yussaiff Ahmed. He appears to be very good.'

'So we are prisoners of Yussaiff Ahmed—Peter Heward that was. What's this place we are in—a dungeon?'

'No—o. It's a delightful little cottage, set upon a hillside overlooking the bay. We have a veranda protected from the sun and——'

'And an armed guard sitting on it.'

'There is a man there. How did you know?'

'I can smell him,' Lawson said sourly.

'Oh!—I can't.'

'No more can I. His sword clinked against something a short time ago. So we lost the frigate?'

'Mr Chandler surrendered immediately after your collapse. He had no other course, apart from sacrificing the lives of his men.'

'Let us hope that their lordships take the same view at our

56

court martial. But you said that *we* have a veranda. How many of us are imprisoned in this place?'

'Just the two of us. I have the next room.'

'A room each, eh?'

Cecilia could not see Lawson's eyebrows raise under the bandages but his tone indicated just that. She coloured.

'And I was sharing your bed because the alternatives were either to rush from my room a dozen times a night or sleep on the floor,' she said spiritedly. 'I tried the floor but the mice are too numerous.'

'Oh!' Lawson grinned ruefully. 'I've been a difficult patient?'

'Not really. It was just that you tried to tear the dressings from your eyes on several occasions and so each time I heard you tossing about I felt it necessary to see how you were.'

'You should have tied my hands behind my back.'

'That was the doctor's suggestion. I compromised by wrapping you in the sheet like a cocoon.'

They heard the crunch of feet approaching the cottage and the sound of the guard on the veranda gathering his things together. It was the change of the watch.

'How often do they do that?' Lawson asked quietly.

'Every hour or thereabouts. This will be the last of the night watch. It is almost dawn. A fierce old man takes over through the day.'

'Old!'

'But fierce—and armed with a nasty looking sword and a brace of pistols. More than a match for Captain Lawson whilst his eyes are covered with bandages, so make the most of the opportunity you have to rest.'

'Does he ever——?'

'I am going to bed, Captain,' she interrupted with a smile, 'and since you are sufficiently recovered to be contemplating an attempt at the guard, perhaps it would be wiser if I went to my own room.'

57

She pulled the bed covers over his shoulders, brushed her hand against his cheek and left him to his thoughts.

The swish of bead curtains, followed by the slither of sandalled feet warned Lawson that he had a visitor some two hours later. The man's breathing was laboured as he bent over the couch and Lawson struggled against a feeling of nausea as his foul breath wafted against his face. Slow fingers unwrapped the bandages. When they were removed the doctor began to pick at a covering of clay over the left eye. Slowly he peeled it away. Immediately Lawson knew that he would be able to see again. He could make out the outline of the doctor's face as it reflected the light from the open door. Fretting with impatience he awaited the removal of the second clay cover.

The old doctor took a pot containing a glutinous grey substance from a straw bag. He scooped out some and oozed it through his fingers before smoothing the cool paste gently but meticulously into the hollow of the eye and under the lids. Then he replaced the clay patch and, to Lawson's disappointment, began to swathe his head in bandages again.

'What about the other?'

The old man went on with his bandaging and Lawson resigned himself philosophically. Evidently the right eye was worse than the left, he thought gloomily as he eased himself onto one side to allow the doctor to examine his thigh.

He had no interest in the thigh wound. He knew it to be nothing more than a tear in the fleshy part caused by a six-inch splinter of wood that he had pulled out himself. It was painful and such an injury had often caused death but Lawson had good healing flesh and he had sustained a dozen similar gashes during the course of his career. The doctor smeared the wound with another of his collection of ointments, gathered his things together and left.

A few minutes later a jingle of spurs warned Lawson that he had another visitor.

'Good morning, John.' Yussaiff Ahmed, immaculate from his

starred headdress to his gleaming boots, advanced to the couch. 'Are you feeling better?'

Lawson grunted.

'I have some very hopeful news about your eyes,' Heward went on imperturbably. 'The doctor is of the opinion that the damage is not serious.'

'Does he know what he's talking about?'

'My dear John! You must not regard the Moors as primitives. I do declare that this old man knows more about doctoring than half a dozen of your ship's surgeons, unless things have changed radically since I sailed with the fleet.'

Lawson grunted sceptically and settled himself back in the cushions.

'Pity you didn't stay with the fleet.'

Heward grinned.

'Had I done so you would have been sweating it out on half pay in that obscure Yorkshire town of yours. Either that or pounding the pavement outside Admiralty waiting for a ship. Don't forget that I was responsible for your commission. How did your orders run now? "You are requested to seek out and destroy the ship commanded by the aforementioned Yussaiff Ahmed." '

Lawson thrust himself angrily into a sitting position.

'You've been going through my papers, damn you.'

'But of course I have, John. Wouldn't you do the same in my position?'

Lawson gradually relaxed as he saw the truth of his words. Anyone with sense would examine a captured ship's papers at the first opportunity. Heward's trespassing was objectionable only because they had known each other in different circumstances.

'I should never allow myself to be in your position,' he grumbled as he settled himself back against the cushions. 'How did it come about anyway?'

'How did what come about?' Heward countered unhelpfully.

'Your being here,' Lawson gestured vaguely, at a loss for words, 'a gentleman accepted as a leader by——'

'Gentleman!' Heward scoffed. 'That's my good old Yorkshire John talking. Seaman, yes. Gentleman, pouff. A man is a man and I made my way here on the strength of that alone.'

'But what of your family?'

'To hell with my family. It was my father who sent me to serve under a madman like Wainwright. He knew his reputation. Then he disowned me when news of my trouble reached England. Now my brothers and sister are sharing my inheritance between them. If I thought I'd half a chance of getting away with it, I'd sail my fleet up the Severn and put a few broadsides into the damned ancestral home.'

He thrust himself from the stool and began to pace the room. Lawson waited in silence. Eventually Heward paused in front of an ornate glass mirror and stared at his reflection. He laughed shortly; an explosive sound without humour.

'I'm behaving like a peevish child. You see what the mention of my father does to me. But you asked me how I became the leader of these merry corsairs. You will surely have heard the first part of the story?'

'Yes! I learned something of it.'

Indeed the whole Navy had heard. It had been the chief topic of conversation for long after the event. Not often had a captain, even one as bad as Wainwright, been knocked down on his own quarterdeck by one of his lieutenants. It had seemed to some that the spirit of mutiny, still feared after Spithead and the Nore, some nineteen years earlier, had at last reached the officers.

'I've no doubt you heard a sadly one-sided story of the business,' Heward said dryly. 'However it's the result and not the cause that'll interest you. I got out of the bilge where Captain, may-he-rot-in-hell, Wainwright saw fit to chain me. I'll not be telling you how, since the man who helped me is, as far as I know, still alive and maybe with a ship of his own. I slipped over the side and swam the best part of five miles to shore.'

'I knew that much,' Lawson said, 'and strange as it may seem, the account I heard and the one that passed around the fleet was not so one-sided as you may think. It's common knowledge that Captain Wainwright ran foul of Lord Nelson over this affair. But how did you come to be received so kindly by the scum of the North African coast? I thought they had a short way with infidels.'

'These fellows will overlook a lot in a good seaman but as far as religion is concerned I am the best Mohammedan of them all.'

'How long have you been a Mohammedan?'

'Since the moment I pulled myself ashore and saw half a dozen fierce looking devils bearing down upon me.'

He took a leather-bound book from a small table and thrust it into Lawson's hands.

'What is it?' Lawson asked.

'That, my dear friend of days long past, is the Koran. Damn me if I can read much of it, but I take it on every voyage. It's my certificate of worthiness if you like. I have my prayer mat like the rest of them and I use it five times a day. Believe me, John, it's far better to beat your head on the deck boards than to have no head to beat.'

'May I see it?' Cecilia asked.

She had entered quietly. Lawson wondered how long she had been there. He wondered also about her voice. She sounded more like a schoolma'am, about to confiscate sticky sweets, than a prisoner. Heward's reply puzzled him even more.

'No. You may not. I bid you both good day.'

He swept from the room with the book under his arm.

'Now what was that about?' Lawson asked.

Before she had the opportunity to speak, Heward was back.

'What became of Jim Saunders?' he demanded.

Lawson suddenly remembered about young Jim. The recollection jerked him to a sitting position.

'God! He was atop the mast when your damned barrel exploded on the fore——'

His voice trailed off as he realised that Heward could know nothing about his midshipman. He had been referring to the boy's father. They had served together as lieutenants on the *Agadir* and Saunders had risked his career by defending a junior officer against his captain, at the enquiry following Heward's escape. He sank back onto his pillows.

'He lost his sight at Trafalgar,' he said listlessly.

'Blinded!' Heward exclaimed. 'The devil take his luck. No one loved the sea more than Saunders. What a tragedy! Now I suppose he's rotting ashore on half pension. You must let me know how I can help——'

The expression on the lady's face halted him in mid-sentence. The lines around his mouth drooped in dismay. He was no longer a leader of murderers and thieves but a very young man, a youth even, painfully conscious of having said the wrong thing.

'I'm sorry, John. I wasn't thinking.'

Cecilia had moved across to the couch. She bent over Lawson and smoothed out the cushions. There were tears in her eyes.

'But have no worries about your eyes,' Heward said with false heartiness. 'They'll be as good as ever in a few days. The old doctor swears there's no permanent damage.—What were you saying about someone being atop the mast?'

'Saunders' son—only child. The sun rises and sets by him. It'll be the end of your old shipmate if he's gone, I can tell you. Must have fallen in the sea I suppose. If he survived the fall, those devils of yours will make short work of him when they find him.'

'Have no fear on that score. If the boy is still alive, I'll see he comes to no harm. The debt I owe his——'

He left the rest unsaid and hurried out. A few minutes later a gong boomed deeply, echoing far across the bay. Then there was the sound of men passing the house, hurrying feet, the clink of steel and the excited chatter of strange tongues.

'There is still some good in him,' Cecilia murmured.

She was sitting on the couch close by Lawson's hand. He reached out and took her arm. She made no attempt to free herself.

'Still? You speak as if you knew him before he turned pirate.'

She looked down at him. Her breast heaved in a sigh. She patted his hand and released her arm. Then she rose from the couch and walked across to the veranda to watch the crowd of men assembling at the quay.

'Yes, Captain. I knew him.'

So Mallory was right, Lawson mused. Not that it was significant any more. The social world of the Navy was small. Heward would have been twenty-one or thereabouts when he had deserted; a dashing young man with family links among the hierarchy of the Navy and Government. He must have rated highly as an eligible bachelor. That had been twelve years ago. The admiral's wife must be about the same age. Maybe they had been lovers. Unaccountably he felt a twinge of jealousy and resentment.

Meanwhile, down at the quayside all work on the ships had been abandoned. The Moors, who had struggled since dawn with a new mast for *Comus*, were either ashore, preparing to scour the surrounding countryside, or scudding across the bay in all directions. The great search was on. Yussaiff Ahmed's promised reward for anybody who could bring back Jim Saunders unharmed, was big enough to keep any three men in luxury for the rest of their lives.

Directing all this activity was Heward. Magnificently mounted on a white horse he cantered from group to group, pointing out the areas he wanted them to search. He looked every inch the leader but it was obvious that his wisdom was being questioned by the two men who followed him. They too were leaders, richly dressed and equally well mounted. Judging by their angry faces and gesticulations, they disapproved strongly of this delay in their preparations for sea.

The ninety British seamen, who had been huddled together on the waterfront under the ready muskets of a dozen villainous-looking corsairs, watched Heward curiously. They had all heard of his introduction on the quarterdeck of *Comus*. Postill, the grizzled old quartermaster who had merely added another scar and a few burns to his body during the action in the bay, had supplied all the details. He had been with the fleet at the time.

'What do you make of this, Mr Barty?' Chandler asked.

'Dunno, sir. But whatever it is, I hope they keep at it. I'd far rather sit in the sun than heave any more damn barrels about. We must have put enough water aboard these ships to keep them three months at sea.'

'I'm going to have a word with this fellow,' Chandler said.

He rose abruptly and attempted to step out of the group. Immediately two guards threatened him with muskets.

'I want to speak to your chief,' he said indicating Heward.

One of the guards prodded him viciously in the chest with his musket and shouted. Heward turned from the two men who had been arguing with him and watched. At last he shouted something in Arabic and the guard reluctantly allowed the young lieutenant to pass. He walked up to Heward, who awaited his approach with expressionless face.

'I think, sir,' Chandler began stiffly, 'that I have the right to know what you intend to do with us.'

Heward's face twitched into a fleeting smile.

'I should be pleased to tell you, if I knew.'

The two pirates with Heward exchanged a few angry words and Chandler required no interpreter to tell him that they had no doubts. Heward ignored them. He smiled down at Chandler.

'You must understand that you are all a deuced embarrassment. If I gave my men a free hand they would cut the throat of every man here, or sell you into slavery. They don't consider you worth holding for ransom. If I leave you behind when I sail, one or the other will certainly be your fate. If I take you with me, I should be forced to watch you twenty-four hours a day. What is one to do with you? I should be delighted if you could offer a solution.'

Chandler was taken aback by his logic.

'Well, sir,' he said without conviction, 'you could perhaps restore yourself out of this situation. With your help we could take these ships while your men are scattered about. There would still be a court martial for you of course but I am convinced that their Lordships would feel kindly disposed towards you. You would certainly be pardoned.'

He would have added to his suggestion but the eyes burning into his were those of Yussaiff Ahmed. The languid Peter Heward had been thrust into the background. Chandler's face blanched.

'You appear to have a very poor opinion of me, Mr Chandler.' Heward's voice was barely above a whisper but there was no mistaking the threat it carried. 'Go back to your men before I have you whipped.'

He kicked his heels into his stallion and cantered away. The others followed him leaving Chandler standing alone. Just as suddenly he wheeled about before he had gone a hundred yards and came back. He pulled his horse expertly to a halt and laughed without humour.

'You're a young fool. Possibly I am becoming an old one. However, you and your midshipman may visit your wounded and make any arrangements you think fit to ensure their comfort.'

He shouted an order to one of the guards who waved his hand in acknowledgement. Then he turned his horse again and galloped away from the bay in the direction of the long line of low hills to the east.

'I don't know what to make of him,' said Chandler to his captain some fifteen minutes later.

65

'Then don't worry yourself about it,' Lawson replied sourly. 'You'll be far better occupied watching for an opportunity to get us out of this mess. How many fighting men has he?'

Chandler looked uncomfortable.

'Perhaps five hundred. N—o, probably not as many as that. Maybe between three and four hundred.'

'Find out, man. Use your mother wit. Watch them carefully. I want you to report back to me tomorrow with a reasonable estimate of their number.'

Lawson's voice had an edge to it and Chandler stiffened.

'Aye aye, sir. Er—will there be anything else, sir?'

Lawson stretched himself meditatively. Now that he had the eyes of his lieutenant to give him a picture of the bay and its defences, a workable plan of escape might emerge.

'Get all the information you can. Pay attention to the rig of the ships in the bay. We may need to get one out in a hurry. Find out where their arsenal is ashore. They must have a good supply of powder, if they are prepared to toss barrels of it about. Check on their armament—shore defences. Ask our men if any of them have knives or weapons of any kind. Have you a list of our wounded?'

'No, sir.'

'Then get one by tomorrow,' he said with asperity. 'I want to know exactly how many men we can muster and who they are. How is Mr Jones?'

'Bearing up quite well, sir, as I understand. I shall go to him as soon as I leave you.'

'Very good. Give him my compliments and best wishes for his recovery. Good day to you.'

As Chandler walked limply out of the building, Barty, who had been lounging under the hostile eye of an aged but formidable-looking guard, eased himself away from the wall, winked impudently into the old man's face and fell into step alongside his senior officer.

'What did he have to say, sir?' he asked.

'Mind your own bloody business,' snapped the aggrieved lieutenant.

He stumped off, leaving the midshipman to follow in his footsteps.

7

FROM the shelter of a wadi on the hillside to the south of the village, another midshipman, gaunt and tattered, lay with two seamen watching the captain's visitors walk away from the house.

'Well?' said Saunders. 'What do you think?'

Thompson lowered the telescope and grinned.

'I reckon the captain's inside those four walls for sure. Mr Chandler looks as though he were sent off wi' a flea in his ear. 'Old on a minute.' He raised the glass again. 'Someone else going in—ah! Food it is this time. What would I give to be sharing it wi' him!'

Jim Saunders sighed. The three of them had fared very badly since they had been pitched into the bay with the fore-mast. Jakes, the other seaman, had tried to surrender but they had prevented him. Then two wandering chickens had been coaxed into the wadi and they had devoured them raw. Apart from that they had eaten nothing in three days. On this sandy stretch of the coast, every man's hand was against them and every small patch of cultivated ground had sharp-eared, savage dogs for its protection.

'What can we do now?' Jakes whined. 'We might as well go down and join the others. At least we'll get somethin' to eat. I reckon that feller on the white 'orse has set his men to look for us. If they come across us up 'ere, they'll make short work of us, I'll be bound.'

'Hold your noise and let your betters do the thinking,' Thompson said contemptuously. 'While we are free we can mayhap do a bit o' good. Once we get down there with muskets ready to blow our heads off, we'll be no better than the rest of them.'

Saunders rolled onto his back and regarded both men thoughtfully. He was a child by comparison but clearly they were looking to him for direction. The more reliable of the two was obviously Thompson. The other was a weak straw who might cause their undoing if they did not watch him.

'As soon as it gets dark, I'm going in to see the captain,' the midshipman said decisively.

Thompson looked at him in astonishment.

'What about the sentry?'

'I'll think of something for him,' Saunders said. 'Now let us rest until tonight. You can keep watch, Jakes. I shall not need you.'

He thrust the telescope into Jakes' hands, turned onto his back and closed his eyes, well aware that both men were watching him intently for signs of weakness and he knew instinctively that if he as much as glanced in their direction they would question his authority. At length he was reassured by the sounds of Thompson settling himself and Jakes scrambling back up the side of the wadi to keep a watch on the harbour.

At sunset Saunders gave up all pretence of sleeping and shook Thompson into wakefulness. Then he joined Jakes.

'Anything of interest happened?' he asked.

The man nodded gloomily in the direction of the harbour.

'They've fed that lot down there. Now they've been locked up again on the ship nearest to the quay.'

Saunders took up the telescope and scrutinised the deck of the *Princess Mary* carefully. It now had its yards crossed and the canvas had been bent on to them, lashed into sausage-like bundles with gaskets. It was not as neat as the Navy would have done it, but it looked ready for sea. Two guards sat on a carronade that had been swung around to command the hatch. Another guard was perched on a bollard, nodding over a musket which lay across his knees.

'A few determined men could maybe overcome the sentries without bringing the whole nest about their ears.'

'What then, sir?'

Saunders noted with satisfaction that Thompson had called him sir; the first time since they had escaped from the frigate. It required only a workable plan to win him over to unquestioning obedience and Jakes would certainly follow his lead.

'Having attended to the sentries we could either bring some of our men on deck quietly or shake out the topsails and work our way from between the other ships and the quay. They'd hear us moving out for sure but by the time they roused themselves, there would be enough of us ready to throw them back over the side.'

'I'm willing to try it,' Thompson said eagerly.

'First I need to see the captain, so I think we'll try an old trick to move the man at the door.'

'Knock him over the head, sir?' Thompson asked cheerfully.

'No, we'd better not hit him. The captain may not agree to our plan. In which case we don't want a missing guard and every man in the neighbourhood searching for him. If possible I shall get in without him being any the wiser.'

' 'Ow do you expect to get past him? He's stood right afore the door,' Jakes jeered.

'Do be quiet!' Saunders exclaimed in annoyance.

The man spat and turned away sulkily. Saunders ignored him and leaned closer to Thompson.

An hour later they rose from the wadi and began to make their way down hill towards the cottage. They had not gone fifty yards before Jakes came hurrying after them.

'What about me?' he whined. 'I'm not staying here on my own.'

Before the midshipman could reply, Thompson had placed one horny hand against the man's face and pushed. He sprawled on the ground.

'Shut up and get back up there,' Thompson hissed viciously.

70

Jakes scrambled away, clearly expecting a blow to follow. Thompson waited for further complaint. There being none he turned to Saunders.

'We can go now, sir, but maybe it would be better if you took your boots off. The leather will crunch the grit and like as not you'll kick a stone or two on the way down.'

Saunders kicked more than a stone or two by the time they reached the cottage and his feet were raw enough to make him wish he had followed the seamen's practice of not wearing shoes on board ship. Thompson had no such troubles. It was he who grabbed the midshipman by the shoulders to steady him whenever sharp flints under the tender parts of his soles caused him to lose his balance.

As agreed they paused at the side of the cottage. The plan was for Thompson to draw the guard away from the door by throwing stones down the hill or, if that were not successful, by allowing himself to be seen. They were about to separate when Thompson seized the midshipman's arm.

'I reckon he's due for relief, sir,' he whispered with the certainty of one long accustomed to weary watches. 'Hark how he's moving about, restless like. We'd do well to wait a bit.'

Thompson proved to be right. A few minutes later they heard someone trudging from the bay towards them. The guard heard him too. He slung his musket over his shoulder and walked around the house to meet him, leaving the two dark figures with an unexpectedly easy approach to the veranda.

The door was secured with a heavy wooden bar which had been simply wedged against it ; a makeshift arrangement to stop a sudden onslaught from the inside rather than for permanent security. It was the work of a moment to remove it and slip through.

'Just holler if you need any help,' Thompson hissed from outside. 'I'll be hiding near by.'

Saunders stood breathlessly in the darkness of the cottage. Obviously he would have to grope his way around and it was possible that there would be a jailer inside. He waited until

71

the relief guard stepped onto the veranda, then using the sounds he was making to hide those of his own, he crept forward until he encountered a wall. He turned left and found himself entangled in noisy bead curtains. No sooner had he slipped through them than he was seized by the throat from behind.

Frantically he kicked backwards but his attacker was ready for him and his stockinged heel made no impression on the man's thigh. Then he felt the life being squeezed out of him and he knew nothing could save him. His senses were reeling when somewhere in the distance he heard a woman's voice shouting. Immediately the cruel pressure on his throat was relaxed and the hands that had been strangling him were supporting his drooping body.

'Jim, lad. Are you all right?' Lawson asked anxiously.

Saunders nodded his head weakly and fingered his throat. Gradually he became aware that he was in a room dimly illuminated by a shaft of moonlight from a high window. Captain Lawson was holding him. The other person, patting his hands and face and easing him out of the captain's arms, was a woman. He allowed her to lead him to a bed listening to her soothing voice and wondering vaguely who she could be.

'Quiet!' Lawson hissed. 'The sentry!'

They waited in breathless silence. The guard outside was now unnaturally quiet. He too was listening. Cecilia's voice must have reached him. After what seemed an age they heard the snick of a flintlock mechanism, followed by stealthy footsteps across the veranda. Now he had changed his mind about the musket and was propping it against the doorpost. The muzzle scraped a few inches and came to rest. There was the unmistakable slither of steel against a scabbard and the easing of the door timbers as the heavy wooden bar was removed. Lawson carefully parted the bead curtains, groped his way to the entrance and pressed his body against the wall, hoping that no ray of moonlight would reveal him when the door opened.

The hinges squeaked and Lawson felt the night air on his face. A blade swept in front of his nose and he knew that he had not been seen. The guard was now within inches of him. creeping over the threshold, testing each step on the creaking boards and restricting his breathing. Lawson's fingers crooked as he tensed himself for the spring that might send the point of the sword through him.

An unmistakable thud announced a change in the situation. The guard lurched forward at the exact moment that Lawson was reaching for him and the two of them sprawled in the darkness. Powerful hands were already at the man's throat but the flesh was unresisting. He had been unconscious before Lawson had touched him.

'Are you all right, sir?' Thompson asked anxiously. 'I felt I had to clobber him when I saw him going in after you.'

Lawson felt an almost uncontrollable urge to laugh. Such was his relief on hearing the voice of a British seaman.

'Who are you?' he demanded as he heaved himself to his feet.

'Thompson, sir, fore topmast.'

'Well, Thompson, if ever we get out of this mess, I'll see that you benefit from this night's work. Now do you keep a weather eye open while I talk things over with Mr Saunders.'

He closed the door on the seaman and turned briskly to Saunders.

'Now we'll have your report, my lad.'

The midshipman had not been wasting his time on the hillside. He unfolded a mental picture of the village and the ships, the powder store and the building which housed the wounded. All the facts that Lawson needed to know were dealt with in rapid succession, including the number of the enemy, estimated at three hundred and fifty. He nodded his head in satisfaction. His nephew was proving to be a good officer. Even his plan to ease the ship away from the quayside was worth considering but Lawson's mind was already dwelling upon other factors that could be brought to their assistance.

'This building where the wounded are housed is in a hollow,

73

you say. Do you think that a blast from the arsenal would reach them?'

Saunders did not need to give the matter any further thought. The possibility of blowing up the powder store had occurred to him and he had spent several hours considering the effects of the blast.

'I think it might just take the roof off, sir, if it touched it at all. Most of the village would be flattened though, provided they keep enough powder there. The ships lying by the quay would certainly be destroyed since they are only fifty yards from the place but *Comus* should weather the explosion. She lies well out in the bay.'

'Good! Go and collect this fellow you left on the hillside. We're going to set our lads free and teach these damned corsairs a lesson before morning.'

'Is this not a very desperate plan that you are embarking upon, Captain?' Cecilia asked quietly when Saunders had left.

'No more desperate than our situation, ma'am. Our lives would be worth nothing if Peter Heward withdrew his protection, or if his authority is successfully challenged, and it's likely to be when they discover that one of their guards has been attacked. We have no alternative other than to strike at once.'

'But you can't even see.'

'You shall be my eyes,' Lawson replied cheerfully.

She sighed.

'Very well, Captain, I shall lead you, but not,' she added emphatically, 'until you are dressed.'

Lawson remembered with a shock that he was attired just as he had been when the sound of the door opening had brought him from his bed; in a voluminous nightshirt. He allowed himself to be led to a seat and, without a word, took the trousers she handed to him. When he had dressed he peeled the patch from his left eye, went to the door and called Thompson inside.

'He's a regular walking armoury, sir,' Thompson said happily as he searched the guard a few minutes later. 'Blest if he ain't a-carrying two pistols as well as a wondrous cruel knife. Then there's the musket out there. Do you take the pistols, sir?'

'No. Give me the knife. The lady will have a pistol.'

A knife for close quarter work would be the only weapon that would be of any use to him. He was going to be very much a bystander in the coming struggle; not even capable of defending his guide, he thought bitterly. She had better be armed—to take her own life if they were recaptured.

'You'd better understand that I will not be able to help you to get rid of these fellows who are keeping watch. I can't see a damned thing apart from a peep of light that's getting in on the port side, and that counts for nothing. So it's up to you, Thompson. Take the guards without a sound and I'll attend to the rest. Allow one of them to give the alarm and we'll have the pack about our ears. Do you understand me?'

'You want me to do it alone, sir?'

'Aye. One man's better than half a dozen for a job like this.'

8

'WE'RE very close to the quay, sir,' Saunders whispered. 'I can make out the top spars of the ships that are lying there. Will you wait with the lady?'

'We'll all wait, except Thompson. He will go on alone.'

The big seaman slipped away into the shadows. Lawson and the others stood where they were, listening breathlessly. There was the sound of the water lapping at the pebbles a few yards to their right and somewhere in the distance the howl of a dog. Otherwise all was still. Cecilia, who had been leading Lawson, clutched nervously at his hand. Automatically he placed his arm around her and she nestled into his shoulder.

'I'm afraid,' she whispered.

He held her closer but said nothing. She had good reason for her fears. Heward would not be able to protect her a second time and there was too big a demand for attractive women for them to allow her the easy escape of death should she be recaptured. She would amuse the pirates until they could get her to Algiers. Then she would be pawed over and sold in the slave market.

'Thompson should be aboard now so we'll creep up on them. Keep low and not a sound. Take care with that damned musket, man,' he hissed at Jakes, who had prodded him in the back.

They crouched almost to all fours and worked their way slowly to the stone cobbles of the quay. There they kept close to the wall of a warehouse until the sound of a cough brought them to a halt. They heard the sentry clearing his throat noisily. He could be no more than forty yards away. He coughed again—a short choking sound this time. Then there was nothing to be heard other than the creaking of a yard and the faint sigh of a breeze through cordage.

Saunders' lips almost touched the captain's ear.

'I think Thompson's taken care of the watch, sir.'

Lawson gripped his arm warningly. There was another sound —a brief scuffle followed by a dull thud and another. Cecilia gripped Lawson tightly and he felt the tremor in her body. She was going to be sick. That second crunch had been someone's skull.

Now the great bulk of Thompson was coming towards them along the quay. They stepped out of the shadows and joined him.

'All clear, sir,' he said quietly. 'Will you go aboard now?'

They climbed on deck and found the hatch cover. It was difficult to move the wedges without a hammer but they managed it after a few minutes. Then they slid the heavy timber silently to one side and Lawson prepared to climb down into the hold. A half blind man would be as good as anyone in that black pit and it was important that a warning about absolute silence should come from the captain. He had descended no more than three steps when the sound of stealthy movement below warned him of his danger. It would be a grim end to the adventure if he were to be strangled in the dark by his own men.

'Mr Chandler,' he whispered hoarsely.

There was a stir and a few whispers followed by a breathless silence. Cupping his hands over his mouth he raised his voice a little.

'This is your captain. I'm coming below to talk to you and I'll have any man who makes a sound tied to the gratings as soon as we get back on board *Comus*.'

If there had been any doubt that the Navy was coming to their rescue, the reference to the grating and the implied flogging would have dispelled it. This was what Lawson had intended. He lowered himself until he was just above their heads.

'We're going to work this ship away from the other two that are lashed alongside.'

'They're full of men, sir,' Chandler said.

'I know, I know,' Lawson growled impatiently. 'You, Mr

Chandler, will take half a dozen strong swimmers and follow Thompson to the magazine. As soon as you see this ship moving away from the quay, break into the building and blow it up —preferably without blowing yourselves to bits.'

'What then, sir?'

'You can get yourself into the water and swim out to *Comus*. We shall have taken it by that time. Get away now.'

'Aye aye, sir,' Chandler replied happily. 'O'Brien, you're about the strongest swimmer we have so no doubt you'll know of any others. Name five and let's get out of here.'

When the magazine party had left, Lawson addressed the remainder.

'There are three hundred men and more in the two ships alongside, and if we make a sound during the next few minutes they are going to pour on deck and cut our throats.' He paused to let the warning sink in. 'I want the starboard watch to stand over the gangways on both ships to make sure that no one gets on deck. Arm yourself with belaying pins or whatever takes your fancy.'

This was more to their liking and he sensed their impatience.

'Mr Barty, you will take charge of these men. The rest of us will be working the ship away from the quay. As soon as you see us getting clear, close ranks and fight your way back to us. If any of you are too late to get aboard, take to the water and strike out for the shelter of the quay. When the magazine goes up you'll need to get out of the way of the blast. Is Mr Postill still with us?'

'Here I am, sir.'

'I'll have you on deck first with your best top men. The rest of you follow.'

Lawson climbed back to the deck where Saunders immediately advised him that Chandler's party had already gone ashore.

'Very good, Mr Saunders. Take four men with you and cast off. If you can do it without setting the other ships adrift, so much the better. Mr Postill?'

'Here I am, sir,' the elderly quartermaster whispered.

'I can hardly see a bloody thing so you'll have to work the ship out on your own. Once you are clear, lay us alongside *Comus*. Let me have a man who can give me an account of what's happening and start us moving as soon as you can.'

Lawson suddenly felt tired. There was nothing more for him to do and he dare not move from where he stood without a guide. Cautiously he groped for the side of the hatch and sat down, wondering what could have happened to Cecilia. She came to him a few seconds later.

'There's a bed in the captain's cabin and I think you ought to be in it,' she said.

Lawson grinned and felt for her hand.

'Sit down, Cecilia. There's nothing I would like better than a long sleep but I have to remain here.'

Even as he spoke he wondered about his familiarity. She was, after all, the admiral's wife. Sit down, Cecilia? He must be getting light-headed. She sat down nevertheless and held his arm while the silent activity of working the ship out went on about them.

'I've got to report what's 'appening, sir,' a seaman's voice said on the other side of him.

'Very well,' Lawson replied cheerfully.

The ship swayed gently under their feet. They were loose from their moorings. Their bows swung away from the land breeze and bumped gently against the ship alongside.

'It won't be long before we hear from them,' Lawson said. 'Are we under way?'

'Nobbut just, sir,' the man replied doubtfully, 'and there's summat stirring down below on t'other ship. We'll be fair pushed to get away wi'out a spot of bother, I'm thinking—sir.'

Lawson smiled at the broad Yorkshire dialect and the hasty addition of 'sir'. The man spoke exactly as his father used to speak and he could have slipped into the same with no difficulty whatsoever.

79

Someone on the ship next to theirs was giving excited orders. There were the scamperings of bare feet, the bang of a pistol and the beating of a drum. Another drum ashore took up the warning and then the sound of battle dominated all others.

'There's a rare to do going on now,' the Yorkshireman said. 'Two of them just got out of yon hatch but that nigger servant of your'n parted the 'air of one of 'em wi' a boat-'ook. T'other one's gone o'er the side. Shouldn't be surprised if our lads couldn't keep this lark up all night.'

There was a crackle of musketry. Lawson did not need his commentator to tell him that it came from the shore.

'Guard against boarders from the quay,' he shouted.

'I think as 'ow Mr Chandler's lot has taken care of 'em, sir. There was a bit of a scuffle just now.—Aye, I can see one of our lads. He's dashing off again back to the arsenal wi' a musket in 'is 'and.'

Their starboard side leaned heavily against the ship next to it and the timbers groaned protestingly as they scraped by. They were getting clear, creeping slowly away from the quay, driven by a land air so weak that it could hardly fill the sails. But it was adequate and it seemed that nothing could stop them.

'Fire ashore!'

Lawson became aware of a dull gleam which grew until he could see the rigging of the ship silhouetted against it. The urge to try the other eye suddenly occurred to him and he felt for the clay covering. Cecilia's hand stopped him. At that moment Jim Saunders arrived breathlessly.

'There's a fire outside the magazine, sir!'

'Very good, Mr Saunders. Mr Chandler has evidently thought fit to employ that method to blow up the building.'

'But the wounded, sir.'

'You have already made clear the position of the wounded, Mr Saunders. They must take their chance with the rest of us. Get every available man to fend off from the quay and the ship that's alongside. It wants maybe one spark in that powder house to blow us all to kingdom come.'

80

Damn Chandler for a fool, he thought savagely. He's counting on the fire having to burn through the door to get at the powder. The door will be full of dry rot and will go up like tinder. What a bloody way to end it all !

In his agitation he had thrust himself to his feet and had stepped off in the direction of the quay. The Yorkshireman saved him from going headfirst down the hatch.

'We've stopped moving, sir.'

'Search the bulwarks for grappling irons,' Lawson shouted. 'See that they've hooked nothing on to our gun ports. Everybody drop what you are doing and find the obstruction.'

'They'd grappled us below, like you said, sir, and our lads has knocked the hooks off but we're still not moving an' there's nowt we can see that's holding us.'

The fire ashore was burning fiercely now and the Yorkshireman's voice had lost its cheerfulness. Suddenly Lawson had an inspiration.

'Look for the for'ard cable. A dozen men over the bows. Tread it under us or pull it clear. Look alive now.'

He linked his arms through those of Cecilia and the seaman.

'Take me for'ard,' he said.

As they hurried over the deck he explained what had probably happened but he was reasoning aloud rather than talking to them.

'There'll be a mooring cable wrapped around our bows. It would have been bone dry when Saunders lowered it into the water and it'll be floating just below the surface. Wouldn't have held us if we hadn't lost the way we had on us—or if we had a bit of wind.'

More than a dozen men had taken the plunge. By now they all knew the significance of the fire, and the water below the level of the quay offered temporary safety. They had found the cable and were dragging it clear. Lawson became aware that the Yorkshireman was pulling at his arm.

'Some of the devils has got out, sir,' he said urgently. 'They've cleared our lads from one of t'hatches and their heathen mates is pouring out on deck. It'll be all up wi' 'em soon.'

Lawson tore his mind away from the fouling cable and the burning magazine to consider the new crisis. There was no point in leaving his men on the pirate ships any longer. They were practically unarmed and it could be only a matter of minutes before they were all cut down. The best plan would be to bring them on board and try to defend the short length of bulwark that still leaned against the port bow of the enemy.

'Mr Barty! Bring your men off.'

A whistle shrilled above the din of the battle and the Yorkshireman resumed his commentary.

'They're coming now, sir. Some of 'em's aboard. Mr Barty is swiping out wi' a cutlass and that nigger o' your'n is giving a good account of 'imself wi' that boat-'ook again. Mr Chandler's back wi' us, sir. Didn't see him come on but he's taken his men and they jumped across to t'other ship. They're knocking 'ell out o' them pirates as is trying to keep our lads from getting back.'

He paused.

'Go on, man. What else?'

'Some o' them pirates has jumped over the side,' he said in wonder. 'Some more's gone now. There's enough o' them to eat our lads but they're just running away like.'

Lawson nodded grimly. The Moors would know how much powder was stored in the magazine. Clearly they did not think that any of the ships had a chance of getting clear in time.

'Mr Chandler and t'others are holding their own now, sir. They're 'aving a rare to do——' He broke off his narrative as the deck trembled. 'We're moving, sir.'

Lawson already knew. He could hear the scraping timbers and the breath of a breeze in the rigging. The increased pressure on the sails and the men on the cable had had their effect. Suddenly they were free and sailing away from the quay.

The wheel came in line with the blaze on shore as Postill changed course to put the two moored ships between them and the magazine. The heavier sails cracked and filled under the influence of a breeze, which was no longer kept from them by the shore buildings, and every man on board seemed to be talking, laughing or just sighing with relief.

'Take me to the helmsman,' Lawson said.

Together they moved aft. There was no shooting. Those who might have fired after them were either rushing for the side and leaping into the water, or valiantly struggling to get their ships away. A splash from the outermost ship announced that they had cut the mooring cable.

'One of them is getting away, sir,' Chandler reported.

Her masts could be clearly seen as she passed the fire. Suddenly she checked and the tracery of her rigging swung in a semi-circle towards the shore.

'What's she up to?' Chandler's voice rose in excitement. 'She's rammed the quay, be damned. She's rammed the bloody quay.'

'My party passed a cable through the pintles, sir,' Saunders said.

'Caw!' exclaimed the Yorkshireman, forgetting himself in his admiration. 'She'll have pulled her bloody rudder off.'

'Keep your damned observations to yourself,' Chandler snarled.

He would have added more but the magazine went up.

At three hundred yards the blast rocked them violently and snapped a topgallant yard. Twin balls of fire soared high over the bay, separated at the highest point of their trajectory and fell into the water. Another reached out in a crazy twisting arc and plunged alongside. These were Chandler's pitch barrels. Men emerged from their cover and looked back at the shore. One of the ships was blazing from stem to stern. The other had disappeared.

'Both ships destroyed, sir.'

Lawson nodded an acknowledgement. He wanted to ask about the hospital building but there was a matter of greater urgency.

83

'Have the men stand by to board *Comus*, Mr Chandler.'

As the lieutenant hurried away he addressed the quartermaster.

'Can you see her, Mr Postill?'

'Dead ahead and coming up fast, sir.'

'Excellent. Just put us alongside.'

His thoughts raced on. Saunders had reported that few men appeared to be on board the frigate and indeed it seemed likely that the main body of the Moors would have been quartered near to the prison ship, ready to deal with any trouble from the prisoners. Those who were there would be watching their approach with guns loaded but it was unlikely that they would fire until they were sure that they were not attacking their own mates. No doubt they would have all guns well stuffed with grapeshot.

'Are you there, Mr Saunders?'

'Yes, sir.'

'Kindly inform Mr Chandler that I want the men well spread out and under cover until we are alongside.'

A voice shouted a challenge over the water. It shouted again, half an octave higher and charged with threat. Now many voices were to be heard and the squeal of gun carriages on deck boards. They were too late. Postill brought his charge cleverly into the wind and allowed it to fall back against the timbers of *Comus*.

Half a dozen guns crashed but the shot had passed under the upper deck and harmed no one. Lawson grinned delightedly. The man in charge was a fool. Those who had just fired from the gun deck would be out of the fight in the first crucial moment. They would have been far better employed manning the carronades and standing by to prevent boarders.

'Tell me exactly what is happening,' he ordered the quartermaster.

Postill's commentary lacked the raciness of that given by the seaman.

'We've got grappling irons well bedded, sir, and most of the lads are aboard.'

There was a tremendous cheer, as the men went into the attack, suddenly lost in the double roar of two carronades. Postill went on but Lawson was listening with only half of his attention. He could hear the exultant shouts and the voice of Chandler directing the battle. That told him all he needed to know. They were getting the upper hand. A few minutes should see the frigate back in the hands of its rightful owners.

'That's about it, I think, sir. Some of the pirates are jumping over the side. There's a few still holding out on the starboard side. It's all over, sir. They've surrendered.'

9

THE first light of dawn was already in the sky when Lawson climbed on board *Comus*. He had sent Cecilia to bed in one of the passengers' cabins on board the *Princess Mary*; the same that she had occupied before Yussaiff Ahmed had captured the ship. Now he had Thompson to help him find his way about, for he could see nothing clearly.

'Have you assessed the damage to the village?' he asked when Chandler reported to him.

'It's a wreck, sir. All the hovels near the water seem to be flat and most of those on the hill are damaged, as far as I can see in this light.'

'What about the place where the wounded were?'

Chandler's telescope swept searchingly to the right, settled then lowered slowly.

'I can see no trace of it, sir.'

Lawson turned abruptly to the sea. Forty men had been in that building. If the hollow had not protected them from the full effects of the blast, he would have their deaths on his conscience for the rest of his life. There was no doubt in his mind that he had done the right thing and any Naval Court would endorse his action, but he had to live with it. Even if he were commended for having retaken his ship and beating an enemy four times his strength, he would still be known throughout the Navy as the man who had sacrificed his wounded.

'Can you see any concentration of Moors?'

'There's no sign of life anywhere, sir.—Yes, there are a few people picking over the debris in the village: women, I think. No doubt there will be plenty lying under cover, waiting for us to go ashore.'

'We must go nevertheless. I will take a landing party to the site of the hospital.'

'But, sir ! You're bl——'

Lawson's one eye silenced him.

'Organise a party of twenty men. Include Thompson and Evans, my servant. Meanwhile we'll stand closer to the shore on *Comus,* so that you can bring the carronades into action if we need help.'

Lawson's plan of action was already clear in his mind. They would go ashore in two boats from the *Princess Mary* and each man would be armed with a musket and cutlass. They would advance in groups of five with fifty-yard intervals. If the first group encountered heavy opposition, maybe they and the five behind them would be able to hold the Moors whilst ten men escaped in one of the boats. In that way he would save a half of his party. He would be with those in front. Without the full use of his eyes he would be of little value in a fight but he could at least encourage those with him to make a stand.

'Landing-party ready, sir.'

Lawson plucked at the patch over his right eye. He would need every bit of light he could get over the next half hour or so. Slowly he peeled the clay back and blinked the ointment clear of the eyelid. He could see. The faces around him had an unreal quality, as though viewed from underwater, but they were visible nevertheless. The right eye was much stronger than the left and it would improve, he knew. His relief was so great that he grinned at the concerned face of his lieutenant.

'I'll take your cutlass, Mr Chandler,' he said gaily.

The men, mostly marines, lowered themselves into the boats. Lawson paused astride the bulwarks and addressed Chandler.

'You will organise the ship so that it can protect itself and the *Princess Mary*. In the event of our running into trouble you will come to our assistance only as far as you can with the guns aboard *Comus* but if you see that the situation is hopeless, you will immediately clear the bay and make for the open sea. On

87

no account will you land a relieving party. Do you understand my orders?'

'Perfectly, sir.'

The captain smiled at the unhappy expression on Chandler's face.

'Don't forget you have a lady on board the *Princess Mary*.'

Ten minutes later the boats ground on the shingle at a point near to where the wounded had been housed. The captain slid over the side into knee-deep water and splashed ashore. The men heaved on the boats.

'Steady there,' he warned as the two boats slid high and dry under the concerted heave of twenty men. 'We may need to get off again in a hurry. Leave the boats so that a couple of men can launch them.'

They were on the outskirts of the village and the ruins seemed to be just as deserted as Chandler had described them. Apart from a lazy curl of smoke from a large heap of debris, and a solitary gull hopping purposefully around a sea shell, there was no movement. Even the hens, which the day before had scratched and fought between the houses, were nowhere to be seen. It was as if every living soul had been annihilated, leaving their broken dwellings as a monument to their stay on earth.

Lawson scowled around him mistrustfully. He knew that the villagers had not been destroyed by the blast. The powder-house had burned too long for that. They would have had ample time to run for shelter before their homes had been flattened. Most of those who had jumped from the ship would have saved themselves too. They would be hiding and watching; waiting for a chance to revenge themselves on those who had landed. He tightened his grip on the hilt of his cutlass.

'First party away.'

Evans, Thompson and three marines followed him as he crunched across the pebbled slope rising away from the water. They were met at the first building by a dog, hostile and bristling but unsure of itself. It barked itself back into the shell of its hovel as they approached, then followed them, still barking,

88

until the sound of the second party sent it hurrying back to defend its master's property.

They reached the rim of the hollow without being challenged and looked down at the building which had housed the wounded. Only the roof and a few feet of one wall had been damaged. It seemed sure that few inside would have suffered from the explosion. Lawson raised his hand and halted the other groups in their tracks. It would be as well to reconnoitre the hollow before concentrating all their forces there. He turned to the three marines.

'One of you remain here in full view of the other detachments. The other two of you can walk to left and right of the buildings. Make sure that your muskets are primed. Evans and Thompson come with me.'

They found the door of the building hanging askew on its hinges. It had not been the blast from the explosion that had done it. A tree trunk, an improvised battering ram, lay on the ground. Lawson's face paled. He knew what he would find within the walls.

'Go in,' he ordered Thompson. 'Tell me what you see.'

Thompson squeezed through the damaged doorway and examined the first of the bodies strewn over the floor. Quickly he passed from one to the next. None required more than a brief glance to tell him that there was no hope. All had been savagely hacked and stabbed. He left the building grey faced, leaned against the doorpost and drew deep breaths of fresh air.

'All dead?' Lawson asked.

'Murdered, sir. Even old Captain Mallory's been hacked to bits.'

Lawson remained staring at the doorway, his face set and drawn. A nervous twitch started in his cheek and he rubbed it irritably.

'If it takes me to the end of my life, I'll see that Yussaiff Ahmed and the men responsible for this, are paid in full.'

'That red coat is a-shouting and a-waving, sir,' Evans called.

A gun fired in the distance. It was a signal from the ship.

'Run,' Lawson ordered.

As the collected party hurried down to the beach they saw horsemen, two hundred or more, descending from the hills to the east. At the same time the rattle of musketry from near by warned them that the survivors of the explosion were rallying. A seaman fell clutching his thigh and a marine sprawled in the sand.

'Covering fire, my lads,' Lawson ordered. 'Second and third detachments, five yards apart and shoot when you see a target. The rest of you get the wounded aboard and float the boats.'

The ten marines remained in extended order facing the land but the Moors had taken cover again. The marine sergeant looked to Lawson for orders.

'Get down to the boats, sergeant.'

'Very good sah,' the man replied with a parade ground salute. 'Brown, 'Iggins, Turner and 'Ope, retire thirty paces at the double and face about.—Not you, McLeod. Face your front.'

The four men ran in the direction of the boats, halted and took open order again with muskets at the ready. The sergeant glanced over his shoulder to satisfy himself that they were indeed in position then turned to the others.

'Now we know whereabouts the enemy is and we can see where our lads is. So all we've got to do is to keep out of the line of fire. About turn. Double march.'

They ran down the slope in extended order. A musket cracked behind them. There was an immediate reply from two of the British muskets ahead. Then they were through their own rear guard and taking up positions along the water's edge.

Now there was work in earnest for the marines, as the Moors, determined to make a kill, left their cover and began to advance on the boats. There were perhaps thirty of them, armed with a variety of flintlock muskets but they were not taking time over their shots, whereas the six marines left on the beach were firing from kneeling positions and reloading with parade ground precision. They were doing tremendous execution and broke off almost reluctantly when the captain ordered them to get aboard the remaining launch.

Bullets struck the water all around the open boat as it got under way. The marine sergeant was hit in the arm and one of his men tried to stand up to return the fire but the captain seized his belt and pulled him down.

'*Comus* will take care of them,' he growled.

As he spoke there was a rushing sound overhead, followed by the roar of one of the ship's guns. The heavy shot exploded the pebbles on the beach in all directions and now the pirates were running back, desperately trying to reach the protecting ridge above the beach. They were climbing into the area that Chandler had reserved for his carronades; the lowest elevation that he dared risk with the spread shot whilst his own men were below the guns. None of the Moors escaped the savage hails of grape that ripped into them.

The captain found the rope ladder that hung in the shadow of the frigate's side and climbed on deck to find Cecilia and Chandler awaiting him.

'Do you want me to engage the horsemen, sir?'

'Just a minute, Mr Chandler. I want to speak to the men first.'

Chandler blew a loud blast on his whistle.

'Those swine ashore have murdered your mates,' Lawson shouted.

There was a burst of angry exclamation followed by dead silence. All the gunners were waiting with grim faces.

'We don't want a haphazard barrage that will give them time to seek cover. We need a broadside. The foremost gun on the starboard bow will aim at the left flank of those horsemen yonder. The aftermost gun of the starboard quarter will take the right flank. The rest of the guns will space themselves sensibly over the whole field. Reload with grape and case shot; faster than you have ever done. Let no one escape. Take aim!'

The tackles squealed protestingly as the heavy guns were slewed around and sighted. There followed a blistering comment from a warrant officer and a hasty alteration of elevation on one of the guns. Then all was still and silent. The gun captains were waiting with lanyard in one hand and smouldering link in the other. Lawson raised his whistle.

'But this too is murder,' Cecilia said urgently. 'Haven't we had enough?'

Lawson glared in her direction and blew hard upon the whistle. The frigate heaved from the shock of the broadside.

The horsemen had reached the village while the captain had been giving his orders. Now they were picking their way over the rubble. Obviously they were landsmen and although they must have seen the fate of the few men half a mile along the shore they evidently considered themselves to be out of effective range. They paid dearly for their ignorance. The first broadside decimated them, cutting broad channels through their ranks and leaving heaps of dead. The guns, loaded at exceptional speed, smashed into the panic-stricken survivors who were hindered in their escape by the rubble at their feet and the wounded and dead, horses and men, on all sides. More fell to add to the carnage. Then it became a complete and utter rout with those still mounted urging their wildly rearing horses over the bodies of their wounded comrades. They dispersed in all directions.

A piercing whistle shrilled throughout the ship. The bombardment lessened and ceased only when Chandler had repeated the blast. He snarled a threat at one of the gun captains then strode red-faced with anger towards Captain Lawson.

'I'm sorry about that, sir. I'll have the gun captains, who ignored the cease fire, in front of you for punishment.'

'Let it rest this time, Mr Chandler. Their rate of fire was excellent. What were their casualties, do you think?'

'Between eighty and a hundred, sir.'

Lawson nodded with grim satisfaction.

'I wish I could have seen it clearly.'

He had been noticing a deterioration in his sight since the first cloud of smoke from the guns had reached his eyes. Now his cheeks were streaming with tears and his vision was so bleared that he was seeing double.

'I don't think Yussaiff Ahmed was there, sir. I examined them closely through the glass but I could see no sign of his white stallion.'

'No, he was certainly not there, or they would have known better than stand so close to a frigate's broadside. He probably knows nothing about the murder of our wounded but his men did it and I'll hang him for it one day.'

Chandler made no comment. His sorrow over Jones's death was genuine enough but it was somewhat lightened by his own promotion. He was now second in command of *Comus*.

'What are your orders, sir?'

'Get a suitable crew aboard *Princess Mary*. We'll set a course for Gibraltar.'

When Chandler had gone about his business, Lawson noticed that Cecilia was standing close by, watching him. He smiled and nodded to her. Her face was white and tense.

'You wish you could have seen it clearly,' she said in a voice charged with emotion. 'I wish I had not seen it and I know it will haunt me for ever. It was brutal, savage and unnecessary. You are just as bad as those who murdered the wounded.'

'The devil I am,' Lawson exploded. 'If those——'

'I don't wish to discuss the matter further with you—or—to discuss anything with you. If you intend to remain on board *Comus*, I should be obliged if you would allow me to sail to Gibraltar in the *Princess Mary*.'

10

THE harbour at Gibraltar was crowded with shipping when *Comus* crept in before a failing breeze and noted that H.M.S. *Impregnable*, the flagship of Admiral Dullant, lay close to shore.

'Start the salute,' Lawson ordered.

Saunders signalled to the master gunner and as the first gun fired he turned the minute glass. He would expect the twelfth shot as the last grain of sand fell. The master gunner would have no use for a minute glass. He would be timing each shot in the traditional manner : 'If I wasn't a gunner I wouldn't be here. Number two gun—fire. If I wasn't a gunner I wouldn't be here. Number three gun—fire.' And he would know that every one of his trade among the anchored shipping would be automatically timing him in exactly the same way.

Midshipman Saunders lowered the telescope with which he had been examining the signals at the masthead of the man of war.

'Our number, sir. We are to anchor to leeward of the flag-ship.'

'Acknowledge.'

Saunders busied himself at the signal lockers. The captain walked away from the group near the binnacle and beckoned to Thompson.

'Can you see the *Princess Mary*?' he asked.

'Just beyond *Impregnable*, sir.'

Lawson nodded with satisfaction. He had been beset with nagging doubts since he had ordered the prize to sail away from them four days ago. Soon it would be in the hands of the prize courts and they could settle any arguments that might arise between the insurance company and the heirs of the dead Captain Mallory. Whatever the outcome, all those on *Comus* would receive their right and proper share.

'Now listen carefully, Thompson. In your new position as Captain's Coxs'n you will be accompanying me whenever I leave the ship. Now you can reckon on my being called away by the admiral as soon as we drop anchor. Do you fully understand what I have told you?'

'Yes, sir. Nobody has got to notice that you can't see so well as before. I've got to do my best to steer you without anybody knowing as what you aren't a-steering of yourself.'

'Good. A whisper here and a touch there. Never direct me by holding on to my arm unless you see that I'm about to fall over the side or something equally dangerous. I can manage fine in daylight on the open deck. It's when I'm between decks that I'll need help. Now inspect the crew of my gig and make sure that it is ready to be lowered smartly over the side.'

The anchor plunged into the sea taking its heavy cable after it. *Comus* fell away from the breeze, jerked once and steadied. A signal gun barked on the deck of the flagship, drawing attention to the string of small balls which were now bursting into flags on the mast.

Midshipman Saunders had no need to examine the signal book. The old sailor with him had warned him that the captain would be ordered to report and they had already looked up the flags that would be used. He scribbled on the signal slate and took it to Captain Lawson.

'Thank you, Mr Saunders. Please order my boat over the side.'

'Give way,' Thompson ordered as soon as the captain had gained his seat.

With the eyes of all the idle men from the anchored shipping on them, the captain's boat crew pulled in unison across the intervening quarter mile of water to the flagship. Thompson, at the tiller for the first time in his life, cleverly navigated around the flotsam and discarded rubbish of a busy harbour to bring the boat in a seamanlike manner to the foot of the entry port.

95

The man in the bows hooked on. Lawson caught at the handrail and swung himself firmly onto the platform. Thompson followed, clutching a waterproof wallet as instructed. This was to be his passport as far as the door of the admiral's cabin. From there the captain would be on his own.

The shrill of boatswains' pipes greeted them as they stepped on deck. Captain Lawson, hand raised in salute at the entry port, saw a line of men under the shade of a thick green awning rigged eight feet above the deck. Two officers in blue coats approached but for the life of him he could not make out which was the senior.

'Captain's to starboard, sir,' Thompson whispered.

Lawson felt the sweat break on his brow. The captain of a ninety-eight gun man-of-war had honoured him by meeting him at the entry port and he had nearly made the mistake of addressing himself to the officer of the watch.

'Welcome aboard,' Captain Hopton said cordially. 'I don't think I have had the pleasure of meeting you before.'

Lawson struggled to see his face clearly as they shook hands but it was gloomy under the awning after the bright sunlight of the bay. He listened carefully as he was introduced to the officer of the watch. Chandler had already told him who was serving on H.M.S. *Impregnable* and he knew none of them.

'Admiral Dullant would be obliged if you would kindly attend him in his cabin as soon as convenient,' Captain Hopton said easily.

Lawson bowed in acknowledgement. 'As soon as convenient' meant immediately when expressed by a rear-admiral. Cecilia, who must have arrived two days earlier, would have told him all about their encounter with Yussaiff Ahmed. He wondered if she had changed her views about the 'brutal, savage and unnecessary' attack on the land force. Not that he had any worries on that score. Any naval officer would have done the same.

'I understand that you have not met the admiral,' Hopton said as they made their way aft, followed at a discreet distance by Thompson.

'Er—no. He was not here when I arrived in the Mediterranean. I have met his wife, though.'

'So I have heard, Captain,' Hopton said with a smile.

The marine sentry outside the admiral's door snapped to attention. Captain Hopton tapped on the gleaming white woodwork, turned the handle and stepped inside.

'Captain Lawson, sir,' he said. 'Admiral Dullant.'

An enormous man with a fat face and weak chin, eased himself from behind a heavy wooden desk and advanced to meet him.

'Welcome to my command, Captain Lawson. We had expected you sooner but no doubt you were delayed by your jury foremast—which my wife neglected to mention.'

Lawson's mind registered briefly the sarcasm in those last few words but he had no time to ponder them.

'Your prize arrived forty hours ago—and what a prize! Whoever buys the *Princess Mary* will pay a lot, I'll be bound. Lucky devils these frigate men, eh Hopton? But do sit down, Captain.'

Lawson found the side of a great leather chair and lowered himself into its depths. He saw the admiral sit behind the desk and realised that they were alone in the cabin.

'First I must thank you for your services to my wife. From what I've been told already, I gather that it would have been all up with her if you had not chanced upon the boat.'

For all the sincerity in his voice he might have been thanking Lawson for seeing his wife home from church on a Sunday morning and since his back was to the light, any sign of emotion on his face was lost in darkness. Indeed the captain could see nothing more than the outline of his head. The admiral leaned forward, clasped his hands together and waited expectantly.

'Perhaps you will start from the beginning,' he said.

Lawson launched forth on his story from the day he had first sighted the boat. He elaborated nothing and left nothing out. Only the account of the injury to his eyes was skimmed over as he tried to give the impression that the loss of his sight had left him with no after effects. The admiral was more concerned with the identity of Yussaiff Ahmed.

'You say that you were temporarily blinded before this fellow appeared on deck, and that you had pads of some kind over your eyes on every other occasion that you spoke to him. Is it not possible that he was merely some Englishman masquerading as Heward?'

Lawson pondered over this question. Cecilia knew damned well that it was Heward. Had she, for reasons of her own, kept quiet about him? He recalled his earlier suspicions, that she and Heward had been lovers. Certainly Heward had engineered her first escape, along with Captain Mallory and the other fellow. He had given them a well-found boat with water and food to last them to Gibraltar.

'We were midshipmen together, sir,' he replied at length. 'I recognised his voice. No!' he added thoughtfully as the details came back. 'I did not. The voice was familiar, but it was not until he identified himself that I was able to place him.'

'Ah!' the admiral exclaimed triumphantly. 'So you have only his word for it that he is Heward?'

A warning bell began to ring in Lawson's mind. The admiral could hardly be as stupid as his question suggested. Obviously he was anxious to lay a smoke screen around Heward's identity.

'It is true, sir, that I did not see him but I felt without question that I was speaking to the same person who had lived with me for a year as a midshipman.'

The admiral rose from his chair and paced his cabin in silence. Eventually he stopped, pursed his lips and looked at Lawson shrewdly.

'I am going to offer you a little advice, Captain, which must never be repeated if you value your career.'

Lawson stared stolidly ahead. The admiral moved closer.

'Forget that this pirate, Yussaiff Ahmed, ever claimed that he was Heward.'

Lawson looked at him in surprise but said nothing. The admiral's voice took on a confidential note.

'We all know our duties, but in the writing of reports we have to be discreet. Some clerk at Admiralty would get hold of the story and it would become tavern gossip throughout London. Lloyds would certainly seize upon it and God help the Navy when they did : a pirate captain trained on His Majesty's ships ! They'd have the First Sea Lord on the rack and likely demand compensation from the government.'

He shook his head and began to pace the cabin.

'Then we'd have trouble from the Hewards,' he went on. 'I need not remind you that they are an influential family both in the Navy and the Government. They would haul you before the highest courts in the country. Their lawyers would dwell upon your blindness and use that one fact to tear your story to shreds.'

He took up the oilskin-covered report that Lawson had laid upon the desk when he had entered the cabin.

'Even if this were accepted, it would not bring Heward one step nearer to justice. It would, however, draw attention to your disability, and that, together with the flurry you'd have caused in high places, would ensure that you would never get another command. Do you understand me ?'

'Yes, sir.'

'Very well, Captain.' He smiled and handed Lawson the oilskin package. 'I look forward to reading your ah—revised report.'

Since the interview was obviously at an end, Lawson bowed and moved in the general direction of the door. After being seated opposite the bright light from the window he found the rest of the cabin to be in semi-darkness. He reached for the handle. The admiral watched him curiously as he groped around, some three feet from the door.

'Obviously your clerk must have written your report,' he said. 'You don't appear to have recovered fully from the explosion.'

'Mr Saunders, one of my midshipmen, sir. My clerk was killed. Saunders is my nephew,' he added significantly.

The admiral smiled and reached for the door handle.

'Then you can impress upon him the need for discretion. Perhaps you and he would care to attend a small social function which my wife is organising for this evening. Have no worries on account of your sight. These things get better quickly and I shall not consider reporting your ah—present difficulties. I too can be discreet.'

'Thank you for your kindness, sir.'

'Until this evening then. I shall look forward to your company.'

He threw back the door with a flourish and placed his hand on the captain's arm. The guiding hand and the brighter light from the door gave Lawson all the direction he needed.

Thompson fell in behind Lawson as he walked away from the cabin.

'There's an officer been asking for you, sir. Here he is now.'

An exquisitely attired lieutenant, with powdered wig and face greeted the captain with a careless tilt of his hat.

'Captain Hopton has expressed the hope that you will join him over a glass of wine before you leave the ship,' he said languidly.

Lawson scowled. The genteel fops who, by the aid of influential connections, found their way aboard the flagships of the Navy were well known to him. During the war, when the Navy had been fashionable, there had not been a ship without its quota of effeminate young men from the 'cream' of society. Like most men who had started with nothing, apart from their ability, Lawson detested them.

'Who the devil are you?' he demanded aggressively.

The young man moved restively, 'like a cat that had its fur stroked the wrong way', as Thompson later described it. A fleeting expression of distaste passed over his face. He withdrew a scented handkerchief from a frilled cuff and sniffed at it.

'Duvalier-Winter, Laurence Duvalier-Winter. A most unworthy lieutenant on this noble ship,' he smiled disparagingly.

Lawson snorted angrily.

'Lieutenant Du—whatever it is—Winter, when you speak to

a superior in rank you will show proper respect. It is customary, I believe, for a junior to hold himself erect and to terminate whatever he has to say with the addition of *sir*. Is that not the case?'

'Yes, sir.'

'Show me to your captain.'

'Certainly, sir.'

The young man bowed from the waist, watched mistrustfully by Thompson, and led the way along the spotless decks.

A number of seamen with wide-bottomed trousers rolled to the knee, were scrubbing vigorously with holystones at the planking of the quarterdeck. As Lawson approached, the men who were swinging water up from over the side, suspended operations and stood respectfully to attention with slopping buckets in their hands. The warrant officer, who had been supervising from a raised hatch, lowered himself to the deck and saluted. When they were clear of the wet patch, Captain Hopton detached himself from the group of officers on the shoreward side and strolled across to meet them.

'I hope this deuced mess has not discommoded you. We're entertaining this afternoon and if it's going to be anything like last time we'll have all the inhabitants of the Rock on board—except the monkeys,' he added with a laugh. 'Maybe you'd like to join us later in the day.'

Lawson mentioned the admiral's invitation.

'Same affair, Captain,' the flagship captain assured him with an airy wave of his hand as he led him to his cabin. 'Mrs Dullant has some sort of a musical evening arranged for after the herd has gone ashore. Old Admiral Heward acquired a reputation in the Fleet as a music enthusiast, as you may remember. Now that he has gone, no doubt she feels that she has to keep it going : family tradition and all that. I'll never forget the musical barges he used to organise on the Thames when he was First Sea Lord. Must have cost him— Are you quite well, Captain?'

Lawson had stopped in his tracks and was staring at Hopton incredulously. He collected himself with a jerk.

'Yes—yes, I'm quite all right, thank you.' He strove to appear casual. 'I was not aware that Cecilia Dullant was a Heward.'

'Oh yes, indeed.' He lowered his voice. 'Her brother was involved in an unhappy business some years ago. Struck his captain and then deserted the ship to escape court martial. You must have heard of it. Most unpleasant for the family and—' he smiled knowingly, 'damned annoying it must have been for her husband. He had looked for advancement from his marriage into the Navy hierarchy, then found his name linked with the black sheep.'

Captain Hopton's cabin was a palace compared with the captain's quarters on *Comus*. It was well furnished, with heavy velvet curtains at the stern window and a silver candelabra suspended from the ceiling. Valuable paintings hung on the bulkheads and on the deck was a carpet that must have cost Hopton more than a year's pay. Lawson barely noticed them. His mind was dwelling upon the information he had just received, and the admiral's advice in the light of it.

'Your good health, Captain.'

They finished their first glasses and a servant refilled them. The cigars were lit. The servant placed a decanter on the table and left them. Hopton settled himself comfortably and waited expectantly for Lawson's story with all the enthusiasm of the professional sailor. The description of the passage through the channel leading to the bay drew forth a cry of admiration.

'Mines be damned! The only time I ever heard of that was against a parcel of Frenchies lying in Brest harbour. Sent three of them to the bottom. Now who was it used them?'

'The *Agadir*,' Lawson prompted.

'That's it!' He banged the table. 'Captain Wainwright of the *Agadir*. The idea of one of his junior lieutenants, so I've heard, but the fellow never got the credit for it.'

Lawson knew that the junior lieutenant had been Heward but he kept it to himself. Hopton might start connecting the two and he had already shown himself to be a man who enjoyed gossip. It would surely get back to the admiral and Lawson had not yet decided what to do about his report.

The advice of a rear-admiral was not to be taken lightly and there was much truth in what he had said. When Cecilia stated positively that Yussaiff Ahmed bore no resemblance to her brother, who would believe a mere frigate captain? The Heward lawyers would certainly make the most of his damaged eyes and no doubt Admiral Dullant would offer evidence to support their case. His last statement on the subject, 'I too can be discreet', had been a threat, Lawson realised. He took the refilled glass, sipped at it, and renewed his narrative.

A tap on the door interrupted him after five minutes. Hopton, who had been listening with rapt attention showed his annoyance.

'Come in, damn you,' he shouted.

The admiral's clerk, a thin, harassed man, dressed in a long blue coat, which accentuated his lack of breadth, opened the door and blinked his way nervously into the cabin. He had a paper which he offered to the flagship's captain.

'From the admiral, sir,' his whispered reverently.

Hopton glanced at it and frowned.

'I'm to let you have two officers and forty men,' he rumbled. 'The officers have been named. As far as the men are concerned you can let me know what you need. I've a lot of young blood who would benefit from service aboard a frigate. Life's too quiet for them here.'

A midshipman hovered behind the clerk in the doorway. The life of the ship was beginning to claim the attention of its commanding officer.

'What is it?'

'The first visitors are putting out from the shore, sir.'

'Damnation! Is it time already?' Hopton exclaimed.

He stood up hurriedly and reached for his sword and hat.

'I pray you will excuse me. It grieves me deucedly to be interrupted in the middle of your fascinating story, but you will understand.'

Lawson, who had risen from his chair, bowed.

'Perhaps you would care to take this note from the admiral. You'll find that the officers mentioned will suit you very nicely, I fancy. Pray use my cabin if you would care to speak to them before you return to your ship.'

He smiled charmingly and bowed in a manner which Lawson could never hope to achieve.

'Mr Newton will remain at your service.'

The midshipman, who was obviously the Mr Newton ordered to remain at the captain's service, looked pained and sucked in air noisily after Hopton had swept from the cabin. Clearly he would rather be at the entry port watching the arrival of the ladies. He changed his weight from one foot to the other, pursed his lips as though to whistle, thought better of it and leaned dejectedly against the bulwarks.

'Come inside, Thompson.'

He closed the door against the midshipman and held out the paper.

'Read out the names of the two officers,' he ordered.

'I'm sorry, sir. I was never learned to read,' he said shamefacedly.

Lawson peered closely at the meaningless blur on the paper. There was nothing for it but to wait until he reached *Comus*. He could hardly ask the midshipman outside to read it for him.

They managed to get the boat away from the side of the flagship before the first of the visitors arrived. As they rode easily over the light swell, Lawson considered the implications of the reinforcements. Clearly the admiral intended that they should continue with their task. That was the part that did not make sense if he wanted to protect Heward. Now that Yussaiff Ahmed's fleet had been destroyed *Comus* could have been sent back, and such an action would undoubtedly have the support of the tax-burdened British people. A frigate cost far too much to be used in a hunt for one man, particularly one who could no longer be regarded as a threat to their all-important trade. There were ships enough—British, French and Dutch—engaged in destroying Barbary pirates.

The sight of Postill at the entry port brought enlightenment. He and several others had heard that Yussaiff Ahmed had been Lieutenant Heward, R.N., and it was quite possible that some of them might even have known Heward in the past. Lawson wondered if the admiral had taken this into consideration and wanted to make sure that no breath of this story should reach England. Whilst *Comus* was under Dullant's command, all reports would of necessity pass through him. He could discount personal letters; the few seamen who could write would have other things to write about than the identity of a Mediterranean pirate. Thoughtfully he climbed aboard.

Lieutenant Chandler had no sooner lowered his hand from a welcoming salute than he offered a list of replacements that would be necessary before *Comus* could go to sea again. Lawson glanced at it and handed it back. There was no point in pretending to read it.

'Bring it to my cabin and be so good as to advise Mr Saunders that he will be accompanying me on board the flagship in two hours from now.'

He strode past the crowd of carpenter's mates who were working with saw and adze on the new timbers on the bulwarks, and paused at an area of deck where a number of men, on hands and knees, were hammering oakum into the deck seams. He sniffed appreciatively at the pitch fumes and listened with interest as a leading seaman berated one of the caulkers in a mixture of pidgin English and some odd language that he could not place.

'Mr Clerk!' he shouted.

The carpenter hurried aft hastily removing a plug of tobacco from his mouth and stuffing it in his pocket.

'Who are these people?'

'The prisoners, sir.'

'Do you find it worth while employing them?'

The carpenter grinned and jerked his head in the direction of the nearest marine guard.

'Aye, sir. They works well wi' half a dozen marines standing over them to see that they gets up to no tricks. Fair exchange too, sir. Marines never could work.'

The captain smiled at the joke. Bantering rivalry between marines and seamen was the usual order of things. It was an indication also that the men were in good heart.

'Rogers is in charge of 'em on account of being able to speak the lingo. At least he sez he can but it sounds more like the Welsh to me.'

Lawson laughed delightedly.

'At least, he is keeping them at it. How long will it be before we're ready for sea?'

'No more'n two days, sir. We've been lucky in the matter of a new foremast. The shipwright has one and a tender will be helping us to seat it this afternoon. Should have the yards aloft by noon tomorrow.'

'Good, Mr Clerk. That's excellent news.'

He went below to his cabin to find that Evans already had a selection of shirts arrayed on the locker. Clearly he had anticipated that the captain would be making several social calls now that they were in a friendly port. Lawson felt them carefully before making a decision.

'I'll wear this one,' he said finally, indicating the most elaborately frilled one. 'Now I'll take my bath.'

Before he had left the flagship he had given orders that a hot tub was to await his return. Evans, who had made it his business to be informed as soon as the captain left the flagship, disappeared for a moment and returned with a tarpaulin sheet which he spread on the boards. Two cook's mates staggered in with a tub of scalding water. One of them remained to add cold water from a large bucket while Evans fussed around the captain removing his clothes. In the midst of this activity, Chandler knocked and entered.

'Read through your list, Mr Chandler,' Lawson ordered, forestalling his apologetic retreat.

Chandler had been thorough, and it was obvious from the number of requirements that he was making the most of the recent action and capture of the frigate to catch up on the back log of replacements. In normal circumstances the Comptroller's staff would not supply a half of it and they would have to make do with patched sails, worn ropes and flaking paintwork. Lawson nodded his approval as he lathered himself in the tub.

'It's fortunate that the Admiralty does not deduct the cost of the damage from the prize-money, eh, Mr Chandler?'

'Yes, sir.'

Chandler watched Lawson, as he scrubbed himself, in fascination. There seemed to be no part of his body that did not bear a scar of some kind. Most of them were obviously sabre cuts but there were others, including a puckered depression just below the collar bone and a wide expanse of gathered red flesh on the other side of his shoulder where a bullet, or shrapnel had made its exit. Lawson looked up suddenly.

'You may read the note on my desk. It's from the admiral about our reinforcements.'

Chandler reached for it eagerly and read it.

'Do you know either of your future brother officers, Mr Chandler?'

'I don't recollect having met Hawbrook, sir, but I do believe that I know Duvalier-Winter.'

Lawson stifled an oath. Duvalier-Winter! The fop who had spoken to him on the deck of the flagship!

'I believe he is senior to me,' added Chandler miserably.

The captain snorted and heaved himself out of the bath tub, swilling water in all directions. Evans stepped forward with a large red towel intending to drape it over his shoulders but Lawson snatched it from him and began to rub himself furiously. The thought of that dandy on board *Comus* was galling.

11

THE deck of the flagship was like a fairground. A score of tradesmen with baskets of fruit and delicacies cluttered up the waist while several boats plied their trade about the ship; their owners apparently trying to under-sell their more fortunate rivals who had managed to get aboard. They were meeting with a great deal of success. Containers of all kinds were being lowered from the gun decks.

Saunders mentioned this curious fact to the captain as they climbed aboard in the fading light of the late afternoon. Lawson nodded and grinned knowingly.

'It isn't for us to tell the officer of the watch his business, Mr Saunders, but if we ever have an affair the likes of this, you'll find no trading going on over the side of my ship. I dare say you'll see many of the baskets being returned with the fruit still in them.'

'That's true, sir,' Saunders confirmed after a moment's examination.

'Can you think of the reason for it?'

Saunders looked over his shoulder as they walked to the quarterdeck. By the time they reached the marine sentries posted to keep the rabble away from the select company assembled there, he had the answer.

'It wouldn't be liquor, sir, would it?'

'That's it, lad,' Lawson said affably. 'Hidden under the fruit. Wouldn't be surprised if a few men are in irons before morning. Now who's this approaching?'

'Good evening, Captain Lawson,' said the flagship captain courteously.

Lawson and his midshipman swept off their hats and bowed.

'May I present my wife.'

'My pleasure, ma'am,' Lawson said.

He introduced Saunders and then cast around for something to say which might amuse a lady. Conversation had never been his strong point. She had no difficulties. Tongue-tied officers, who had spent all their lives at sea and therefore away from the conventions of society, were no strangers to her. Skilfully she set about drawing Lawson out of his reserve.

He vaguely heard Saunders being introduced to a midshipman from the flagship. Then Hopton was sent off to find his wife's wrap and Lawson was left alone with her. It soon became evident that she was not really interested, nor even understood the answers to her questions about the action in the bay, but she was fascinated by the part that Cecilia Dullant had played.

'Fancy shutting you up *to-geth-er* in his house,' she said savouring every syllable. 'Surely you'd think that even a savage would have some sense of the proprieties of things. How fortunate for Cecilia that she has not led too sheltered a life. I mean—this chasing across Europe on her own would surely have taught her to rely upon her own resources and perhaps given her a certain—philosophy, don't you think?'

'I really hadn't thought about it, ma'am.'

'La, Captain!' She tapped him teasingly on the shoulder with her fan. 'I'm sure that you must have given—Cecilia, my dear! Captain Lawson was just telling me about your exciting experiences.'

Cecilia gave her a wintry smile and turned to Lawson.

'I am delighted that you were able to come this evening, Captain.'

Lawson bowed.

'My pleasure, ma'am.'

'I'm sure that you two will have lots to discuss,' Mrs Hopton said conspiratorially, 'and there is James, gossiping with my shawl in his hand. He's completely forgotten——'

She swept away to join the group with her husband.

'Our adventures have given the Gibraltar society something to talk about and the people here are bursting with impatience to be introduced to you, so I had better take you around. Before I do, I want to say that—I am very sorry that I made a scene on the deck of your ship. I have had time to think about things and I realise that your world of war and—killing and being killed, must have given you a very different set of values from those which I have gained in my—in this,' she indicated the elegant throng on the quarterdeck, with a contemptuous gesture, 'sort of existence. I am sure that any captain would have done exactly as you did and I hope that you will forgive my outburst.'

Lawson bowed, completely at a loss for words. She looked at him quizzingly, then smiled briefly.

'Come! You must meet everybody.'

She took him by the arm and led him from one group to another. They were mostly naval and army officers, government officials and their wives. All plied him with questions about the action against the Moors. This was a welcome change from the usual conversation of the 'Rock' society.

'Did you actually see this dreadful man?' asked one thickly powdered, stout dame eagerly. 'Rumour has it that he was an English officer at one time.'

Lawson sensed the disquiet in Cecilia at his side. If he were to tell this crowd that Yussaiff Ahmed and Heward were the same, the story would be all over the Navy in no time.

'See him? No, ma'am, but I would confirm that he speaks English like an English gentleman.'

A deep gong interrupted the excited discussions that followed his last words. The musical evening was about to begin.

Coloured lamps had been hung at various points over the rapidly darkening scene. In the centre of the deck, gathered about the wheel, which had been draped with the flag, were a dozen musicians busily tuning their instruments.

'Do you like music?' Cecilia asked, leading him away.

'Passionately ma'am.'

'Then we shall sit together. I cannot abide people who regard music as a background for conversation.'

She led him to a secluded seat by the lee rail and sat down. A waiter hovered with a tray of drinks and a marine whisked a small table in front of them. They settled back comfortably and waited for the concert to begin but there was a further delay because the players had not enough light to read their music and more lamps had to be found.

'There is one of the more colourful members of Gibraltar society,' Cecilia said suddenly. 'The tall gentleman in black talking to the army officers. We knew him years ago in England.'

Lawson saw a man so tall and thin that he thought his eyes must be playing tricks again. He was standing with his head almost touching a lamp that had been slung seven feet above the deck and he was obviously expounding upon some weighty subject by the solemn shakings of his head and the gesticulations of his hand. He was dressed in funeral black, relieved only at the cuffs and collar by the white of his shirt.

'Well, Captain, what do you make of him?'

'A preacher?'

She laughed.

'A preacher to be sure, but not of the gospel. His theme is the criminal folly of the government in abolishing slavery.'

Lawson looked at her in astonishment.

'That is Sir Harry Doolan, or Bristol Harry to his intimates of days gone by. No doubt you have heard of him.'

'Indeed I have,' Lawson said. 'One of the wealthiest slave traders in England. What on earth is he doing here?'

'Why I believe that he is the gentleman to whom you must apply for your stores. He is employed by the Admiralty on the Comptroller's staff. It is common knowledge that though he was amply compensated for the destruction of his business, he very quickly lost every penny in unwise speculation. He is now something of a permanent fixture in the ever-changing Gibraltar society and though he bores everybody to distraction he is still invited to every function because his goodwill is essential to ships' captains in need of supplies.'

Lawson nodded understandingly. The guardians of government stores, both in the Navy and Army, were men conscious of their power and very quick to take offence. Many a captain had gone to sea with rotten meat and weevily biscuits and had every request for essential equipment refused, because some high official on the Comptroller's staff had been left off a guest list or slighted in some way.

'It is considered to be an intellectual exercise to speak to Sir Harry and steer him clear of the evils of Wilberforce and Clarkson,' Cecilia added with a laugh.

At one point, the stout lady, who had asked Lawson about Yussaiff Ahmed, was persuaded to sing. She did extremely well with her first song and she was just about to start on another when a disturbance somewhere forward of the quarterdeck bore out the truth of Captain Lawson's earlier words to Saunders. One of the seamen was demanding admission to the quarterdeck to 'entertain the gennellfolk' and a 'marine bastard' was stopping him. There was a scuffle and amid it a drunken voice singing some tavern ballad, obviously in a desperate last-minute attempt to convince those on the quarterdeck that they were missing something of quality. It was a disjointed effort, suggesting that someone was trying to clap their hands over his mouth. Then the song ended abruptly in the middle of a long drawn out 'darleeeng'.

Lawson grinned boyishly at Cecilia.

'The Master at Arms has just got to him.'

Cecilia reached forward and touched his arm. She regarded the scarred face, dimly illuminated in the yellow light of the lamp, with wonder.

'You should smile more often, Captain.'

The rest of the evening passed quickly. They had refreshments followed by more music and then came the time for Cecilia to leave the ship. Lawson escorted her to the group surrounding her husband and realised with a shock that this was the first he had seen of the admiral and he had monopolised his wife's company for three hours. This would give the Mrs Hoptons of the Gibraltar society something to gossip about.

The admiral was evidently not going ashore, Lawson noted. Cecilia had joined the ladies of the Governor's party. They clustered about the entry port thanking their hosts and saying their farewells. When most of them had descended to the waiting launch, Cecilia turned back to Lawson.

'Will you call upon me the day after tomorrow?'

'I should be delighted, ma'am.'

'Then I shall expect you early in the afternoon.'

The launch pushed off. The ship's officers gathered for a last glass of wine together on the open deck before retiring for the night. Admiral Dullant went to his quarters in the aftermost part of the ship and Lawson began to look around for his midshipman, wondering why the admiral chose to live aboard when he had a beautiful wife ashore.

'Ah, Lawson! There you are at last. Been trying to get you on your own all even'n' but you've been better occupied, you dog.'

Captain Hopton nudged Lawson and leered drunkenly into his face.

'Wouldn't mind being occupied myself with our Cecilia,' he whispered confidentially, 'but old Dullant's as jealous as the devil, even though he's no use for her himself.'

Lawson's angry protest was halted by the last few words. He waited breathlessly.

'He's been watching you all the time—when he wasn't keeping an eye on his mistress,' he added with a roar of laughter.

'Mistress?'

'Oh come, dear fellow!' he hiccuped loudly. 'You must have heard of the admiral and Lady de Vere?'

'No.'

'He's been faithful to her for years. The more so, since he married Cecilia,' he added with a laugh.

He beckoned to a steward, forced another drink on Lawson and had his own glass recharged.

12

CAPTAIN LAWSON slept late the following morning. When he left his cabin the sun was already above the rim of the sea, casting a tracery of long shadows across the deck and on to the still water beyond. He sniffed appreciatively at the freshness of the new day, passed a cursory glance over the occupants of the quarterdeck, then placed himself alongside the wheel and fixed his eyes forward. This had been his practice ever since the frigate had left the bay and naturally it had caused no surprise whilst they had been at sea. Now they were lying at anchor, when no officer was required to be in charge of the watch, his stance and concentration caused a few eyes to be turned curiously in his direction. They were not to know that he was testing his sight.

On the day that they had retaken *Comus* he had discovered that he could see reasonably clearly as far as the mainmast. Daily his vision had improved until the forecastle had taken on a definite shape and he could discern the lines between the planking on both sides of the well. Then there had been a halt to further improvement and he was beginning to believe that his eyes would never recover from the powder burns.

A gay laugh attracted his attention. Several men were spread out along the newly hoisted main yard on the foremast. He tried to make out what they were doing but they were outside his effective range. Chandler approached, noting the screwed-up eyes with sympathy.

'Reeving new futtock-shrouds, sir. Mr Saunders is in charge.'

'Very good, Mr Chandler. We shall need to check all our cordage whilst we are here. What of the new replacements? Have they arrived?'

'Half an hour ago, sir. Your new clerk was with them. I believe that the officers are on their way over. A boat put out from the flagship a few minutes ago.'

Lawson noted the mournful expression on Chandler's face and knew the reason. During the course of the previous evening he had learned that Chandler was junior to both of the officers from the flagship. Duvalier-Winter would be first lieutenant and Chandler would once again be third. Obviously Chandler had made it his business to look up their seniority.

'Your time will come, Mr Chandler,' he said with a smile. He walked a few paces and added musingly, 'Not quite as quickly as it did for some of us during the war, but it will come nevertheless. Courage and prudence can give a man as much advancement as a privileged birth.—You have proved that you have courage.'

Chandler looked up quickly. The omission seemed to imply that he was lacking in common sense. Lawson's eyes were on the approaching boat, now almost under their stern.

'It would be imprudent to discuss with your brother officers the general belief that Yussaiff Ahmed and Peter Heward are the same,' he said at last. 'At least that is the view of the admiral and our future careers lie in his hand.' He turned suddenly and faced Chandler. 'We shall take Yussaiff Ahmed one day. Then he will be hanged. Meanwhile nothing can be gained by talking about it.'

Lawson's lower jaw jutted aggressively and his eyes sought Chandler's. The lieutenant stared at him, then nodded abruptly.

'I shall say nothing, sir.'

The boat hooked on and Lieutenant Duvalier-Winter swung himself gracefully onto the companionway and climbed aboard. He was joined in a moment by the more heavily built Lieutenant Hawbrook. The captain acknowledged their salutes and introduced Chandler. Whilst they were exchanging courtesies he quickly appraised the newcomers.

Duvalier-Winter did not appear to be so much the dandy as he had the day before. He was still elegant but not foppishly so. No handkerchief dangled from his cuff. The cut of his jacket was not so extravagant. Hawbrook was his opposite : a regular John Bull of a man whose round face would have not been out of place at a country fair. His well worn, faded jacket indicated that he had little, if anything, beyond his pay as a lieutenant. Lawson's heart warmed to him.

'I should like you to wait upon me in my cabin as soon as—' he was going to say as soon as convenient but checked himself when he remembered his own reactions to the admiral's request on the previous day—'as soon as you have attended to your gear.'

He smiled fleetingly and turned away. He wanted to take in more of this delightful morning air before returning to his cabin.

His idling steps took him forward to where the work was going on aloft. He paused at the foot of the newly stepped mast and looked up. The cheerful shouts from above died as the men became aware of their captain's presence. He decided to join them and was reaching for the ratlines when a thin wisp of a man in a dark suit caught his attention by clearing his throat noisily a few feet away.

'Who are you?' Lawson demanded brusquely.

The man uncoiled himself from the stork-like stance he had adopted and sidled closer. He looked earnestly up at the scarred face of the captain and adjusted his coat before replying.

'If you please, sir, I am Savage, your new clerk.'

Lawson's face twitched. A more unlikely name could hardly have been found for the poor creature blinking nervously in front of him.

'Well, Mr Savage, I'll pass the word when I need you.'

'I've brought the mail with me, sir.'

Lawson scowled.

'Yes, Mr Savage. Later.'

'Personal mail as well, sir,' he persisted.

'Go to hell !'

The clerk scuttled off but the damage was done. Lawson's

sunny mood had evaporated and he forgot his intention to go aloft. Letters from home interested him as much as any man but he was certainly not going to examine them now. They would wait and the clerk would wait for him to deal with the official stuff until he had spoken to the replacements.

'Officer of the watch,' he shouted.

Midshipman Barty hurried forward, gulping down the last of an orange he had been surreptitiously eating. Hastily he wiped his mouth on the sleeve of his coat.

'Sir,' he said and belched.

Lawson's face darkened.

'You are disgustingly untidy, Mr Barty,' he snarled. 'Unless you mend your ways, you are going to be a very sorry young man for the rest of this commission.'

Barty mentally cursed the clerk whose importunities he had seen.

'I'm very sorry, sir.'

'Call up the new people.'

'Aye aye, sir.'

Barty hurried away, leaving the captain to stump around the deck. Not a sound came from the yard above. The carpenter and his mates worked silently with the prisoners casting apprehensive glances in his direction. The numerous parties around the decks bent industriously over their tasks. Even the noisy gulls seemed to have sheered off. Suddenly Lawson saw the humour of the thing and smiled to himself. By the time the newcomers had assembled he had almost recovered.

The officers had joined him and together they walked along the lines of men, with Lawson pausing from time to time and asking questions of those who interested him for one reason or another. Most of them were young, but there were a few grey beards among them; gunners and tradesmen with years of ship experience behind them; sound men who stayed in the Navy because they knew no other life. Hopton would never have parted with them in wartime. Lawson was very impressed.

'It would seem that you have brought a fair body of men with you,' he said when the inspection was over.

Duvalier-Winter smiled charmingly.

'I should hardly call them fair, sir. I daresay they're as unwashed as the next.'

Captain Lawson's brows contracted. He glared belligerently at his second in command. Chandler and Hawbrook tried to look as though they had not heard the remark.

'I was referring to their general air of competence and not to the cleanliness of their bodies. However, since you claim that they are unwashed, I should be obliged if you would personally supervise their immediate ablutions. I will no more tolerate dirty bodies on my ship than—I will permit powdered faces. Do I make myself clear, Mr—Winter?'

'Perfectly, sir. But my name is——'

'I don't give a damn what your name is. Carry out my orders and report to my cabin when you have finished.'

His eyes burned into those of the lieutenant as if daring him to make a reply. There being none, he snorted and strode off, remembering when it was too late to go back, that he had intended to welcome the men with a special speech which he had prepared during a sleepless hour the previous night.

Evans had witnessed the whole business and he now knew enough about his master to get both himself and the clerk out of the cabin before Lawson reached it. Consequently the captain was alone when he closed the door behind him.

'Damn the man,' he muttered as he dropped into the chair behind his desk.

There was the mail before him; the official stuff on the right and two letters, which were obviously personal, on the left. He recognised both envelopes as belonging to a batch he had bought for his sister on his way home during his last visit and if there had been any doubt the smell of lavender would have removed it. All her belongings were surrounded by lavender bags. He peered at the writing but could make nothing of it; perhaps later he would manage with a reading glass. Meanwhile there were the dispatches to deal with. Most of them would be unimportant but there might be something that needed prompt attention.

'Sentry!' he shouted. 'Send for my clerk.'

Whilst he waited he pondered the problem that now faced him. It would be a long business replying to the official mail even supposing he were able to read it with the aid of a glass. Not all of these letters could be entrusted to a clerk. Some of them could be intended for the eyes of the captain only, and it would be a court-martial offence to allow Savage to see them. Obviously Jim Saunders must go through it first. When the clerk arrived he would reprimand him for not placing official mail under lock and key and then send him off until later.

A tap on the door announced the return of the sentry. He stepped smartly inside and came to attention.

'Beg to report, sir. Your clerk is having a bath. The new lieutenant said 'e can't come yet, sir.'

Lawson's jaw dropped in surprise. The marine stared fixedly ahead.

'He can't come yet?'

'Beggin' your pardon, sir. That's what the gennelman said, sir.'

The captain thrust himself out of his chair. He clutched the desk, his knuckles showing white, and glared at the sentry. Then he charged across the cabin and out through the open door onto the deck.

'Mr Winter!' he shouted.

Duvalier-Winter was over by the port side watching forty or more naked seamen trying to dodge the jets from a number of hosepipes whilst they lathered themselves. He glanced in the captain's direction then casually turned back to the public washing. Lawson's eyes blazed.

'Mr Winter!' he roared.

The lieutenant detached himself from the rail and sauntered over.

'Did you want something, sir?'

The veins on Lawson's neck swelled visibly and his face grew purple. His great hands clenched and he thrust his face close to Duvalier-Winter's.

'Why the bloody hell do you think I called you?' he ground through clenched teeth. 'What the blazes do you think you are doing?'

He pushed past the lieutenant and strode forward to the forecastle.

'Belay that,' he ordered the men with the hoses.

As the jets were turned away, the unfortunate men stood dejectedly looking at him. For the most part they were spiritless; dumb animals crushed by the discipline of the navy, suffering yet another indignity. Yet a few eyes flashed resentment. Lawson sensed the rebellion, but it was not this he feared. A frigate needed proud men. Browbeaten lickspits could never make an inspired fighting force. On an impulse he began to unbutton his coat.

'Mr Du-vallee Winter.'

'Sir?'

'Shall we join the men in a bath?' he asked loudly. 'That is an order which you will obey,' he added in a whisper, 'and if you value the future control you will need to lead these men, and will look as though you are enjoying it.'

As the two officers began to strip, Chandler and Barty advanced.

'May we share your bath, sir?' Chandler asked.

Lawson nodded his approval and they too began to strip off their clothes. The stolid Hawbrook looked on in astonishment for a moment, then hurriedly fumbled with his cravat. A few minutes later, Saunders, high up on the yard, witnessed the unusual spectacle of the ship's officers being subjected to a hosing on the foredeck before a crowd of happy seamen.

'Ladies coming, sir,' a topman warned the midshipman with a grin. 'Over there.'

A long low barge, such as had brought most of the visitors out from the Rock to the flagship the day before, was approaching leisurely. Seated in the cushions and shading themselves from the sun under multi-coloured umbrellas, were three ladies and a small boy. One of the party was Cecilia Dullant.

'Avast there at the pump,' Saunders shouted to the men below.

As the jets drooped away the captain looked questioningly about him. It was Chandler who spotted the boat. The men at the oars were grinning. The ladies were finding something of interest in the opposite direction.

The deck was cleared in seconds. Saunders scrambled down from his perch, jerked his coat straight and waited at the entry port, as the only officer available to receive the visitors.

The boat hooked on but the ladies made no attempt to rise. Cecilia smiled up at the midshipman.

'Good morning, Mr Saunders. Captain Hopton's son expressed a desire for a boat trip around the harbour and since the weather is so glorious we decided to accompany him.'

'Would you care to come aboard, ma'am?'

One of the ladies giggled.

'No, thank you. Pray convey our respects to your captain.'

The boatmen pushed off and as they got under way again the small boy's voice came plaintively over the water.

'But why can't we go? They've finished their bath.'

Meanwhile Lawson and Duvalier-Winter were facing each other across the width of the captain's table. They were both naked except for the towels which Evans, with his growing imperturbability had provided. Lawson rubbed himself vigorously as he spoke and his lieutenant looked thoroughly subdued as he listened with the towel around his waist and shoulders still gleaming wet. His fine clothes, which he had clutched at as he had bolted, were strewn along the path of his flight. Only his trousers were with him and they lay crumpled at his feet.

The cold water and the lieutenant's immediate compliance with his orders had somewhat mollified the captain. He sensed what an ordeal it must have been for Duvalier-Winter to strip on the deck. Nevertheless he was still annoyed and spoke his mind.

'Have I made myself clear?' he concluded.

'Perfectly, sir.'

'As for your having to take a bath before the men,' he rumbled as he reached for his shirt, 'that is not a part of your duties. You can make a complaint to the admiral if you wish, without fear of reprisals on my part.'

'It is not my intention to take the matter further, sir.'

'So be it.—You will find that the men will think no worse of you for having been hosed. The main thing is that they will feel no bitterness now. They will consider themselves to be part of a family and that is important in a fighting ship.' He paused then added thoughtfully, 'Treat men like curs and that is how they will behave in the face of enemy. Give them a chance to develop dignity and confidence and they will conquer the earth. —The man who gave me that bit of advice, Mr Duvalee-Winter has more sea victories to his credit than any sailor in the British Navy.'

13

As Captain Lawson sped over the bay in a newly acquired gig, he experienced an unusual feeling of complete contentment with his world. The troubles of the previous day were behind him. A third of his crew were on shore leave and the remainder were working happily with the thought that their turn would come over the next two days. Even Midshipman Barty, having dispelled the cloud that had lain over him by volunteering for a bath on the open deck, had been given permission to go ashore. Peacetime was not so bad after all, the captain reflected. Had they been at war, he would not so readily have left his ship under the command of Lieutenant Duvalier-Winter. Nor would he have been able to allow so many men away. Indeed the pressed men would be kept permanently aboard and a marine guard would have to be rowed around the ship after dark to make sure that they did not swim for it.

An old man, pockmarked and swarthy, heaved himself to his feet as the captain's boat approached the quay, and called for the seaman in the bows to throw a rope. The bowman ignored him. With neat judgement he stepped ashore, made fast his painter and took the stern rope from Thompson before the boat lost its way. The old man scowled and stood back.

Lawson looked at him doubtfully after he had left the boat. 'The admiral's house,' he demanded briskly. 'Do you know where it is now?'

'Si, Señor Captain. You follow me.'

He led the way through a crowd of market women with baskets of fish, fruit and merchandise of every description. With little prospects of selling anything to the well dressed officer in their midst, they nevertheless cheerfully called out at him and thrust their goods under his nose. A host of barefooted, ragged children, who had been squabbling and playing in the dust, scrambled to their feet with whoops and laughs to join in the fun. Lawson was brought to a standstill as they danced playfully around him, begging for money. He felt in his pocket and found some small change, then his guide came back and cleared the way with curses and flailing hands.

The disturbance seemed to be of great interest to a bearded man of barrel-like proportions, who was wearing the cocked hat and blue tunic coat of the merchant captain. His small eyes had glittered and the thick sensual lips had twisted into a sneer when Lawson had been brought to a halt. Now as the guide cleared a way through the market crowd, he followed at a distance.

Eventually they came to a pair of wrought iron gates set in a high wall. The Spaniard pushed one open and pointed to the house, an ugly box-like building with flat roof and slatted green sun visors at the windows. The garden was overgrown but a recent attack had been made on the weeds on both sides of the drive and a fork stood in freshly turned earth around the entrance porch.

Lawson dropped a silver piece into the man's crooked hand and smiled ruefully at his gasp of astonishment. He never knew how much to tip these people. Evidently he had overdone it again.

'Gracias, Captain. I wait for you. Take you to very fine place with beautiful ladies and good wine.'

He tested the coin between his teeth and grinned speculatively at Lawson's retreating figure. Suddenly his throat was caught from behind and he was thrust back against the wall. Eyes wide with fear he stared at the bearded face of the man who held him. The merchant captain's lips curled contemptuously.

'See here,' he said, thrusting a golden guinea under the Spaniard's nose.

The old man's face twitched nervously but greed was already struggling with the terror in his eyes.

'It could be for you.'

The grip around his throat was relaxed. He gulped in air noisily and awaited the conditions.

'Go in the garden and hide in the bushes. I must know to whom the Kapitan speaks. When you hear something of interest to me, you can have three more guineas.'

The Spaniard's head nodded eagerly.

'You wait here, señor?'

'Nein. I wait in the Royal George. Go now.'

The old man peered through the gates, paused, then scuttled into the bushes. The merchant captain listened for a few minutes, then flipped the gold coin, caught it neatly and dropped it into his pocket before retracing his steps down the road.

Lawson had reached the house by the time the Spaniard, creeping along the back of the hedge, had reached a position of vantage. The man was just in time to see the broad shoulders of his quarry disappear through the open door. He waited, biting his nails in disappointment.

The Spanish woman who had admitted Lawson seemed worried as she relieved him of his hat and sword and led him to a small room cluttered with pottery, swords and tapestries of Moorish workmanship.

'Please wait, sir. I'll see if m'lady will receive you.'

'She is expecting me.'

'Yes, sir, but she has just received some disturbing— She is not very well, sir.'

She backed out of the room in some confusion and closed the door. Lawson thoughtfully picked up an elaborately worked sword but it held no interest for him. His mind was turning over what the woman had been about to say, 'she has just received some disturbing—news.' It could hardly be anything else but from where could she have had news? Certainly nothing from England had arrived over the last two days unless she had some private overland communication; a highly unlikely possibility. Could it have been 'some disturbing—gossip—the admiral and his mistress?'

A movement in the bushes just outside the window caught his attention. Perplexed he walked over the thick carpet and looked out. There was no one to be seen. He wondered if his eyes were playing tricks again. He was still watching when Cecilia came in.

She came close to him and took his hand. Lawson became aware of her perfume and realised that the room, with its musty smell, had not often been visited by her. Her next words confirmed this.

'I see you are seeking relief from this dull place, Captain. I can't imagine why Marie brought you in here.'

'I hope you are feeling better, ma'am. Your woman told me that you are not very well.'

She smiled brightly; too brightly. There was a suspicion of a tear.

'Come, let us leave this depressing room,' she said impulsively. 'I have reserved the only reasonable patch of garden for your visit. Perhaps you can give me an opinion on the roses for I am undecided what to do with them.'

She led the way through a large drawing room to french windows which opened onto a veranda festooned with climbing roses. Lawson blinked in the bright sunlight, misjudged a rose tendril and became entangled.

'Ouch!' he exclaimed as a thorn scratched his head.

'Don't move or it will pull threads out of your coat,' Cecilia warned. 'Let me help you.'

She eased the thorns carefully out of the cloth, then stretched to dab at the blood spot on his brow with her handkerchief. She overbalanced and leaned heavily against him. Lawson's arms reached out to steady her and, instead, held her to him. He looked down into her eyes. She smiled mischievously and disengaged herself.

'Well, now that you have had a close look at the roses,' she said brightly, 'what do you think I ought to do about them?'

'Cut them down, ma'am.'

'You think they have been neglected too long?'

'I don't know about that. It's just that my head has some kind of attraction for them. My sister has them all over the porch at home and I'm damn— I can neither get in nor out without them trying to scratch my eyes out.'

'Do you always stay with your sister when you are at home?'

'Whenever I have the opportunity to go north, ma'am. I have nowhere else.'

'You were never married?'

'Yes. I had a week of married life, followed by two years at sea; the old familiar pattern of the average sailor's life. Some wives can stand the strain. Mine couldn't.'

'Oh! I'm sorry.'

'Nothing to be sorry about, ma'am. We were both well satisfied I believe, in the end.'

Her face lightened in a fleeting smile and became solemn again. Lawson watched her carefully. Clearly something was troubling her.

'Look, ma'am,' he began awkwardly, 'when I arrived, your maid said, or almost let slip, that you had received some disturbing news. Now if this is the case, and I can be of any help, I should be very pleased. If not, perhaps you would prefer me to curtail my visit on this occasion.'

'Don't go!' she said quickly. 'Please don't leave me.'

She placed her hand on his arm and looked up at him. There was urgency in her eyes and a certain tenseness about her that Lawson found disturbing. His embarrassment was so obvious that her face relaxed into a smile: a slow fond smile that set his pulses racing.

'And don't call me ma'am,' she reproved with mock severity. 'It sounds so formal after our—adventures together.'

She squeezed his arm. He covered her hand with his, then drew her gently towards him. They stood for a moment looking into each other's eyes before he kissed her.

His kiss was gentle, almost apprehensive. She remained in his arms, close to him, looking up into his face. Her eyes were filled with a curious mixture of maternalism and physical desire. She ran her fingers through the curling hair at his temples, half shrugged herself free, then drew his lips down to her again.

The second kiss broke down her reserve completely. She clung to him, moulding her body into his, responding to the growing fire of his passion with all the ardour of a long neglected wife.

A rustling sound in the bushes froze Lawson into rigidity. Cecilia, who had heard nothing, looked at him questioningly, a hint of fear in her expression. Lawson thrust her aside suddenly and strode across the veranda. Immediately the Spaniard broke cover and ran with short darting steps through the garden. Lawson hurled himself after him, plunging into the clinging thorn with a roar of rage.

Less than sixty yards separated the fleeing spy from the gate and he had already covered a third of that distance before the captain had disentangled himself but he was being overtaken rapidly and his eyes were wide with fear. As the great figure of his pursuer loomed over him and the powerful hands were reaching out, he darted desperately to one side. There was a glint of steel. Lawson's hand swept down to dash the knife away but he misjudged it. The blade slashed his forearm and grated against his ribs with a shock that caused him to lose his balance and sprawl in the undergrowth. The Spaniard fled, leaving his knife where he had dropped it.

Cecilia sent for a doctor, despite Lawson's declared intention to attend to himself. The doctor arrived promptly and cast a brisk professional glance at the captain as he sat on the veranda gripping his forearm to stem the flow of blood.

'A glass of wine would not come amiss, I think. Meanwhile we'll have the coat off you to see what sort of a mess you are in.'

Cecilia gasped at the sight of the gash. Then her eyes widened in alarm when she saw that the front of his shirt was soaked in blood. The doctor cut away the linen to reveal a long shallow slash on the left side of the lower ribs. He examined it curiously before turning back to the arm.

Whilst the man was stitching and dressing the wounds, Lawson had a good opportunity to examine him. Cecilia had introduced him as Thomas Fairweather. The name was familiar to Lawson but he could not remember where he had heard it before. It fitted in with that part of his life that he had spent tramping the streets of London waiting for a ship.

He judged him to be in his late fifties. He was sturdy rather than fat, though his face was inclined to be fleshy and gave the impression of being wider than it was because of the enormous side whiskers which framed it. Lawson disliked side whiskers and being a man of prejudice, he regarded all who wore them with disfavour, but there was something likeable about this man. He had a quiet air of competence and a firm touch. His eyes, as far as Lawson could see, were shrewd and intelligent. Suddenly he became aware that they were directed questioningly at him.

'Well, Captain, what do you make of me?' he asked with a smile.

'I beg your pardon.'

'You've had a preoccupied expression on your face ever since you heard my name. But you can't remember where you've heard it before so, like the normal intelligent person I think you are, and well used to assessing men, you've been busy fitting me into a category.'

'I have been doing no such thing, sir,' Lawson said sternly.

Fairweather smiled charmingly.

'I should like you to know all about me, Captain. You see, I am wanting you to do me a favour and you'll not be granting it otherwise.'

He patted the chest bandage into place.

'There, that should heal nicely, leaving you with another scar to join the others. I'm not so sure about the arm though. I rather fancy you might have a little difficulty in moving the first and second fingers. Time alone will tell. The human body is a wonderful machine, Captain. We can take it to pieces and examine every part of it. We can see how it works and sometimes we can repair a bit of damage but our successes in the end depend upon the ability of the living flesh to heal itself.'

Suddenly Lawson remembered where he had heard the name Fairweather before. The man had been involved in the trial of a notorious body snatcher and murderer. The whole of London had been buzzing with the details of the trial and Doctor Fairweather's house and laboratory had been burned to the ground. Fairweather was watching him enquiringly, a twisted smile on his lips.

'Now you remember where you have heard my name before, Captain, and you are wondering why a rogue like me is permitted to remain in Gibraltar.'

'Damn it, sir. Are you claiming to be able to read my thoughts?'

'That is the last thing I would wish to do,' Fairweather replied quietly. 'Perhaps I am so used to people condemning me for my research that I have become too sensitive about my past. Whenever I sense that I am in disfavour I immediately assume that the unfortunate business in London has been remembered against me. Silly, really, I suppose. It might only be my side whiskers that are giving offence.'

Lawson looked at him in astonishment. Could the man read his thoughts? This seemed uncanny.

'What is this favour you mentioned?' he demanded brusquely.

Doctor Fairweather washed his hands in the bowl that Marie had brought and smiled ruefully.

'I fear that you are not in the right mood to grant favours. However, I must ask you now since I am not likely to be offered another opportunity. Before I do ask, I should like you to know a little more about the unhappy business that drove me temporarily from London.'

He walked across the veranda to the table where Cecilia had placed a decanter of wine, and poured two glasses. Lawson joined him, took the offered glass and sat down. Fairweather sipped at his own appreciatively and pulled up a chair on the other side of the table.

'I am an anatomist, you understand. The study of the human body has obsessed me since I was a youth and I believe that some of my discoveries have been of value. The teaching of the Church makes it devilish difficult for the anatomist to obtain subjects and so he must, of necessity have dealings with some very odd characters. Rand, the murderer, was one of these, but of course I knew nothing of his murders until he was arrested. His trial and the publicity that followed caused me to leave England.'

He shrugged and took a sip of wine.

'I had intended to travel abroad anyway, as soon as the war ended. Professor Surborg in Hamburg has made some interesting discoveries, so has Doctor Testa in Milan. There was also Bogatti in Rome, but he has recently died. All have been engaged in research on the human eye and since my own father became blind for no accountable reason at the age of forty, this particular field has interested me more than any other.'

He looked keenly at Lawson who waited attentively.

'Today I think I know more about the causes of blindness than any man in Britain.—Believe me, Captain, I am not boasting. I am full of humility because I know so little.—Perhaps you will, by now, appreciate the nature of the favour I am about to ask you.'

Lawson said nothing. Fairweather leaned forward urgently.

'It is common knowledge that you were blind for several days after the explosion on your ship. I should be very interested to see the effect on your eyes.'

'My sight is as good as ever,' Lawson growled.

Fairweather smiled sympathetically.

'I appreciate the need for absolute secrecy, Captain. No one will ever know the results of my examination.'

'I tell you that I have no trouble,' Lawson replied angrily.

Fairweather shrugged, poured wine into Lawson's glass and refilled his own.

'Your health, Captain,' he said, raising the glass to his lips.

Lawson reached out automatically but checked himself as he

realised Fairweather's intentions. A moving tracery of shadows from the rose tendrils lay across the table. This, together with his defective sight, caused him to see several outlines of his glass. Evidently Fairweather had noted his uncertainty each time he had taken it. His hand fell back and he glared at the doctor.

'How long will your examination take?'

The man rose to his feet, a smile of pleasure rather than triumph on his face.

'I will call on you tomorrow on board your ship. I ought to see your wounds anyway. Will the forenoon suit you?'

Lawson considered the proposal. He had no wish to advertise the fact of his impaired vision but the officer of the watch would learn that he had been wounded and since they had no surgeon on board they would expect him to arrange for one to call.

'Very well, Doctor. I will expect you on board as early as you please.'

At that moment Cecilia rejoined them. Fairweather bowed courteously and left. Lawson took Cecilia's hand.

'I must go. Perhaps we can find this Spaniard before dark and I think it important that we should find him. There will be blackmail notes otherwise, for there can be no doubt that he saw us.'

Cecilia smiled bitterly.

'Does it matter?' she asked.

'No—o. Except that I should want to be the one to tell the admiral, if you wish him to know about us.'

She kissed him impulsively, then turned away and stared pensively over the garden.

'He—was not hiding in the garden to spy on an unfaithful wife. There are bigger things at stake.—Just before you arrived I received a letter demanding twenty thousand pounds for the life of someone I hold very dear.'

'Ransom!'

'My brother—Peter Heward. You did know.' She shot him a quick appealing smile. 'We were always together as children. Now he is a prisoner of the Moors. They blame him for our escape and the loss of the ships. They have discovered that he is the son of a wealthy family.'

'They can't seriously hope that you will pay twenty thousand pounds.'

'I will, if I can find the money in time.'

'But—but his life is forfeit anyway. There's not a sea-faring nation in Europe that wouldn't hang him if they caught him. I'm sorry—but you do understand his position.'

She had covered her face with her hands. Lawson reached for her and at his touch she broke down and sobbed uncontrollably.

'It isn't just death—it's torture. If they do not receive the money in two months, they threaten to send his—ears.'

Lawson held her and stroked her hair as one would a child. His face was thoughtful. Chandler's report, he recalled, had suggested that there were two leaders under Yussaiff Ahmed's command who had challenged his authority at the time he had dispersed his men to search for Jim Saunders. It was possible that they had seized control. Having done so, it was unlikely that they would take the risk of releasing him. Rather would they play Cecilia along for as much as they could take from her and kill Heward in the end.

'There would be no sense in paying them,' he said gently. 'They would bleed you white and they daren't let him go. He knows too much.'

'Then what is to be done? Could you return to the bay and release him?'

He shook his head doubtfully.

'It's unlikely that they would keep him there. But even supposing they have and we were able to take him, there would still be a court martial and he was under sentence of death before he turned to piracy.'

She drew away and looked up at him incredulously.

'But you would not bring him back here. You could land him in France, or allow him to escape.'

Lawson frowned.

'I should do no such thing, m— He must pay for the deaths of my men and no power on earth could persuade me to do otherwise.'

She stepped back as though he had struck her, stared at him whitefaced for a moment, then ran into the house.

14

Down at the quayside Lawson found Thompson driving off a crowd of dockside urchins. They were standing at a safe distance baiting the coxswain when Lawson, with face as black as thunder, strode through them from the rear. They scattered to right and left and then paused to watch him step aboard the boat.

'Back to the ship,' he ordered abruptly.

He propped himself in the stern cushions with a scowl on his face. Thompson stifled the pleasantry he had been about to utter and with a few curt words ordered the boat away from the quay. The tattered children watched silently as the moorings were cast off and the boat was sent forging across the choppy waters of the bay.

'She led me on, damn her,' Lawson thought furiously. 'Prostituting herself to get me to help her brother and no doubt loathing every minute of her contact with a common sailor. To hell with her and all her kind.'

By the time they reached H.M.S. *Comus*, he had decided upon his future plans. They would go back to the bay and if Heward was there they would take him and hand him over for court martial. He would be the principal witness and the high and mighty Heward family would have to face up to the skeleton in their cupboard. First he would have to obtain permission to leave harbour and if the admiral guessed his intention, permission would not be given.

'Will you require the boat again, sir?'

Lawson looked at his coxswain thoughtfully. Thompson and the others would have seen the Spaniard. Quite apart from the probability of blackmail, the man must be brought to justice for attempted murder.

'You will remember the old man who met us at the quayside?'

'Yes, sir.'

'Go back and spend the remaining hours of daylight searching for him.'

He swung himself from the boat and turned to look down upon the interested boat's crew.

'Let every man go ashore who claims that he can recognise the fellow. If you find him, arrest him and bring him to me. Here, take this.'

He handed several silver pieces to the surprised Thompson.

'You will need to go through the taverns,' he added by way of explanation. 'If any man makes a fool of himself or refuses to obey the orders given by my coxswain, I'll have him in irons for a week.'

He glared threateningly at the upturned faces, jerked his head in a gesture of dismissal and climbed on board *Comus*. By the time he had reached his cabin, the boat with its light-hearted load of seamen was already half way back to the shore.

Evans, grinning in welcome, pulled off the captain's shore-going shoes and replaced them with the canvas slippers he wore habitually when in his cabin. The stiff tunic coat with its expensive gold braid was eased from his shoulders. When the Negro saw the bandaging on the forearm, his eyes opened wide and he clucked anxiously. The captain ignored him and, stretching himself on his cot, closed his eyes obstinately. Suddenly he remembered the unopened mail.

'Ask Mr Saunders if he will kindly report to my cabin,' he said wearily.

By the time the midshipman arrived, Lawson had laid out all all the dispatches and slit the wrappings.

'Sit down, lad,' he said. 'Most of this will be routine stuff and I can't be bothered to wade through it all with a reading glass. Just set aside the paper work that will be handled by my clerk and read the rest to me. I can trust no one else with the know-ledge that I am having trouble with my eyes.'

Only one letter was of real interest to Captain Lawson. A merchant sea captain called Kettelmann was suspected of mix-ing piracy with his legitimate business and he was believed to have had dealings with Yussaiff Ahmed.

'I know that name,' Lawson said.

He searched his memory. The name was German. That much was certain but he had known many Germans when he had been based on the Baltic and the North Sea. He cast his mind back to the time he had stayed as a guest of the Graf von Oldenburg. They had spent every day on horseback, hunting wild pigs and deer, or driving their mounts through the marsh lands around the Jade Büsen in search of fowl, and all the time expecting to run into a patrol from Napoleon's regiments, stationed not forty miles away in Delmenhorst. One of the party had surely been called Kettelmann.

Suddenly he had it : Friedrich Kettelmann, captain of a privateer. Lawson had come into contact with him again a few months later at a council of war on board the flagship at Lübeck and they had followed up with a hectic night in the town.

'A giant of a man,' Lawson said reflectively, 'with a fund of crude stories and a loud coarse laugh. He was a vicious rogue. There was a vivid scar running down one side of his face. Not your neat little duelling snick that the German takes pride in, but a full-blooded slash that must have cut through the bone and would have killed most men. He spoke tolerably good English. In fact I think he said that his mother came from England.'

'I do believe that one of the guests on board the flagship answers that description, sir !' Jim exclaimed.

'Indeed !' Lawson sat up sharply. 'How old would you say he was?'

'About fifty, sir. Head and shoulders above everybody else but he was very stout also. He spent most of the evening telling a group of army officers about his adventures during the war. I heard a little of the conversation and I would say that there was most certainly an accent that was not English.'

'The scar? What about the scar?'

'He wore a beard. That might have concealed it,' Jim replied after a moment's hesitation. 'But he had an unusually loud laugh, sir,' he added hopefully. 'Possibly you heard him.'

Lawson rubbed his chin thoughtfully. Kettelmann would be somewhere in the region of fifty and it was quite possible that he had put on a lot of weight with his advancing years.

It seemed a long shot but the means of identification were close at hand.

'Ask Mr Duvalier-Winter if he will kindly attend me in my cabin,' he said suddenly.

It was a diffident, somewhat uneasy first lieutenant who presented himself a few minutes later. Lawson wasted no time over preliminaries.

'You would know something of the guest list for the affair you had on the flagship,' he said. 'I want to know about the big man with the beard.'

'There was a fellow with a deucedly attractive wife. He is something in the Governor's service. Can't for the life of me remember . . .'

'A sea-going man,' interrupted the captain. 'I shouldn't think he had a wife with him.'

'You wouldn't mean the German fellow?'

'Who was he?' the captain demanded tensely.

'I can't remember, sir. One has great difficulty in getting one's tongue around those foreign names.'

'Was it Kettelmann?'

'No, sir. Certainly not that,' replied Duvalier-Winter, becoming more matter of fact when he realised that his captain had something on his mind of more importance than a social evening. 'Perhaps Mr Hawbrook might be able to remember him. He spent some of the evening in his company. Didn't care for the fellow myself.'

'Did you notice a scar on his face?' demanded Lawson.

The lieutenant answered without hesitation.

'The very devil of a scar, sir. He's tried to conceal it beneath his beard but it's clear enough. The whole of the left side of the jaw has been cleft.'

Lawson thumped the table.

'Kettelmann!' he exclaimed.

He took up the letter which Jim had just read to him and thrust it into Duvalier-Winter's hands. The second in command read it briefly and replaced it on the table. He waited expectantly.

'I do believe that this German captain is the man referred to in that dispatch. The name by which he is known at the moment is of no importance. What can you tell me of him?'

The lieutenant appeared apologetic.

'Very little, sir. He is master of a fine ship. She's also well armed unless her lower gun ports are false. He arrived spectacularly enough just a few hours before you. He had a pack of small craft at his heels when he was first seen from the masthead of the flagship. The lookout had reported the gunfire some fifteen minutes earlier and most of us witnessed the running battle that took place.'

'Battle?' queried the captain.

'A fleet of dhows, sir. Came out after him whilst he was lying becalmed. He managed to hold them off for an hour until a breath of wind enabled him to get under way. The admiral sent for an account as soon as he dropped anchor.'

Lawson considered the news. It was quite possible that Kettelmann had been attacked. Rival pirates were just as likely to try to take his ship as they were to capture legitimate traders. It was also possible that he had arranged a dramatic approach to justify his being at Gibraltar should Cecilia start looking for the ship which had brought the message about her brother.

'What is the name of his ship?'

Duvalier-Winter considered for a moment.

'*Die Reichmacher* or something like that.'

'Maker of riches,' mused Lawson.

He sat for a moment in thought, drumming his fingers on the desk top.

'Go ashore, Mr Duvalier-Winter,' he ordered abruptly. 'Learn all you can about this German captain and his ship. I want to know how often he comes here and where he trades. Make your enquiries as discreetly as possible if you value your life. Before you go, instruct the watch to inform me at once of any activity aboard *Die Reichmacher*.'

'Yes, sir.' The lieutenant looked surprised.

'Have a pistol in each pocket of your coat.' He grinned wryly. 'It'll play the devil with the set of the shoulders but you may find the precaution worth while.'

'Very good, sir,' Duvalier-Winter replied soberly. 'Supposing I discover something to justify this fellow's arrest?'

'Send a message back to me. You'll need someone reliable. Get Barty or——'

'Mr Barty has the watch, sir,' Saunders volunteered.

Lawson smiled. Jim Saunders clearly wanted to go. It was the sort of adventure that must appeal strongly to a boy.

'Mr Saunders will serve as your messenger,' he said.

He nodded in dismissal and turned to replace the papers in the box.

IT was almost dawn when Duvalier-Winter reported back. Lawson, who had spent half the night awaiting the return of Thompson, was asleep. He awoke quickly enough when the marine sentry knocked on the door of the cabin and entered with a lamp. A bedraggled first lieutenant followed.

'Well?'

'Success and failure, sir,' drawled the second in command with some return of the languid manner that had so infuriated Lawson earlier.

'Give me the details,' he growled.

'I found a fellow who claimed he had sailed with this German captain. A fellow with a prodigious thirst. As long as I plied him with drink he was prepared to tell me stories which, if true, would make the piracy charge insignificant.'

'Where is he?' demanded the captain.

The lieutenant eased the collar of his jacket from his neck and Lawson noticed for the first time that he was wet. Indeed, when he looked closer, he saw that the man was soaking.

'That is the failure part of my report, I'm afraid,' replied the lieutenant. 'He gave me the slip. Having said that he would return with me on board *Comus*, damn me if he didn't knock me on the head and pitch me over the side of the quay.'

Lawson smiled despite his disappointment. He felt that he now knew more about his second in command. The languid manner which he affected was to hide his embarrassment. It was likely that the unknown informant had merely led him along for the sake of the drink. He had obviously no intention of giving evidence. Probably he had none to offer.

'Perhaps I can take a party ashore at first light,' added

Duvalier-Winter. 'I should like to make his acquaintance again.'

'I doubt if you would find him,' replied Lawson dryly. 'I suppose you saw no sign of my coxs'n and his party whilst you were ashore?'

'No, sir.'

'Very well. Go and get some sleep.'

He nodded his head in dismissal. The lieutenant turned to go, then paused at the door.

'Several seamen were arrested for murder during the night, sir.'

'Where were they from?' Lawson demanded urgently.

'Can't say, sir. I was involved with this fellow at the time. Someone came in with the story that there had been a fight and a Spaniard had been knifed.'

'Damn!' exclaimed the captain.

'You don't think that our men are involved, sir?'

'Change your clothes and report back to me,' ordered the captain. 'Tell the sentry to pass the word for Evans.'

Evans arrived breathlessly, buttoning up his coat. He found the captain looking around for his shore-going shoes.

'Shave,' ordered Lawson.

The negro disappeared instantly. Lawson found his shoes and buckled them on. He was reaching for his shirt when there was a knock on the door and the marine sentry entered. He clicked to attention and saluted.

'The officer of the watch sends his compliments, sir, and wishes to report that the German ship is weighing anchor.'

Lawson dropped his shirt and hurried out on deck. In the chill light of dawn, he stood poised at the head of the companionway, his hair blowing in the fresh breeze. A senior midshipman was officer of the watch but Hawbrook had already joined him. He offered the captain his telescope. Lawson waved it aside.

'I should be obliged if you would keep her under observation, Mr Hawbrook. Report her movements exactly.'

Evans fussed around with the shirt, whilst Hawbrook focused on the departing vessel.

'She's under way, sir,' he reported. 'Mainsails and topsails, and they are shaking out the topgallants on all three masts, sir.'

Lawson gnawed his lower lip. It was probable that many of the questions he needed to ask about Peter Heward could be answered by the captain of *Die Reichmacher*. For a moment he considered ordering him to heave-to, then decided against it. Even if the captain were Kettelmann, he had no evidence against him. The Admiralty letter had merely stated that he was suspected of piracy. He could hardly arrest him on suspicion.

'She'll pass very close to us if she holds her present tack, sir,' said Hawbrook, watching the approaching ship intently.

Lawson grunted and turned to retrace his steps to his cabin. When his shoulders reached the level of the deck he stopped and looked up at the officer of the watch.

'Don't appear to be too interested in her, Mr Hawbrook,' he cautioned.

He found Duvalier-Winter below and beckoned to him to enter his cabin.

'I'm going over to the flagship shortly. You will accompany me in the boat and then go ashore to see the Provost Marshal. Tell Mr Hawbrook that the ship must be ready to weigh anchor when we return.'

Duvalier-Winter, who had been looking forward to a leisurely breakfast and a restful morning after his activities of the night, sighed. Lawson shot him a quick glance and was about to add a rebuke when the irate voice of Hawbrook was heard on deck.

'Damn you! Keep your distance.'

Lawson ran to the foot of the companionway leading to the quarterdeck, then checked himself and listened. At the same time the deck heaved gently as though from the wash of a ship passing close by. There was a roar of laughter that took him back over the years; the unmistakable laugh of Friedrich Kettelmann. Lawson turned away and smiled grimly to himself.

Whilst Evans was busy applying the soothing warm water and lather, Lawson listened to the sounds of an awakening ship and considered the problems before him.

It was most likely that the men who had been arrested were those under Thompson's command. Clearly his first job must be to obtain their release. Then he would ask for permission to leave harbour to keep an eye on Kettelmann. Once he was clear of the Rock and free of the control of the flagship, he would return to the bay to try to find out who was holding Peter Heward. More than likely Captain Kettelmann would be able to supply the answer.

'That'll do,' he grumbled irritably as Evans poised with a razor. 'Get my coat.'

He pulled at the white cloth around his neck and dabbed at his face. If he could obtain the release of his men quickly and get the admiral's permission to leave, there was a chance that he would reach the pirate base before Kettelmann had time to get clear of it. His thoughts raced on to the action that would follow if he found *Die Reichmacher* in such an incriminating situation. Then he smiled at his assumption. Probably Kettelmann had no intention of going near the bay.

'Call away my boat,' he ordered the sentry.

On deck Hawbrook was carefully plotting the course of the now distant ship. Chandler was supervising a party engaged in bending the great anchor cable onto the foredeck capstan and keeping an eye on a chain of men who were passing ball shot to the racks alongside the guns. Aloft, midshipmen were carrying out a last-minute check of the cordage. The captain took note of all this activity as he joined Duvalier-Winter in the ship's launch.

By the time they reached the platform below the entry port on the flagship, he had explained to his first officer enough about the Spaniard's activities to justify the release of Thompson and the men with him.

'Tell the Provost that they were acting under orders. If he refuses to release them, demand an escort of marines, and claim your right to hold them as prisoners. I want them on board the flagship for questioning.'

The boat headed for the shore. Lawson climbed up through the entry port to be met by the officer of the watch.

After a delay of some thirty minutes, he was admitted to the great stern cabin to find Admiral Dullant at breakfast. The senior officer waved courteously for his early visitor to join him.

'I have something of great import——'

'Later, Captain,' the admiral interrupted. 'Pray try some of these kidneys.'

Lawson sat down and reached for the dish. Since the admiral was obviously not prepared to listen, he might as well eat. Quite possibly there would be little opportunity later. In any case they would have to wait for the return of Duvalier-Winter.

At length Admiral Dullant leaned back in his chair, dipped his fingers in a silver water bowl at his elbow and dried his hands. Lawson gulped down the last morsel from his plate and waited for permission to speak. The admiral selected a tooth pick from a glass container on the table and indicated with a nod that he was ready.

When Lawson had finished his recital, the admiral rested his great head on his hands and stared pensively at the table for several minutes.

'I wonder what this Spanish fellow was seeking at my house?' he mused.

Suddenly he raised his head and looked keenly at Lawson.

'Very likely he had robbery in mind, sir,' Lawson lied. He was convinced now that the Spaniard had been in the pay of Kettelmann.

The thin clerk entered and handed a slip of paper to the admiral.

'Well, Captain,' said the admiral, rising from his seat. 'Your men have arrived on board. It should be interesting to hear what they have to say.'

He reached for his cocked hat.

'As for your German captain.' He paused and fiddled with the gold braid of the hat, 'he may not be this fellow referred to in the dispatches but his leaving harbour without paying his respects makes him out to be either damnably rude or exceedingly guilty. That is a problem for you to solve and I need not tell you that it is one which is fraught with danger. If you act precipitately you are likely to earn the extreme displeasure of the Admiralty.'

Lawson bowed in acknowledgement and followed the admiral out of the cabin and on to the gleaming quarterdeck.

A group of midshipmen, taking their navigation lesson under the first officer, bent their heads studiously over their books as the admiral appeared but Dullant ignored them. His eyes swept the great deck until they came to rest on a group of sorry looking seamen huddled before the foremast under the eyes of half a dozen armed marines.

'Have the coxs'n brought to me,' the admiral ordered the fresh-faced officer of marines standing attentively a few yards away.

He removed a compact telescope from an inner pocket of his tails, extended it and focused the glass on the horizon. For several minutes he searched the sea whilst Thompson, escorted by two marines, was brought to a halt at a respectful distance.

Lawson searched the man's face and could see no guilt there. Thompson was naturally embarrassed but he was still the same honest sailor who had so impressed the captain by his action in the bay, and by his competence as coxswain. Whatever had happened, Lawson felt sure that this man had not let him down.

The admiral turned from his survey of the sea, closed his glass with a snap and twitched his lips into a humourless smile.

'I doubt very much if you will see your friend Kettelmann again today,' he said.

He turned to the coxswain and thrust out his weak chin. Hard eyes studied the unfortunate man.

'The full story,' he ordered curtly.

Thompson shuffled his feet awkwardly. His hands were

bound behind him and he found difficulty in speaking without them.

'We was sent out under orders from the captain, sir,' he began, with a little bob of apology to Captain Lawson.

'I know all about that,' the admiral answered testily. 'I want to hear of what happened in the brawl that resulted in the death of this Spanish fellow. Was he the man you were looking for?'

'Yes, sir. It was him all right. We'd just asked him to come along wi' us when the trouble started. I'll swear it was none of our men that did for him, sir.'

'How can you be sure?' the admiral's brows lowered fiercely.

'We was dragging him out, sir, when they came at us. A dozen or more wi' a big officer as had a bushy beard, egging 'em on. Two of 'em came straight in wi' knives and the old man gave a sort of spluttering cough and fell down.'

The admiral turned to Lawson and raised his eyebrows significantly. Lawson looked at him steadily. Dullant remained for a moment in thought, then turned sharply to the officer of marines.

'Release this man and the others,' he ordered abruptly. He turned back to Lawson and led him a little way along the deck, out of hearing of the officers. 'There's a lot more to this than meets the eye, Captain. I think that the sooner we take a look at this fellow Kettelmann, the better.'

'Have I your orders to sail, sir?'

'You have more than that. On the testimony of this coxs'n of yours, you have orders to halt *Die Reichmacher* on the high seas and to question the captain and his crew about the murder. I don't suppose it will be any good but at least it will give you the opportunity to get on board without a protest being raised by my Lords at the Admiralty.' The thin lips parted in a smile. 'Now make ready for sea. I will send written orders to you within the hour.'

Lawson took his leave and hurried to his waiting launch. The first lieutenant and the reinstated Thompson awaited him.

'I'll send the boat back for the others, sir,' Duvalier-Winter said, indicating the newly released seamen who were looking wistfully down from the side of the flagship.

Lawson nodded absently. Already his mind was on the tasks ahead. If Hawbrook had attended to his duties, they needed only the written orders from the admiral before they could get away from Gibraltar—and Cecilia. She had been at the back of his mind all the time and he needed action to get rid of her. Kettelmann, he felt sure, was involved in some way with Peter Heward's captivity. Possibly he had Heward chained below. In which case the capture of *Die Reichmacher* would complete two of the frigate's tasks. Then would follow the displeasure of the admiral and certainly the hatred of Cecilia when he handed over her brother to the authorities.

Comus loomed above them. Lawson found the handlines of the platform and swung himself easily out of the boat. The second lieutenant met him on deck.

'We sail on one hour,' the captain told him. 'Are we ready?'

'Yes, sir,' affirmed Hawbrook. 'But there's a doctor by the name of Fairweather on board. Says he is expected, sir.'

Fairweather, who had been waiting in the background, moved forward and bowed.

'I hope that I am in good time, Captain.'

Lawson frowned. He had completely forgotten that he had agreed to see the man.

'Pray come to my cabin,' he said after a moment's hesitation. It would not do for his first lieutenant and the others to know the real purpose of the doctor's visit.

He strode aft. Fairweather, with a slight bow to the curious Duvalier-Winter, followed at a distance.

Savage was busy with correspondence when the doctor and the captain entered the cabin. He bobbed to his feet and began to bustle about with a sheaf of papers awaiting signature.

'Out!' ordered the captain unceremoniously.

The little man's jaw dropped in astonishment. He indicated the letters in front of him and made as if he would remonstrate but the scowl on his captain's face made him think better of it.

He scuttled around the table and hurriedly closed the door behind him.

'You too,' Lawson added, turning to his servant.

Evans slipped quietly away.

'Now, Doctor,' he said when they were quite alone. 'I regret that time will permit only the briefest examination. I am ordered to sea and will be leaving within the hour.'

He began to strip off his coat but Fairweather made no move to open the small case that he had brought with him. Lawson looked at him expectantly. The doctor smiled and lowered the case to the deck.

'Since yesterday I have been thinking a great deal about going to sea. I feel in need of a change and I understand that you have no surgeon.' He paused and looked at the captain speculatively. 'Do you think that I might sail with you?'

Lawson heaved his jacket back on to his shoulders. His eyes sought those of the doctor for a moment. Then he nodded briefly.

'Delighted to have you, if you can gather your things together and get them aboard immediately.'

Fairweather smiled and picked up his bag.

'I'm sure that you will have much to do before you weigh anchor. My examination will wait until it is convenient for you.' He paused by the door. 'I had already taken your permission for granted. All the things I need are in the bumboat which brought me out from the harbour.'

The captain's eyes hardened in anger, but before he could say anything the cabin door was thrust open violently to admit a very harrassed looking first lieutenant.

'What the devil,' shouted Lawson, transferring his rage to Duvalier-Winter.

'Young Saunders is missing, sir.'

'Missing?'

Lawson's face drained of colour, and he clutched at the desk behind him.

'He did not report back to the ship last night, sir.'

149

Suddenly Lawson remembered that he had sent Jim ashore with Duvalier-Winter. In the excitement of hearing about the arrest of Thompson he had forgotten all about the midshipman. He felt rage against his second in command surging up inside him but with an effort he restrained himself.

'The facts,' he demanded tersely.

Duvalier-Winter was plainly nervous. Already he knew something of the bond of affection that existed between his captain and Saunders.

'I sent him back to the ship, sir, when I realised that it was going to be a drawn-out affair at the inn. He wasn't serving any useful purpose and it seemed a pity to keep him from his cot. There were lots of boats plying for trade on the quayside and there would have been no difficulty about his getting somebody to row him out.'

'What time was this?' rapped Lawson.

'About midnight, sir.'

Lawson snatched a pad from his desk and wrote rapidly. Then he tore out the sheet and thrust it at Duvalier-Winter.

'Have this signal sent at once to the admiral.'

The first lieutenant hurried from the cabin.

The doctor went to follow him but paused with his hand on the door.

'Is there anything I can do?'

'Leave me alone.'

Lawson slumped behind his desk and forced himself to consider the problem in a rational manner. His first impulse was to take half of the crew from *Comus*, and rush ashore, but as he thought about it he realised that such action would be foolish. The military could search the Rock far better than seamen. They would know every possible hiding place. *Comus* would be better employed in setting the same course as *Die Reichmacher*. Possibly Kettelmann had something to do with Jim's disappearance and the longer *Comus* delayed her sailing, the less chance they would have of finding him.

16

A N early morning mist, damp and impenetrable, clung to
the dark surface of the water on all sides of *Comus* as
she lay idly boxing the compass. It hung about the deck,
eddying with each gentle movement of the ship, now making a
channel, revealing stern and bows, now marshalling its wreaths
between port and starboard until the man at the wheel could
scarcely see the binnacle in front of him.

Lieutenant Chandler, hunched miserably in his deck coat,
turned tired eyes to the patched sail hanging dejectedly from
the yard above him. Disinterestedly he followed the course of
the muffled seaman heaving himself to invisibility up the starboard ratlines to the small look-out platform at the masthead,
appropriately known as the 'tops'. There the man would feel
that he was no longer with the ship. Below him would be the
rootless shrouds and perhaps an occasional glimpse of the upper
yards; around him a dense blanket of bone-chilling greyness. So
he would remain in dreary isolation until the sun climbed out
of the sea to thaw him out, fully half an hour before it would
perform the same service for the rest of the ship's company.

Naval regulations demanded that he should be there before
dawn. Captain Lawson, through the officer of the watch, had
impressed upon him the necessity for a sharp look-out. It was
important that the frigate should know at the earliest possible
moment if any vessel had joined company during the night.

So it had been every morning since they had left Gibraltar,
The mist had given way to oppressive heat which had not been
relieved until around six bells of the forenoon watch when the
ovenlike Sahara had begun to suck in the air from round about,
causing strong north-westerly breezes in the Mediterranean.

Lawson had followed the same course that he had taken in his search for Yussaiff Ahmed. In Oran there had been no sign of the ship commanded by Kettelmann. The bay where *Comus* had been lost and retaken, was already far to the west and his search there had been fruitless. Now, three weeks after leaving Gibraltar, he knew no more of the whereabouts of Kettelmann than when he had left the Rock. There were other reasons for his sour expression when he emerged from his cabin fully one hour before his accustomed time.

'Mr Chandler,' he said testily in response to the young man's greeting. 'I should be obliged if you would find some other way of inducing warmth to your feet.'

'Sir?' the third officer's raised eyebrows expressed his astonishment.

'For the past two hours you have been stamping on the deck above my cabin.'

The new black patch over his right eye danced with the angry movement of his face and the left eye glared at the younger officer. Chandler shot a quick glance in the direction of Midshipman Barty, who had been keeping the watch with him and was now absorbed all too closely with the binnacle. Later he would give Barty something to think about. Meanwhile, since he had charge of the deck, he would have to take responsibility for the noise that had disturbed the captain.

'I'm sorry, sir,' he said.

'Ship ho!' came a thin call from the masthead.

'Upon which quarter, you bloody fool?' Lawson roared at the invisible figure aloft.

'Port bow, sir, there's a masthead stickin' out of the fog an' no more 'n a cable's length away.'

Lawson's eye swept across the deck to Barty, now waiting attentively.

'Get up there,' he ordered abruptly with a jerk of his head.

Barty ran for the rigging of the mainmast and heaved himself off the deck. Lawson paced thoughtfully backwards and forwards over the damp boards, then swung around.

'Call all hands, Mr Chandler.'

There was a faint chance that the ship lying becalmed so near to them might belong to Kettelmann. The odds against such a possibility were incalculable but that was not going to stop the captain, in his present mood, from rousing the ship's company some thirty minutes before the accustomed time. Later he would regret his action and allow them to lounge about in the afternoon sun in recompense. At the moment he felt no sympathy for them as they hurried bleary eyed, from below. Thompson, the coxswain was among the first. He hurried aft for orders.

'What the devil is Barty doing up there?' Lawson demanded peevishly.

Chandler raised his speaking trumpet but before he could hail the midshipman's voice reached them.

'Nothing visible at the moment, sir.'

The mist had swallowed up the neighbouring ship again and they could only wait until it cleared but Lawson felt the need for activity.

'Kindly bring the glass from my cabin and join me aloft,' he ordered Thompson.

He strode forward into the mist, past the mainmast and on to the ratlines leading to the foremast tops. Thompson, complete with telescope, reached him before he had climbed more than twenty feet above the deck and thereafter leisurely followed his captain.

Lawson could normally ascend the mast as quickly as most seamen of his age but now the wounds in his arm and chest bothered him. By the time he reached the lubber's hole at the foot of the tiny platform he was only too pleased to scramble through. Thompson, who would normally have taken the more dangerous course around the outside and thought nothing of it, prudently followed his captain.

The view from the masthead was exciting. Lawson's bad temper evaporated as he looked about. It was like a fairyland. Billowing clouds like a vast snowfield, lay below them, tinted with gold from the rising sun. They could see for miles in all directions and everywhere it was the same; a rolling, living sea of mist beneath a glorious sky.

Lawson turned to Barty and the seaman standing on the mainmast tops sixty feet away. He felt a ridiculous urge to wave to him but Barty pointed away to his left.

'There she is, sir,' he shouted.

A masthead could be seen clearly for a moment. Then there was nothing. Lawson trained his glass and waited. The mist swirled away again revealing the top twenty feet or so of two masts which swung idly around to reveal the tip of a third, much lower than the other two. It was not a full rigged ship out there. It was probably a barque. Disappointed he gave Thompson the telescope.

'Keep her under observation,' he said and lowered himself through the hole.

Back on deck the crew was following the normal morning routine in the absence of further orders from the captain. Duvalier-Winter, who had relieved Chandler, raised his hat as Lawson approached.

'Send the men to breakfast as soon as convenient,' Lawson ordered.

He walked the deck for ten minutes, casting glances from time to time over the port side. At last he turned to go below.

'Mr Duvalier-Winter,' he called from the head of the companionway. 'If this mist should clear before I return to the deck, I should be obliged if you would kindly instruct Mr Hawbrook to take a boat out to that vessel. They might have some useful information.'

'Aye aye, sir.'

Evans had breakfast ready below. Lawson sat down eagerly enough. He was hungry. The climb to the top of the mast had given him an appetite and the sliced beef and eggs in front of him looked good.

As he was finishing his meal, there was a tap at the cabin door and Doctor Fairweather entered. He had none of the diffidence of the usual ship's surgeon about him as he strode into the cabin. Lawson looked at him tolerantly. He had learned to respect him over the past weeks.

'Coffee?' offered the captain, indicating the steaming pot on the table.

'Thank you, no,' replied the doctor, 'but I should like to take a look at the eye when you are ready!'

Lawson finished his coffee, rose from the table and carried his chair over to the brighter light of the stern window. Fairweather bent over him, peeled back the dressing beneath the patch and wiped away the evil-smelling glutinous mass that had lain under it. Lawson's eye blinked open. For a moment he sat perfectly still, allowing his eye to get used to the light. Then he realised he could see everything in the cabin clearly. The doctor, watching him closely, noted his excitement and smiled. On impulse, Lawson pulled a sheaf of papers from his pocket. He examined the top one and found that he could read it without difficulty.

'Wonderful!' he exclaimed joyfully. 'It is almost as good as it was.'

Fairweather nodded in satisfaction.

'We'll leave that eye uncovered now and work on the other. This salve has done no more than speed up the process that nature had begun. I have no doubt now that your sight will get steadily better until in perhaps six months' time you will be able to see as well as the next man.'

He began to uncork a pot which he had brought with him but a movement of the ship had already brought Lawson to his feet.

'It will have to wait until later,' he said. 'There's a breath of air out there.'

On deck the mist was dispersing rapidly and the frigate's gig with Hawbrook sitting in the stern was already being rowed over to a barque which lay, still partly obscured, some three hundred yards away. Duvalier-Winter joined the captain.

'The barque is under way, sir,' he said, offering his telescope.

Lawson took it and held it to his newly uncovered eye. The first lieutenant was right. There was no perceptible bow wave but there was no doubt that the vessel was moving. She was evidently finding more wind than *Comus*. As he watched he saw the mainsails fall into place on the yards and the great spanker boom on the mizzen-mast swing over to leeward. Hawbrook was going to have a hard time getting up to her.

'Ask them to heave to,' Lawson said.

The signal flags raced out on a halyard, running at sixty degrees from the deck. In the absence of wind they were not fully extended but they would be seen clearly enough from the barque and even if their message were not understood, it would be evident to the captain that the frigate wished to communicate.

'Fire the signal gun,' ordered Lawson when the barque showed no sign of heaving-to.

The little brass gun on the poop barked out its warning but still the barque continued on its course. All those on the frigate's quarterdeck, well aware of the significance of this drama, waited breathlessly. Lawson hid his growing excitement behind his speaking trumpet and hailed the guns.

'Mr Chandler, I'll have a shot across her bows and I should be obliged if you would attend to it personally.'

Hawbrook was out there in a small boat and in direct line. A faulty charge could send the ball crashing into him.

A faint sighing in the shrouds announced that the breeze had reached them. The topgallants cracked and filled. The heavier mainsails stirred and sagged again but the ship had steerage. Lawson looked over the water to windward and noted the disturbed surface with satisfaction. He would not have to rely on Hawbrook's report. There was going to be enough wind to put the frigate alongside.

The dull boom of the bow chaser drew his eyes back to the barque. He waited anxiously for the fall of the shot. If Chandler had made an error he might see the ball flying along the deck of the barque doing untold damage.

'Dead ahead, sir,' Duvalier-Winter reported.

Lawson nodded. It had been an excellent shot, though a little nearer than he would have sent it. A spout of water and been thrown up within ten yards of the running craft. He smiled grimly when the bows came around. The captain of the barque knew better than to run from a frigate.

Hawbrook's boat reached the barque and hooked on. The lieutenant evidently felt justified in boarding it since its captain had ignored the signal to heave to. Lawson focused his glass on deck and waited for his junior officer to appear. Meanwhile *Comus* was easing her way nearer. The boat's crew would have very little rowing to do by the time Hawbrook had finished asking his questions.

'A bunch of cutthroats, if ever I saw one,' Duvalier-Winter remarked.

Lawson nodded. He had been observing the crew closely through the glass. Each of them carried a weapon of some kind and although the flag of France drooped from the stern, most of the men seemed to be Moors.

A movement aloft attracted Lawson's attention. A man was sliding down the foremast stay from the tops. It was Thompson, who had been left at the masthead when the captain had gone for breakfast. He hurried aft and approached Lawson just as Hawbrook's boat was leaving the barque.

'Begging your pardon, sir,' he said, 'but the captain of that ship was mixed up in the fight that killed the Spaniard.'

Lawson searched his face for any sign of doubt.

'Are you sure?'

'Yes, sir. An' there's them as was with me that night as will be able to bear to the truth of the matter.'

'Bring them to me,' ordered the captain. He turned to Duvalier-Winter. 'Clear for action as quietly as possible. The lives of our men in the boat depend upon your silence.'

He paced the deck with studied slowness to hide the excitement he felt. If this man were one of the henchmen of Kettelmann, what was he doing commanding a French merchantman?

He studied the craft carefully. *Marguerite* was her name. Certainly the barque had not lain in the harbour at Gibraltar while *Comus* was there.

'Well?' he demanded of the seaman brought aft by Thompson.

'It's 'im yer honour,' confirmed the man. 'I just seed 'im through the glass. An' there's another fellow as was there. 'E came in wi' a knife an' I clobbered 'im. Begging your pardon, sir.' He knuckled his forehead.

'Thank you,' said the captain. Now that the story had been confirmed he knew how to act.

They were less than a hundred yards away but the barque was already filling her sails on her new tack. Hawbrook's boat grated at the entry port.

'Run out the guns!'

A startled Hawbrook hurried aft to the accompaniment of squeals from the iron wheels of the gun-carriages.

'She seems to be in order, sir,' he said urgently.

'I've no doubt that she does, Mr Hawbrook,' replied the captain, 'but we're going to board her all the same.'

He hurried forward to the crew of the long gun.

'I'll have a shot across her bows.'

They heaved on the tackle and skidded the great gun over. The gunner bent over the sights then stepped back and jerked the lanyard. The flint-lock mechanism clicked but the spark did not catch. Quickly he stooped, took the slow match from the bucket, blew it into life and thrust the glowing end into the vent. The gun roared back against the restraining ropes and enveloped the men about it with pungent smoke.

Splinters flew from the bow as the shot glanced off. The gunner had not considered the advance of the barque in the interval between misfire and the actual shot. Lawson scowled. If Thompson had made a mistake there would be serious trouble when the matter was reported.

He was not left long in doubt. The gun ports along the starboard side of the barque opened with the precision of a man of war and the black muzzles of thirteen guns slid forward. Lawson smiled in satisfaction. He was definitely on to something here. No ship so poorly armed would dare to show fight against such odds unless the alternative were something much more frightening.

'I should think that the hangman will be busy when we land this lot,' he said to Duvalier-Winter.

'Piracy, sir?'

'Aye,' growled the captain. '*Marguerite* is a prize, or I'm a Dutchman. The original crew will very likely be battened below.

Suddenly the thought occurred to him of what would happen to the prisoners between decks if he allowed his gunners to pour in a broadside.

'Mr Chandler,' he called. 'You will direct your fire aloft when given the order.'

'Aye, aye, sir.'

The side of the barque suddenly became obscured with smoke as her guns fired together. There was a rushing sound overhead and a great deal of cracking. The lower top-sail yard on the mizzen-mast suddenly folded up in the middle and hung drunkenly. At the same time a gash like a question mark appeared in the mainsail. They were using chain shot and the gunners of the barque had evidently been given the same orders as those on board *Comus*, but for a different reason.

Their only hope of escape lay in temporarily crippling the frigate.

Lawson signalled to the waiting Chandler. The next moment the deck heaved from the thundering broadside of the frigate's guns. The foremast of the barque was seen to jerk forward at the foot and fell back against the yards of the mainmast behind. It had been severed ten feet from the deck. For a moment it held, tangled in the rig, then slowly it toppled, tearing away the yards which had fouled it, and plunged with a mighty splash over the side.

'My oh my!' Hawbrook exclaimed.

Duvalier-Winter was more voluble.

'Marvellous shooting! Excellent! Damn me if I ever saw better.'

Lawson was looking up at the mass of sails above. They were hanging slackly with not a breath of air to fill them. Already the frigate had lost its steerage and was beginning to yaw. Soon the main armament would not be able to bear.

'Boats away,' he ordered his first lieutenant. 'We'll have to swing her around.'

The first guns to be reloaded were already firing independently at the barque but they were not going unanswered. Puffs of smoke were blossoming from all along the side of the smaller ship. The pirates were not going to give up without a struggle. Several crashes forward announced hits. One of the deck carronades hurtled back on its carriage to crash against the foremast, leaving a trail of blood across the deck from the unfortunate man who had been dragged with it. A blast of air from a passing ball made Lawson stagger backwards. He heard a smash behind him and turned in time to see Postill falling to the deck with a part of the wheel protruding from his side.

'Damn them!' Lawson exploded. 'They're giving a better account of themselves than I expected. Have those guns silenced, Mr Hawbrook. If there are any prisoners below decks, they'll have to take their chance.'

The gig which had carried the second officer across to the barque was still in the water. Already it had taken a light cable and was pulling valiantly to bring the bows around but it was doing no more than check the drift. Now it was being joined by the much larger launch. Soon the frigate would be hauled back into its most formidable position.

A hail of musketry struck the water all around the gig. Lawson saw one man fall forward and focused his glass on the larger boat. Thompson was at the tiller. Lawson hoped that his coxswain would have had the sense to get the broad hulk of the frigate between him and the enemy but he had no time to watch him. The ship was claiming his full attention.

The wheel had not been badly damaged. Only the forward spokes had been shattered. The cable which passed around the drum was apparently still operating the rudder but it was useless anyway until they had a passage through the water.

The port guns, firing at their maximum angle owing to the position of the frigate, ripped into the side of the barque. With professional satisfaction, Lawson noted the gaping holes level with the gun ports. There would be chaos there. The bursting timbers would create havoc. However, some of the barque's guns still operated; three of them let loose their shot as Lawson watched. He waited for the iron to arrive but nothing came.

'The gig's gone,' said Duvalier-Winter.

Lawson glanced over the starboard side. The launch, struggling to take the slack out of a heavy cable, was alone. A few planks and the bobbing head of a solitary swimmer were all that remained of the other boat. Then a ball from the barque bounced on the sea behind the launch, skimmed over the heads of the crew and went on for another half dozen leaps like a flat stone thrown across the surface of a pond.

The guns of the frigate roared out with renewed energy and the last of the heavy armament on the starboard side of the barque became silent but there was still a lot of musketry from the deck and from the yards of the mainmast. The men on the barque were making a last determined attempt to stop the launch before it could swing the frigate into its most effective position. Their efforts were in vain. Already the royals and the topgallants were filling. *Comus* did not need to be pulled around. She had steerage.

Quickly the frigate reduced the distance between them. The barque had cleared away the wreckage of its foremast and was under way but with the absence of one third of its canvas it could not hold its lead against its pursuer.

'Stand by the carronades,' ordered Lawson as they slid towards the barque.

'Ready with the grapnels,' shouted Duvalier-Winter from the waist.

The rest of the men from *Comus* waited tensely under the protection of the port bulwarks armed with cutlasses and pikes, ready to swarm over the side. Hawbrook and Chandler crouched with them while Barty had charge of the men who were manning the yards eighty feet above the deck. The coxswain was absent from his post. He was well astern, sprawling in the bottom of the launch where a musket-ball had laid him.

Lawson knew that Thompson had been hit. He had seen the launch swing as his body had fallen against the tiller. Then he had taken a cutlass from the master at arms and fixed his eyes grimly upon the barque. The pirates were going to pay for him. They were also going to pay for Postill, who had been taken down to the orlop deck. As the distance between the two ships slowly dwindled the captain moved impatiently over to the port side and positioned himself ready to jump.

The musketry, which had crackled incessantly during the approach, suddenly stopped on board the barque when the first of the grappling hooks bit into its timbers. Lawson raised his hand to give the order to the carronades but there was no target for them. Every man on the deck opposite was under cover. The *Comus* men heaved on the lines bringing the two ships together. Then a voice, loud and clear, called out to the frigate.

'We surrender!'

Lawson flung his cutlass to the deck in disgust and stormed away, leaving the taking over of the barque to his second in command.

17

THE crew of the captured vessel were herded on their own foredeck while Chandler and Hawbrook searched below. Lawson looked them over and decided that the big man in a grey tunic coat was their leader.

'Bring that fellow here,' he ordered.

'I'll have an explanation of this outrage, Captain,' the man said. 'I'm an Englishman and I find it hard to believe that one of His Majesty's ships has turned pirate.'

Lawson controlled himself with an effort.

'An Englishman, is it? Well, you'll soon be dancing on an English gallows as a special privilege.'

'And what would be the charge?'

Hawbrook had returned to the upper deck. He shook his head in response to the captain's questioning look. There were no prisoners below. For a moment Lawson wondered if he had made a mistake. Then he remembered how quickly the barque had gone into action.

'I'm arresting you for piracy and for firing upon a British ship.'

The man smiled faintly but his eyes were watching Lawson closely enough.

'Piracy?' he replied scornfully. 'Your lieutenant has examined my papers and found them in order.' He indicated the devastation about him. 'This is my answer to the other charges. I have too few men, too few guns. I merely attempted to defend myself against your attack.'

'There is also the murder of the Spaniard at Gibraltar to answer for.'

The man started and there was a brief flicker of fear in his face but he recovered his poise in an instant.

'I don't know what you mean.'

Lawson smiled grimly. Thompson had been right. It was now only a question of time before the ship's papers were proved to be false.

'Can I speak to you a moment, sir?'

'What is it, Mr Hawbrook?' Lawson asked his eyes still on the pirate.

'The launch has just come alongside, sir, and there's something on board that you ought to see at once.'

The captain gave the lieutenant a sharp glance and followed him aft. The launch lay under the stern of *Comus* and close to the side of the barque. The wounded were being swayed aboard and Thompson had already gone. The thing of interest lay in the bows—a body with a bag tied around the legs.

'Stabbed to death and dropped over the side, sir, from a gun port, along with half a dozen others while *Comus* was creeping up to her. The other bodies went under at once but there is a hole in the bag around this fellow's legs. Looks like the ballast has fallen through. They were so set on getting rid of the bodies out of sight of *Comus* that they forgot about the launch cutting across their stern. Thompson gave orders for this one to be brought aboard.'

'Thompson?'

'Yes, sir. Wounded in the back. He was conscious when he was brought aboard.'

Lawson turned away suddenly and walked back to the master of the barque.

'You murdering swine.'

The man's face twitched nervously but he tried to carry it off nonchalantly.

'What is it now?' he asked with an air of boredom.

Lawson's fist clenched and his eyes blazed with anger.

'Put this lot below in irons,' he ordered. 'No, leave this one.'

he added, when they reached out for the Englishman. 'Take him on board *Comus* until I am ready for him.'

'On your feet,' the master at arms shouted.

The prisoners were hustled along the deck. Of the twenty or so villainous-looking creatures who had escaped the action, six perhaps were Arab. The rest consisted of the sweepings of the Mediterranean ports. A fat, greasy-looking fellow with a beard was pleading with the seaman who pushed him towards the hatch. He cringed away from the master at arms and cried aloud when he was cuffed back into line.

'Take note of that man,' Lawson ordered. 'I want him separated from the rest.'

The ship stirred in the freshening breeze and the timbers groaned against the side of *Comus*. Lawson craned back his head to examine the towering pyramid of sails. The topgallants were flapping noisily and the mainsails were stirring.

'Mr Duvalier-Winter,' he called across to the frigate. 'Make ready to stand off.'

As the men rushed to the cables binding the ships together, Lawson climbed on to the bulwark of the captured vessel and reached for the rigging on *Comus*.

'You will take command here,' he called down to Hawbrook. 'Follow a parallel course to *Comus* at a distance of half a cable. When you receive a signal from us, bring that greasy coward out on deck and threaten to hang him from the yardarm if he refuses to answer your questions. Meanwhile we shall be arranging a little show on *Comus* for his benefit. You know the sort of questions to ask?'

'Kettelmann's whereabouts, sir?'

'Aye! Kettelmann, Yussaiff Ahmed and anything else he has to tell you. If I'm not mistaken he will volunteer all the information we require. You can keep Mr Chandler with you and forty men.' He paused and looked about him. 'Take the carpenter and some of his mates. You'll need them.'

He stepped easily over the gap between the restless ships and landed on the frigate's deck.

'As soon as the prize crew is aboard, you can stand off,' he told Duvalier-Winter. 'I'm going below to see the wounded.'

The scene which met Lawson's eye on the orlop deck was painfully familiar.

Bending over a rough table, his tense face lit by the yellow light of oil lamps, was Doctor Fairweather. Beneath him, his pale cheeks glistening with sweat, and his eyes wild with fright, lay one of the victims of the recent action. His legs were tied to the table and three surgeon's mates held him down. As the doctor poised with a knife, the poor man gasped in horror and tried to roll onto his side, but relentless hands forced him back against the board and held him. Lawson turned away.

This was the worst part of war. Action on an open deck, with death and mutilation on all sides, was nothing to the horrors of the surgery. Here was a torture chamber, a hell, through which all the wounded must pass, on their way to long convalescence or death. Later, in four or five days' time, there would be the stench of gangrene to add to the smell of oil lamps and sweating bodies. Then there would be more amputations, as the surgeon tried to separate rotting flesh from good. Too often the sailmaker would take over from the surgeon, and the whole of the ship's company would be assembled to pay their last respects to the remains of a shipmate.

'Where is my coxs'n?' Lawson asked of one of the surgeon's mates, bandaging a young marine.

'Here I am, sir,' answered a faint voice in the darkness.

The captain unhooked a lamp from a low beam and picked his way carefully among the wounded on the deck. He found Thompson lying on a rough bed of straw. He was deadly pale but he smiled bravely enough. Blood-soaked bandages swathed the upper part of his body.

'Have you been there yet?' Lawson whispered, indicating the table under the pool of light.

The boatswain bit his lip and shook his head. At that moment a long-drawn-out scream came from the man under the knife. Thompson's teeth clenched and he took a deep breath.

Lawson gripped his arm and squeezed reassuringly.

'It's not as bad as the noise would have you believe, lad. He'll have that musket-ball out of you in no time and you'll be back on duty in a week or so. Then you can look for promotion for you've done an excellent job of work.'

He smiled and moved on to have a word with every man still able to listen. He found Postill, grey faced and unconscious, just as they were taking him to the operating table.

Doctor Fairweather shook his head doubtfully in reply to Lawson's questioning glance, and bent over the wound which was just under the ribs on the left side. The surgeon's mates had sheared off the splinter before they had brought him below. The stub, less than an inch across, was firmly embedded in the torn flesh and congealed blood.

'The bleeding has stopped anyway,' Lawson said.

'The external bleeding has stopped,' Fairweather corrected, 'but a man can bleed to death and not a drop spilt outside. Do you know what lies there?'

'The stomach?'

'The liver.—It will be dripping blood at this moment.'

'Can't you stitch it up?'

'Aye I could do that. I've stitched many a one. It's a common enough injury. The trouble is that the patient rarely lives for more than a week afterwards. They go bad inside. Don't ask me why. Better brains than mine have wrestled with that problem without success.'

He took a scalpel and made three neat incisions around the stub. Then he began to work the flesh away from the jagged edges, delving deeper with fingers and blade until his assistant was able to ease the splinter clear.

It was four inches long and as sharp as a pike. Fairweather examined it closely. It was important that none of it had been left inside. Meanwhile the assistant was mopping at the open wound with a piece of cotton gauze that had lain on the table, his fingernails red from the blood of previous operations.

The surgeon turned to the man on his right, who was

engaged in dipping the points of some instruments in a bowl of hot charcoal.

'Are you ready?'

'Yes, sir.'

Fairweather bent over the wound again, singled out the largest of the blood-vessels and tied them off. Then he took the hot forceps from the bowl, held the instrument near his face to test the heat, and probed into the gash. There was a sizzling sound and a thin spiral of smoke as he gripped the end of a small artery. Lawson's nose wrinkled in disgust when the smell of burning flesh reached his nostrils but he watched fascinated whilst the doctor deftly sealed one blood vessel after the other until the bleeding had stopped.

'Now we'll see, as far as we able, what damage has been done inside. You'll notice that the blow broke the bottom rib?'

Lawson nodded.

'That stopped the force of it. He'd have been dead within minutes otherwise.'

'There doesn't seem to be any blood coming from the liver,' Lawson said.

'Not yet, but you'll notice that the chisel-shaped point of the splinter followed the lines of the muscle instead of tearing across them. Now the shock has caused the muscle fibres to close the wound on the inside. Watch.'

He pulled the inner lips of the wound apart. Blood flowed sluggishly through the aperture. He examined it closely and pressed on the patient's abdomen with his elbow. The flow increased. He inserted his finger and explored carefully inside.

'It is as I thought,' he said at length. 'The liver has been punctured but not too deeply. There's still a chance.'

He wiped his hands carefully, removed a large gold watch from his pocket and checked Postill's pulse against it.

'Doesn't seem to have changed much. We'll stitch him up and let the liver take care of itself.'

'How will you know if it isn't taking care of itself?'

'The heart will have to work harder as the blood supply gets less. We'll check his pulse every fifteen minutes or so. If it suddenly speeds up, I shall have to go inside.'

Having set the broken rib carefully and stitched the muscles into place around it, Doctor Fairweather drew the outer flesh together with deep sutures and tied his knots. He left the rest to his assistants, having instructed them to place the patient in a bed with the foot eighteen inches higher than the head.

'That will give his vitals a good share of what blood he has left,' he explained to Lawson, 'and with luck the viscera will slide back against the liver and close the cut in the right lobe.'

Medical science could do no more for him. Postill's recovery would now depend upon the healing properties of his flesh and the ability of his constitution to fight against the poisons that had entered his body during the operation.

Duvalier-Winter met the captain on deck.

'Mr Chandler found these papers, sir,' he said, offering a package. 'The last entry in the ship's log was made four days ago.'

Lawson glanced over the water at the barque. Hawbrook was keeping at the distance he had ordered.

'Thank you,' he replied. 'I'll see the prisoner.'

The pirate captain had been tied to a grating fixed upright against the bulwarks. His feet hung clear of the deck and all his weight was borne by the lashings about his wrists.

'Cut him down!' he blazed in anger at the guard.

He would have added more but the mocking grin on the face of the prisoner checked him. No doubt he had given the master at arms good cause for ill treatment.

'Who are you?' Lawson demanded when he had been cut loose.

'Call me Smith,' the man replied, rubbing at his wrists where the thongs had bitten deep. 'Smith of London Town. That's as good a name as another for the hangman.'

Lawson tried to weigh the man up. It would be difficult to obtain information from him about Kettelmann's movements and if he were to volunteer any, it would probably be a pack of lies to lead the frigate away from the pirates' rendezvous. Far better to get this rogue below decks and concentrate upon the wretch held on board *Marguerite*, he thought.

'Strip the coat from him.'

The prisoner's mouth opened in astonishment but he had no time to voice a protest. Willing hands seized him and wrenched the grey tunic from his shoulders.

'Now I want a volunteer to be swung to the yardarm. Who fancies a flight through space for a pound of tobacco?'

A tall, loose-limbed seaman allowed himself to be nudged forward by the others. He grinned and knuckled his forelock.

'I'd be after trying it, sir.'

The captain's eyes twinkled. O'Brien, the swimmer, would suit his purpose very well. He was several inches taller than the prisoner but that would not be noticeable from the barque.

Lawson explained what he wanted and a stout canvas sling was quickly fashioned and stuffed with waste cloth. O'Brien stepped into the sling and had it secured around his legs and under his armpits. Rope was passed under the sling, with an extra length attached to the main rope as a reserve if the sling should break under the strain. When all was ready, O'Brien was dressed in the grey coat so that the rope passed out between his neck and the collar.

'Make the signal,' ordered the captain.

Two tiny balls, which had been bent on to the halyard in readiness, raced aloft to burst and flutter their message across to the barque. Lawson waited for the acknowledgement and then turned to the Irishman.

'Do you understand what I want you to do?'

'Aye aye, sir. I'm to dance all the way up and then lie as still as if I was atop the gallows at Tyburn.'

Meanwhile on board the barque, the cringing seaman was being dragged on to the deck where Hawbrook, looking as forbidding as he knew how, awaited him. A seaman stood by with a rattan cane whilst another held a noose. The fat man's startled eyes followed the line from the noose to the yardarm and jerked back to the deck where three seamen were holding the descending rope in readiness.

'Look, sir,' said Chandler suddenly, pointing over the water.

All eyes on the deck turned in the direction of the frigate in time to see a dancing figure in grey swing to the main yard. There he kicked for a moment and then hung limply. O'Brien had given the performance of his life.

Hawbrook gaped. He had been warned that there would be an exhibition but had not expected anything so realistic. Making an effort, he adjusted his face to the role he was playing and swung back on the prisoner before him. The man's eyes, still fixed on to the hanging figure on the yardarm of the frigate, were bulging in terror.

'String him up,' ordered Hawbrook with a gesture to the man holding the noose.

The seamen crowded round but the prisoner slipped through their arms and threw himself sobbing at the lieutenant's feet, calling upon all the saints, in a mixture of crude English and Spanish, to bear witness that he had never had anything to do with piracy.

Hawbrook warned Savage, the clerk, to stand by with pen and paper. Then he began to ply his questions.

The information poured out of the wretched creature. Indeed, he would have betrayed the innermost secrets of his heart to escape being hung from the yardarm like the Englishman.

Savage wrote steadily and when he had finished, the man made his mark, which in turn was witnessed by the officers and the clerk. Then the prisoner, under escort, was transferred to the frigate and Hawbrook awaited further orders.

He had not long to wait. Signal flags raced above the deck of the frigate to stream out in the freshening wind within a few minutes of the Spaniard arriving aboard. Hawbrook hastily called away the hands from their work at the damaged gun ports and ordered them to man the braces to bring *Marguerite* around on a new tack. The chase was on.

The wind lasted throughout the afternoon and despite the

reduced sail area on the barque, the two ships made good speed across an empty sea. With the setting of the sun came the calm and Lawson signalled for the barque to work her way alongside. Now was the opportunity to perform the ceremony of burial.

Six bodies, stitched in sailcloth and each with a heavy shot at the feet, lay on the gratings. Over on the barque were fifteen more. Many sea captains would have pitched the dead pirates unceremoniously over the side. Lawson allowed four of the prisoners on deck to witness the burial service. They stood in front of the prize crew still in their irons, under the watchful eye of Hawbrook.

Lawson's voice carried easily over the decks of the two ships as he read out the service. It was a service with which he was well acquainted and normally he could read it dispassionately but on this occasion the thought that he would probably be reading the same service again on the following days depressed him. There were several seriously wounded men below decks who would surely die during the night, and they might expect the first of the gangrene harvest in about four days' time.

After the burial Lawson resolutely turned his mind to the tasks ahead. There was much to be done. In the frenzied activity of the next few hours he would have no time to dwell on the wounded. A new mast had to be stepped on the barque and new yards fitted. Useless guns had to be stowed where they could not get in the way. Most of the work would have to be done in the dark because dawn might find them alongside Kettelmann's ships.

The frightened prisoner had given much useful information. Kettelmann was hunting with the pack. No longer was he trying to conceal his piracy under the cloak of the trader. It was as if he had become aware of the dispatch from the Admiralty and had decided that nothing could be lost by showing himself in his true colours. Three more vessels sailed with him, a brig, a dhow and a full-rigged ship called *La Reine Noble*. This was as powerful as *Die Reichmacher*. Together they would be superior in fire power to a ship of the line and individually would have twice the speed and manoeuvrability. They would be more than a match for a frigate, even when assisted by *Marguerite*. No one could have blamed Lawson if he had run for reinforcements rather than set course for Algiers where he had learned they would rendezvous.

Something else drew the captain. The informer had been with Kettelmann at Gibraltar. In response to Lawson's questions, he had admitted that a 'young gentleman' had been taken as prisoner on board *Die Reichmacher* just before they had sailed.

18

THE stepping of a jury foremast in the barque would have been difficult if there had been any wind. As it was, the frigate was able to do the hoisting as the two ships lay side by side in the dead calm. Slowly, the mast, one of the spare main yards from *Comus*, was lowered into place and fished to the jagged stub of the mast which had been shot away. Shrouds were quickly lashed into place and ratlines firmly secured. Then, as always, came the night breeze, rushing out from the distant North African coast. Reluctantly Lawson gave orders to cast off and stand away. The barque would have to hoist its own yards on to the new mast and it would have to perform the task whilst close-hauled on a starboard tack. They must take advantage of every breath of air if they were to arrive in time to block Kettelmann's route into Algiers.

Doctor Fairweather climbed wearily on deck as the ship got under way. His eyes were red rimmed and his face sagged with the strain of the day. He looked very old. Lawson walked to meet him and took his arm to support him against the list of the ship.

'All finished, Captain,' said the doctor. 'I've done all I can. Now it depends on the flesh.'

'What about Thompson and Postill?'

The doctor rubbed his eyes and yawned.

'I think they'll do nicely if their wounds don't poison. I managed to get the ball out of Thompson though I had a devil of a time. It had bounced off the ribs and passed under the scapula. Well, good night, Captain.'

'Good night,' replied Lawson. He thoughtfully watched the man disappear down the campanionway to his cabin. If the

Navy had employed more like him and fewer blustering butchers there would not have been so many for the sailmaker during the war.

He stood by the weather side watching the phosphorescent waters of the Mediterranean slip by. The sky was a mass of stars, now dimmed by the brightness of the moon as the dark clouds rolled away. The sea gleamed with a silvery light bringing into stark relief the silhouette of *Marguerite* with her jury foremast and newly set yards, as she surged through the swell. Few men could do other than love the sea in such a mood. Lawson found himself thinking about Cecilia.

She had broken into his thoughts frequently since Gibraltar, particularly when he was alone in his cabin, and each time he had driven her out, usually at the cost of hours of sleep. Now he allowed himself the luxury of recapturing the memory of her passionate kiss and the warmth of her body against his. He needed her badly, he realised, more than he had needed any person before.

Midshipman Barty, who was sharing the watch, broke into his dream.

'There's a ship out there, sir,' he hissed excitedly.

Away on the starboard side, at a distance of perhaps a mile, sails gleaming dully in the light of the moon, was a full-rigged ship on a parallel course to *Comus*.

Lawson threaded his arm through the starboard ratlines to steady himself and brought his telescope into focus. His examination told him no more about her than he had seen with the naked eye. Then he caught the glimpse of another sail lying just beyond the full blown canvas of the ship under observation. There were at least two vessels. Neither carried navigation lights.

'Bring her round a couple of points to starboard, and have the lamps masked,' ordered Lawson.

Barty repeated the order to the wheel and rejoined the captain.

'There's another sail, sir !' said Barty.

'Yes,' replied the captain, vaguely wondering how the youth could distinguish, without the aid of a glass, the rig of the ship that lay beyond the one he was observing.

'Almost dead astern,' continued Barty.

'What!'

Lawson lowered the glass and followed the midshipman's pointing hand. Astern and slightly to starboard, at a distance of barely half a mile, the sails of a third vessel could now be seen.

'What do you make of her?' demanded Captain Lawson, thrusting the telescope into his hands.

Barty focused carefully.

'A brig, sir. Making full sail on the same course as the other.'

The captain took the telescope and closed it thoughtfully. Kettelmann had a brig in his company, if the informer were to be believed. Further, the whole fleet was on a direct course for Algiers with only nine leagues to go.

'Rouse the ship,' he ordered decisively. 'And do it as quietly as you can.'

Whilst the watch was turning the ship's company out, Lawson took a lamp and waved it over the port side. That was the prearranged signal for the barque to close. He waited, hanging over the rail, whilst *Marguerite* loomed nearer. Together they raced over the gleaming water, with less than ten yards separating their bulwarks and with their yards almost touching. Lieutenant Hawbrook came hurrying on deck, stuffing his shirt into the top of his trousers.

'Mr Hawbrook,' said Lawson in almost confidential tones. 'I want you to clear for action as quickly and quietly as you can. The ships out there will probably be none of our business, but there is just a chance that they may be the ones we are seeking.'

He swung back from the rail to find the men assembling amidships in various stages of undress and pulling their clothes about them. The boatswain was in the middle of the crowd getting them into some sort of order.

'That will do,' said the captain. 'They can hear what I have to say to them from where they stand.'

He placed himself in front of them with legs braced and hands thrust behind him. The men waited in silence.

'I hope that I have not disturbed your sleep unnecessarily,' he began. 'I have reasons to believe that the ships which lie to starboard are the ones we are seeking.'

There was a murmur of excitement.

'If that should prove to be the case,' he went on, 'we shall shortly find ourselves fighting against odds.'

He paused to allow the information to sink in.

'We have the advantage of surprise, however, because even if they have seen us, they will not be aware of our intentions and they may possibly mistake us for their own. It depends largely on you. I want you to clear for action as quietly as you know how and if and when we engage the enemy, I want you to do your duty as British seamen should.'

One seaman began to cheer but he was quickly silenced by those about him. Then the dark shadows on the deck dispersed rapidly, each man to his own job with the quiet determination and eagerness that Lawson had hoped for.

'Please God, let it be Kettelmann,' he muttered.

The moon was now obscured by cloud and nothing was to be seen except the bow wave of the nearby *Marguerite*.

Evans appeared out of the darkness with the captain's pistols. Lawson pushed them into his belt and turned to his second in command.

'I believe the first ship to starboard may be *Die Reichmacher*. There's another beyond it and a brig astern. We are on a converging course and unless they go about, we should meet up in forty minutes or less. I intend to get in close. The first broadside should be directed at their gun ports. Then each gun can be fired independently at whatever takes the gunner's fancy. But no gun, now mark this, no gun, must be aimed below the level of the gun decks. Do you understand me?'

'Yes, sir.'

If Jim Saunders were aboard *Die Reichmacher*, he would probably be chained on the orlop deck below the waterline. He would be safe unless Kettelmann's ship went down or unless— The memory of the murdered men in the hospital building suddenly filled his mind. He forced himself to concentrate upon the approaching battle. He had a plan of action, that, if successful, would disable the ship without pounding her to bits.

'Mr Barty!' he called. 'Pass the word for the sailmaker and his mates. Tell them to bring all the scraps of tarpaulin they can find. We're going to try something different tonight.'

Duvalier-Winter followed him across the broad deck but Lawson said no more. His mind was busily working out the details of the plan he had conceived.

At last the sailmaker and three mates emerged, each carrying a great bundle of cloth. They advanced aft with expressions of surprise on their faces.

'Put them down there and listen carefully,' Lawson said.

The four sailmakers, Barty, Duvalier-Winter, the men at the helm and those manning the nearest carronades, waited curiously.

'Have you ever made a rag football?'

They looked at each other in astonishment.

'Is it not a simple matter of tying a bundle of rags into a ball, sir?' the sailmaker asked doubtfully.

'Make six of them out of this tarpaulin. Each will have a one-pound bag of gunpowder in the heart of it and when finished should be about two feet in diameter. Lash them securely.'

'Aye aye, sir.'

Thirty minutes later, Midshipman Barty raced silently along the length of the deck to the captain.

'She's there, sir,' he whispered excitedly.

Lawson peered into the darkness. The moon was still obscured by layers of dark cloud. He could see nothing.

'Abaft the beam, at about two hundred yards, sir.'

'Very good,' replied Lawson. 'You may now take up your position aloft and await my orders.'

For a moment he considered the advisability of going round a couple of points to bring the frigate in to her more rapidly. He glanced at the sky. There was an open patch in the cloud to windward of the moon. In a few more minutes he would be able to see the ship. They would also be closer. Then he could perhaps make certain that it was *Die Reichmacher*.

Suspended above the racing water on the starboard side of the frigate, Barty made himself comfortable astride the main-yard on the mizzen-mast : a yard that had been stripped of its canvas. He held a line in his hand and three others were looped through his belt. The four lines stretched across the width of ship to the port side of the same yard where the sailmaker and his three mates sat, each clutching a canvas ball. Between the four was a seaman with a smouldering link in a covered bucket. When given the order he would ignite a ball. Barty, on the opposite end of the yard, would swing it like a great pendulum over the side and drop it with its line on to the enemy deck. In this way Lawson hoped to set fire to *Die Reichmacher*'s sails and cripple her with the minimum amount of damage to the hull.

Suddenly, as if the heavens were working on the side of the frigate, the moon broke clear. The ship, which had been running ever closer to *Comus*, was revealed in all her glory less than a hundred yards away.

'It's her, sir,' whispered a seaman excitedly. 'That's the ship which nigh on rammed us at Gibraltar.'

Lawson nodded in acknowledgement but he had to be sure. Anyway, for the completion of his plans he had to stand in much closer.

'Put her over,' he ordered the men at the helm.

They were slightly ahead and with the wind now on their beam, even with the lower mizzen mast stripped bare, they were rapidly closing the gap. The barque followed in their wake.

'Halloo,' came a cry from across the water. At the same time, concealed lamps were hurriedly revealed.

Lawson smiled grimly. As expected, they were not in the least prepared for attack. They believed that this was a chance encounter which might lead to a collision. If such were the case, they were shortly to be disillusioned.

'Get ready to bring her round,' cautioned Lawson. 'Steady! —Now!'

He had timed it beautifully. When it had seemed that he must run across the bows of the other ship, when every man on board *Comus*, from the first lieutenant down, was biting his nails in anxiety, the frigate had been brought neatly towards the wind to fall off with her yards almost touching those of *Die Reichmacher*.

There could be no mistake about her identity. Her name, inscribed on the bows in ornate Gothic script, could be read easily and if there had been any doubt, there was Kettelmann, beard and nightshirt streaming in the breeze, cursing them for a lot of landlubbers in his native German.

Lawson smiled grimly and gave the order. The next moment he staggered as the frigate heaved to the shock of twenty-four guns fired as one. In that mighty eruption of flame, four hundredweight of iron had smashed into the pirate ship at point-blank range.

The captain waited for the smoke to clear from the narrow trough between the two hulks before ordering the carronades into action. They swept the decks opposite with their deadly hail, adding to the confusion and the din and the smoke of the attack. Then the first of the main armament to be reloaded fired again, followed immediately by another, followed in turn by a ragged fire, as the slower served guns got off their second shots. From now until the engagement ended, the sweating gun crews would have no respite.

Lawson swung away from his position by the rail and hailed the men above on the mizzen main yard.

'Now!' he shouted.

Immediately a spark appeared, a spark which swung round and round, becoming brighter and brighter, until it burst into flames, revealing itself as a blazing link in the hand of a seaman.

Lawson watched anxiously as the torch was applied to the first of the bundles of tar-impregnated cloth. Much depended upon the efforts of these men aloft. If one of the balls were to explode prematurely, it would be dangerous for *Comus*.

The first tarpaulin ball was afire. The sailmaker dangled it for a moment to give the flame time to engulf it and then allowed it to fall. Down it plummeted. Barty, forty feet away, heaved on the line and directed the flaming arc out over the ship's side, high up to the top of its swing and released the rope, just as the blazing mass was in line with the belly of the enemy's mainsail.

It hit the taut cloth in a shower of sparks and slid ineffectively down to the foot of the sail and on to the deck. There it exploded hurling burning rags in all directions, illuminating the deck and the men who rushed forward to put out the fires. Lawson looked around expectantly at the quarterdeck carronades. This was their opportunity to wreak a terrible toll.

The second pendulum of fire swung out to the pirates. This was more successful. As Barty released it at the top of its swing, it curved in a falling arc and jammed itself in the ratlines within a few feet of the mainsail.

'Stand off!' Lawson ordered the helmsman. As the bows eased away Lawson watched the burning ball in fascination. A man had scrambled up ·from the deck and was poking futilely at it with a boat-hook. Then suddenly he lost his nerve and retreated hurriedly. Even before the ball exploded there was no hope for the canvas. A great tongue of fire was already reaching out across the wide expanse of .cloth, and soon the whole of the mainmast from mainsail to royals had become a roaring pillar of flame.

There was an excited shout from the men at the wheel. Lawson tore his eyes from the sight before him to find fire on his own deck. The sailmakers had had an accident with the third fire ball. The rope holding the package together had burnt through before it reached the bottom of its swing and the flaming contents had been spewed just behind the wheel housing. The captain sprinted across to the blazing rags strewn across the deck.

Somewhere in that ten-foot spread of fire was a compact ball of gunpowder. He shielded his eyes against the fierce heat and stinging smoke and searched. Then a lithe figure dropped from the ratlines, swooped with the speed of a hawk and emerged on the other side of the fire with a glowing bundle in his hands. It was Barty. Lawson watched him with bated breath as he ran to the side and flung it overboard.

As *Comus* fell away, flashes from Kettelmann's ship announced that some of his gunners had recovered from their surprise but it was a feeble reply to the terrible barrage that was still ripping into it. Most of the guns along the port side must have been smashed or dismounted. Others would have lost their gun crews. *Comus* would have sent her to the bottom with little difficulty if she could have stayed but other things were claiming her attention.

Marguerite, trapped between the brig and the dhow, was in dire trouble. Her already weakened timbers were being pounded from both sides. The remaining vessel of Kettelmann's fleet was a full-rigged ship which could only be *La Reine Noble*. It had circled the blazing pile in a wide arc, and was returning at speed with the wind behind it, bent on revenge for the fright it had received.

Lawson noted her wild approach with grim amusement. The captain of the ship was throwing caution and good sense to the winds, by interposing his broad bulk between *Die Reichmacher* and the punishing guns of the frigate. He was obviously trying to gain time for Kettelmann but he would have done far better if he had gone to the other side where he would have had some room to manoeuvre. After one brief exchange of shots he would be obliged to run on, and there would be some delay before his ship could cast her weight on the side of the other pirates.

The guns of *Comus* reached out for the newcomer but they drew forth no reply. Clearly the pirate captain was waiting to deliver his broadside.

'Wait for it, carronades,' bellowed Lawson as one of the squat pieces behind him hurled its spread of shot uselessly across the water.

The best opportunity for the lighter carronade was yet to come. Soon the enemy would be starkly revealed against the burning canvas and glowing masts of *Die Reichmacher*. Then the blasting grape shot would tear into those on the open deck. The pirates were going to pay heavily for their captain's mistake.

The heavy balls from the frigate's guns smashed into the approaching bows of *La Reine Noble* with increasing fury but her advance could not be halted. She swept into the gap and presented the whole of her silent starboard battery.

'Now for it,' breathed Duvalier-Winter, his face twitching nervously.

'Holy Mary, Mother of God!' whispered one of the helmsmen.

Lawson heard them both but he had long perfected a formula guaranteed to preserve an outward calm in such a situation. 'Breathe deeply and repeat to yourself, God save the king,' he had been advised as a midshipman. Suddenly the air he had inhaled escaped in a snort of indignation. The tall man on the quarterdeck of the enemy ship was surely Yussaiff Ahmed.

Could he have sunk so low that he would write a ransom note to his own sister? Lawson asked himself. Now he had raised his arm. Was he waving? Damn his impudence. The arm fell abruptly and the dark silhouette of *La Reine Noble* erupted.

Vicious spouts of flame raced along her length, blossoming into balls of fire to illuminate the two ships and the narrow strip of water in between. She had fired her broadside.

A section of the bulwarks five feet from Lawson smashed into splinters, but the ball, fired at a high trajectory, passed harmlessly overhead. Other parts of the frigate were not so fortunate. A great gap had appeared just forward of amidships where several balls had converged to smash down the wall of timber between two gun ports. A gun had been torn from its mounting on the foredeck, and in the waist several men were struggling to lever a carronade off the crushed legs of a screaming gunner.

'That was very foolish of him,' Lawson said to Duvalier-Winter. 'I should have expected something better. If he had fired as soon as his guns had been able to bear, he would have got away twice the amount of metal. As it was, each gun fired only one shot to our three. None of his gunners had time to reload.'

Duvalier-Winter said nothing. He was not aware that Yussaiff Ahmed had been trained by the Royal Navy, but in any case he was more concerned with the jagged sliver of wood sticking out of his arm than he was in the lesson on tactics.

'Ready to go about,' Lawson warned, but his shout was lost in a tremendous cheer.

'Her mast has gone,' someone cried.

Lawson turned in time to see the mizzen-mast of the ship they had just engaged, plunge into the sea. He grinned, then recovered himself.

'Ready to go about, damn you,' he roared.

The frigate swung around into the wind and over on to the other tack.

'Meet her—steady.'

The acting quartermaster looked at Lawson in some alarm. The frigate's bows were directed at the dhow.

'Hold your course,' Lawson ordered sharply.

Shot smashed into *Comus* and ploughed along her decks but she rushed on inexorably. Now the dhow's helmsman was spinning the wheel desperately to bring his charge around but he was too late. With a sickening crunch and tearing of timbers the bows of *Comus* crashed into the broad beam of the pirate vessel and held. The two of them swung, locked together whilst the frigate's carronades poured in a withering fire upon the crowded deck. Then the wind, helped by the swell, eased *Comus* away. She fell astern with her sails taken aback, leaving the stricken dhow to the darkness and the sea.

19

THE frigate's starboard guns were now shooting at the brig but Lawson was not watching the results. All his attention was directed over the port side where *La Reine Noble* should reappear out of the night at any moment. There had been ample time for her to clear the wreckage of her mizzen-mast and Yussaiff Ahmed would be sure to return.

A seaman, his face blackened and his clothes soaking, ran on the quarterdeck. He tried to catch the captain's attention and at last, in desperation, he shouted above the din of the guns.

'The ship's on fire.'

Lawson swung around as did all the crew of the nearby gun. Few things were more dangerous than fire in a wooden ship. They stared at the man. He twisted his hands nervously.

'If you please, sir, Mr Clark said I was to report that the ship is on fire.'

'Where?' demanded Lawson tensely.

'In the cable tier, sir. Mr Clark says it must have been the wads from the dhow's guns when we went into her.'

Lawson considered the information. Certainly the guns of the dhow had been close enough to hurl their wads into the bows after the ball had smashed an opening. There they would have smouldered and fanned into flames as the frigate had got under way. The bulkheads, thickly coated with pitch, would soon be a blazing inferno if the fire was not checked.

'Very well,' said Lawson at length. 'Tell Mr Clark that I am sure he is equal to the situation and if he needs more men he can have them.'

The ship might be burning under their feet but the captain

dare not leave the deck whilst they were in action. Their fate could easily be decided for want of an instant decision.

An outbreak of firing from the frigate's port side battery announced that Yussaiff Ahmed's ship was on its way back. Lawson found the outline of her sails against the background of the thickening clouds but he could not discern the hull and wondered if his own gunners could.

Now the forward guns of the pirate ship were replying to the frigate's barrage. Bright spouts of flame sprang out of the darkness but there was no following crash announcing a hit on *Comus*. Lawson remembered the previous engagement of one broadside and smiled to himself. Evidently Heward knew his business after all. If this was the best his gunners could do, he had been right to control their fire. But he had made a serious error in approaching *Comus* at this angle. He was sailing bows on, into the muzzles of twenty-four guns and he would be able to bring only his bow guns into action. Obviously he had underestimated the distance that *Comus* had travelled since they had parted company. He would have intended to close from dead ahead.

Now the terrible bombardment was forcing *La Reine Noble* to present her broadside. She was swinging around slowly in the failing breeze at one hundred and fifty yards, when obviously they would have preferred to be closer. She settled on a parallel course and the guns along her starboard side crashed into action.

Comus was in a dangerous position. There was the brig to starboard and *La Reine Noble* to port. If they kept their distances Lawson would have no real anxiety but he knew that Heward would not allow the contest to be decided on gunnery alone. Already they had begun to close and there was no room for *Comus* to go about, even if there had been enough wind to complete the manoeuvre. Soon they were at fifty yards and the smoke from the guns of the three vessels, punctuated by leaping flame, merged into billowing clouds over the narrowing strips of water.

'They're going to try to board, sir,' Duvalier-Winter shouted above the noise of the battle.

Lawson waved an acknowledgement. Under the circumstances Heward would be a fool to do otherwise. He knew that he could not compete with the frigate's gunnery and since neither *La Reine Noble* nor the brig could bring more than a half of their armament to bear upon the frigate, the one craft could improve upon the fire power of the other two. On the other hand, if the pirates were able to board *Comus*, there would be hand-to-hand fighting against overwhelming odds.

'What the devil has become of Hawbrook and the barque?' Lawson fretted irritably.

A great cheer from the men of the starboard battery sent Lawson hurrying across the deck to see what had happened.

'What is it?' he demanded of Duvalier-Winter.

'Don't rightly know, sir, but the brig is falling off. It isn't going to close with us.'

'Beggin' your pardon, sir,' said a voice in the darkness, 'but I think as 'ow the barque is on t'other side of the brig.'

'Have you seen her?' demanded the captain.

'No, sir, but I seed a bit of gunfire for'ard o' the brig, and then the next time it were coming from just amidships of her, like as if whoever was firing was on the opposite course. Then it seemed, the brig sort of checked and began to fall off. I reckon that Mr Hawbrook 'as grappled her and he's pulled her bows across the wind.'

Lawson recognised the voice of the Yorkshireman who had given him the commentary when they had been making their escape from the bay. He had formed the opinion at that time that he was a sensible man. His suggestion now was quite possible and there appeared to be nothing else to explain the action of the brig. *Marguerite* would be unable to tow the larger craft away but since the brig was close hauled and the barque had the failing breeze behind it, Hawbrook would certainly cause the other vessel to fall off. He grinned delightedly. Whilst he was served by men capable of showing such courage and imagination, he need fear no odds. Now *Comus* had only Heward's ship to worry about for the next few minutes.

'Cease firing with the starboard battery,' he ordered Duvalier-Winter. 'We'll have those gunners aft, ready to throw these swine into the sea.'

'Aft, sir?' queried Duvalier-Winter, but Lawson had gone.

The captain gathered a dozen men from the guns and gave them orders which sent them running across the deck. Then he studied the ship creeping towards them. Not a man was to be seen but there would be plenty crouching behind the bulwarks, ready to leap on to the decks of the frigate as soon as the gap closed. The frigate's gunners were making the most of this last minute and they were receiving very little in reply. Lawson grunted with satisfaction as a section of the enemy's bulwarks some six feet in length disintegrated in a shower of splinters. The men who had been sheltering behind it would most certainly be out of the battle.

'If we could hold them off a little longer, we'd pound them to pieces,' said Duvalier-Winter, appearing at Lawson's side.

Lawson nodded absently. He was judging the distance separating the two ships and the angle of approach. Already the men he had instructed were positioned, ready to carry out his orders.

The first grapnel hurtled through the air and bit into the frigate's timbers.

'Axemen!' shouted the first lieutenant.

At the same time, a heavy three-pronged hook swept him off his feet, and skated over the planking to wedge itself against the mounting of one of the carronades. He scrambled up and drew his sword to cut it free but the captain stopped him.

'Leave it,' he ordered. 'I want their grapples aboard.'

Heward watched in amazement as the men from the frigate's quarterdeck carronades began to hurl their own grapnels over the water to bite into the stern of *La Reine Noble*.

'Now, hard a-starboard,' Lawson ordered the helm.

As the frigate responded slowly, he turned to Duvalier-Winter.

'No sense in letting them dictate the terms,' he said conversationally. 'They are anxious to come alongside. We can't sail out of their reach, so we have arranged for them to come stern first.'

Axemen had cleared away the clinging lines from all places forward and two great spars were being secured amidships to fend off. If the pirates were to come alongside it would have to be stern first. Instead of the hordes sweeping over the side along the whole length of the frigate, they would now be obliged to attack on a very restricted front where their numbers could not be used to full advantage. Meanwhile the heavy port side guns continued to hurl shot across the wedge of water.

'They're on fire!' screamed an exultant voice from somewhere in the waist.

So was *Comus*, Lawson remembered with a shock, unless Clark had been able to put it out. The blaze across the water seemed to be nothing more than a small deck fire. It would soon be doused but it would occupy Heward's attention for the next crucial minute and perhaps he would not notice the changing angle of the two ships.

'Ready now, carronades,' he warned.

The stern of *La Reine Noble* was swinging slowly around, exposing the length of her deck to the aftermost guns of *Comus* and bringing into line all the pirates crouching behind the bulwarks, clearly illuminated by the glow.

Heward suddenly saw the danger and shouted a warning. One of the men under the guns' muzzles screamed in terror and leapt to his feet. The others scrambled over each other to save themselves but they were too late. The wide-mouthed carronades engulfed them in flame as they hurled their hundreds of musket-balls across the deck.

Most of the frigate's crew were now clustered in the stern with pikes and cutlasses but there was no immediate attempt to board. Twenty or more of the pirates were sprawled in the scuppers where the grape shot had laid them. Others were dazed with shock but Yussaiff Ahmed was driving them to the attack and rallying the others. Now they were pouring up from below and dropping from the rigging, confident of their ability to overwhelm the inferior numbers on the frigate.

Yussaiff Ahmed was one of the first to board. He leapt over the bulwarks with his sword at the ready and was immediately attacked by a marine. Lawson rushed across the deck and almost reached him but the press of boarders soon swept him away and the next moment he was fighting for his life.

A half-naked negro was swinging a scimitar at Lawson's head, whilst on the other side of him a pikeman was trying to stab under his guard. He fired his pistol full into the man's face whilst fending off the wild slashes of the negro. Now he parried a thrust and darted inside with the point of his sword. His opponent fell back coughing blood.

Flares had been ignited by the pirates, and musketeers on *La Reine Noble* were firing whenever the opportunity presented itself but it was unrewarding work for the most part. The light was too uncertain and the press too close. They would have been far better employed if they had been able to get on to the frigate's deck but the narrow strip of stern in contact with *Comus* was their only bridge and it was already jammed with their frustrated comrades.

The two ships, still lashed stern to stern, were now paying off in opposite directions under the influence of a breath of wind. The angle between them had widened to almost a hundred and eighty degrees and they must soon drift together with the starboard side of the frigate against the port side of the pirate unless immediate action was taken. They might also damage their rudders and *Comus* would need to be manoeuvrable to keep out of trouble when *Die Reichmacher* re-entered the battle.

Lawson saw no point in continuing the hand-to-hand fighting. The superior numbers of the pirates must tell once they had cleared a way for the rest to get a foothold.

'Close your ranks,' shouted Lawson. 'Drive them over the side.'

Other voices took up the cry. The tempo of the defence increased. The defenders hurled themselves savagely on to the pirates and swept them back. Lawson was wherever the fight was thickest; lunging, slashing, punching; giving no quarter and shouting encouragement to his men. Few could have withstood such an onslaught. The motley crowd who had boarded the frigate were used to the feeble resistance of merchant ships and had no stomach for this kind of fighting. Quickly they fell back. Now they were jumping back over the bulwarks, landing amongst their swarming mates, still clamouring in the stern of their ship. It would have been a complete rout but for a pocket of resistance around the aftermost gun, where a few pirates were fighting fiercely. Lawson was forcing his way towards them when a blast of scorching flame hurled him on one side. Heward had fired the frigate's quarterdeck gun and an eighteen-pound ball had torn through the British seamen. By the time the captain had picked himself up and beaten the fire from his clothes, Heward and the last of his men were back aboard their own ship.

Lawson was not sorry that the action was over. It had been a very near thing. If the pirates had held out until Yussaiff Ahmed had fired the captured gun, they would probably have been able to clear the aftermost part of the frigate and establish a bridge for their mates.

Now the British seamen were thronging the bulwarks, waiting for the order to carry the battle on to *La Reine Noble*. Lawson blew a furious blast on his whistle just in time to stop a few of the wilder ones from jumping.

'Cut her free,' he ordered.

They axed the cables and the gap widened. No new grapnels came over the side. The enemy had had enough. They wanted to escape into the friendly darkness to lick their wounds before resuming the attack.

'All guns will fire as soon as they can bear,' Lawson ordered.

As the frigate wallowed slowly around on the oily swell, the grey mist began to settle about them shutting them off from the pirate ships and silencing the newly commenced bombardment for want of a target. The situation that Lawson feared had come about : they were becalmed in a fog.

'They'll think twice about coming back,' Duvalier-Winter said with satisfaction.

Lawson rubbed at his eyes, red rimmed from lack of sleep and the smoke of the battle. He leaned out over the bulwarks and peered into the darkness for some time before replying.

'He'll be back,' he said, 'and Kettelmann will attack for sure. He has no alternative. He can't escape and he's not fool enough to wait until morning. He'll probably have his boats out, towing what's left of his ship. They'll be creeping up on us now, and *Die Reichmacher* will be as effective as *Comus* until we get a breath of wind.'

Duvalier-Winter looked apprehensively over his shoulder.

Lawson paced the deck thoughtfully. It would soon be dawn. If they could keep well clear until there was enough wind to give them steerage, they would engage *La Reine Noble* at five hundred yards and sink her. Then *Die Reichmacher* and the brig would be at his mercy. Kettelmann would not be able to hoist much canvas on his charred mast and spars and he could hardly outsail *Comus* whilst under jury rig. Hawbrook, on the barque, would also lend his weight to the battle, if he had not gone down.

Die Reichmacher and *La Reine Noble* must now be working on compass bearings taken from the flashes of the guns. The best thing for *Comus* would be to move as far from her present position as possible.

'Hoist out the boats. We're going to tow,' Lawson ordered abruptly.

There was far too much noise, Lawson thought. Axes were being used to cut away wreckage. Deep down in the bowels of the ship, carpenters were hammering baulks of timber into place to strengthen the weakened planking and, at a lower pitch, filling in the momentary lapses in the general racket was the asthmatical sighing of the pumps. The din would travel far over the water.

'Stop that!' he shouted suddenly. 'I want absolute silence.'

The hammering dwindled and died as the captain's order was relayed throughout the ship. Now only the sound of the pumps remained and the squeak of block and tackle as the last of the three boats was lowered over the side. One of the carpenter's mates, his face blackened and his clothes wet and dishevelled, appeared out of the darkness.

'Yes?' demanded the captain.

'The fire's out but there's a mortal lot of damage, sir. Mr Clark asked if you would kindly inspect the stem when you have a moment to spare, sir.'

'Very well. I'll go down immediately.'

He called Duvalier-Winter over. 'I'm going below to inspect the damage for'ard. Make just enough clearance to ensure the efficient working of the guns. The more noise we make, the easier it will be for the enemy to find us. I want half a dozen reliable men stationed about the ship with their eyes and ears open. We don't want them to surprise us.'

'Aye aye, sir.'

20

THE carpenter and his mates were up to their waists in water hammering a canvas covered plug into a six-inch shot hole. The captain waited outside the circle of lamp light until the spurting jets of sea were reduced to a trickle, before he edged his way along one of the broad bow ribs just clear of the water. Now he was above them.

'Are the pumps gaining, Mr Clark?'

The carpenter waded across the deck, removed a long dead pipe from between his teeth and held his lantern high.

'Aye, sir. They're doing fine at the moment,' he said, peering up at the captain, 'but mayhap they'll have more than they can cope with once we get under way. The stem's gone, sir.'

He indicated the damage, clearly revealed in the glow of the lamp.

'Shot through and through, sir,' he said with a shake of his head. 'It took a knock when we rammed the dhow and then the fire did it no good.'

Lawson examined the fire-blackened slab of adzed oak which rose from the keel to form the bows, and upon which most of the main timbers of the ship depended. It was a yard thick and would seem to be indestructible but some of the shots from the dhow had torn great chunks from it and one had punched a hole completely through. This, together with the collision, had caused a split along its length.

'I've seen the like of it afore,' rumbled Clark, 'when I were a boy on board the *Valiant* in '75. The timbers'll start working if we get any kind of a wind and then we'll be hard put to keep the sea out.'

'How did you manage on *Valiant*?'

'We went down, sir,' replied Clark dolefully.

'Oh!' Lawson found himself grinning despite the seriousness of the situation. 'Well, we're not going to go down on *Comus*. You'll have at least two hours without wind, if the weather follows the pattern of the past week. I shall be very surprised if an enterprising man such as yourself cannot accomplish something in that time.'

He was about to go when he remembered Yussaiff Ahmed.

'The ships we attacked are lying somewhere close by and likely trying to find us, so I should be obliged if you would make as little noise as possible.'

On his way back, a groan in the darkness reminded him that he was within a few yards of the thin bulkhead that separated the wounded from the rest of the orlop deck. It seemed days since he was last there and it came as something of a shock to realise that it had been but a few hours before. There was no time for him to pay a visit. Doctor Fairweather would have his hands full with the recently wounded, and those who had been operated upon earlier would be either sleeping off the effects of exhaustion and laudanum, or dead. Lawson climbed wearily back to the quarterdeck. The next hour or so might see them all at the bottom of the sea.

The blackness of the deck had been relieved by the grey light of dawn but the mist was thicker than ever and visibility was only a few yards. The captain looked keenly at his men in passing : huddled outlines crouching around the guns, haggard with fatigue, but tense and watchful nevertheless. The pumps had been stopped and the ship was unnaturally quiet. Only the occasional creaks of the top spars, as they swung idly in the gentle swell, were to be heard.

Duvalier-Winter was in a state of agitation when the captain reached him and it was with obvious relief that he relinquished his responsibility.

'I think that they are with us, sir,' he whispered.

Lawson nodded. He had suspected that to be the case when he had noted the attentiveness of his men.

'Have you seen them?'

'Sir!' hissed Barty from two yards away. 'There it is again.'

Lawson and Duvalier-Winter followed the direction of his pointing finger. Fifty yards away the bows of a ship's boat and the white foam from the threshing oars could be seen. It remained for the space of three or four strokes before it was swallowed up in the fog.

'Hard a port,' Lawson hissed to Duvalier-Winter. 'Have the towing parties informed of the change of course.'

The boat appeared again, much closer than before.

'It's not towing, sir,' Barty whispered. 'There's no cable astern of her.'

At that moment the boat's coxswain saw *Comus* and shouted.

'Take aim,' Lawson ordered the carronades on the starboard quarter.

The cast iron wheels of the carronades squealed as they were skidded sideways across the deck boards. Lawson hesitated. The shadowy figure in the stern of the small boat had put the tiller over and his bows were pointing towards the frigate, in line with the muzzles of the carronades. A white flag drooped from its transom.

'That's the captain of *Die Reichmacher*, sir and—,' Barty's eyes opened wide in astonishment, 'Mr Chandler is with him.'

Lawson considered this new development. It seemed that either the barque had gone down or it had been captured. Could it be that Kettelman, realising the futility of his position, was about to come to terms? Grimly he watched the boat as it hooked on.

Lieutenant Chandler was the first on deck. Kettelman followed heavily and stood panting by the rail. He was clearly out of condition and it was obvious from his appearance that he had taken an active part in putting out the fire on his ship. His clothes were charred. One of his hands was heavily bandaged and the great beard was badly singed down the right side. Gone was the arrogance he had displayed in Gibraltar Harbour but hatred was there, a hatred that was consuming him and blazing from his eyes as he turned from his quick survey of the frigate to stare at the captain.

'You will observe that I have returned one of your officers,' he said in a strong guttural accent.

Lawson ignored him.

'Your report, Mr Chandler, if you please.'

The young lieutenant gave him the facts, precisely and ungarnished. It was as Lawson had expected. The barque had gone and the survivors had been taken from the water by Kettelmann.

'We sank the brig though, sir,' said Chandler as an after-thought. 'She went down shortly after we filled.'

The captain's brooding face jerked into a grin at this un-looked for piece of good news.

'That was well done, Mr Chandler. Now we have only two lame ducks to worry about.'

'And I think, sir, but I'm not sure, that the ship you engaged is taking herself as far away as she can get.'

'*La Reine Noble*!' Lawson exclaimed incredulously.

He glanced quickly at Kettelmann but the man's face told him nothing. If this information were true, the German needed desperately to bargain with *Comus*. *Die Reichmacher* was doomed.

'You will have some proposals to put to me,' Lawson said.

The man heaved himself away from the bulwarks and scowled into Lawson's face.

'*Ja*. I propose to set your men free.'

'The terms.'

'You will sail away and leave me to my repairs. Your gallant Mr Hawbrook, and the twenty men who are chained with him, will be given my launch with provisions after I have reached Algiers.'

'And if you are attacked?'

The German captain spread his hands and shrugged his great shoulders.

'Your people would go down with *Die Reichmacher*. Men in chains cannot swim.'

Lawson glared at Kettelmann whilst his mind worked furiously on the problem. The pirate's logic was unassailable. If he were to surrender there would be the gallows for him and most of his crew. He would fight until his ship sank under him and even the most sanguinary optimist would hardly expect him to cast off the chains from his prisoners should that happen. To save his men, it would be necessary for Lawson either to board *Die Reichmacher* or accept the conditions. Kettelmann sensed his thoughts.

'I have three hundred men and more aboard my ship, including those from the brig. You could hardly expect to carry odds of three to one. If you were foolish enough to attempt it, I feel sure that my men would hang their prisoners from what is left of my main yards. They don't feel kindly disposed towards you, Captain.'

'The mist is thinning, sir,' warned Duvalier-Winter, 'and there's a breath of wind.'

Lawson looked about him. He needed time to think. Kettelmann seemed to be in a position to dictate terms. *Comus* must either accept them or condemn Hawbrook and the others to death. For a moment he considered discussing the problem with his second in command and then he rejected the idea. The responsibility was his and his alone. He had to make a decision. At the best he could only gain better terms.

'Ship ho !' came the warning from the masthead.

Barty sprang for the ratlines, not waiting for the captain to give the order. Lawson watched him for a moment making his rapid ascent and then turned to his first officer.

'Keep this man here,' he instructed Duvalier-Winter and climbed after his midshipman.

From the masthead, which he shared with Barty and the man who had reported, Lawson could see the bare masts of Kettelmann's ship quite clearly. They were only a cable's length away. Beyond, at a distance of perhaps two miles, in a clear patch of water with all sails set, was *La Reine Noble*. Clearly it was abandoning *Die Reichmacher* to her fate. Lawson closed the telescope and thoughtfully descended the mast.

There was something odd about this. Heward had never been one to run from a fight, and his attack in the bay had proved that he had lost none of his natural courage. Why then was he sailing away? Could it be that high intrigue among the hierarchy of the pirate state made Kettelmann's disappearance desirable? Heward's ransom note to his sister showed him to have become a man without scruples. Whatever the reason, it had placed the frigate in a strong position. Lawson now knew what line of action he must take.

The expression on Kettelmann's face clearly indicated that he was aware of Heward's desertion.

'Your comrades have left you,' began Lawson. 'They are sailing for the safety of Algiers as fast as the breeze will permit.' He paused to allow the information to sink in. 'A bird in the hand is better than two in the bush and *Die Reichmacher* is very much in my hands. The fact that some of my men are held on your ship does not affect the situation in the least.'

'You would condemn them to death?' sneered Kettelmann.

'If necessary.—However, there is another possibility.'

Kettelmann waited.

'Before we discuss terms, what have you done with the midshipman you captured at Gibraltar?'

'He is on board *La Reine Noble*.'

'You're a liar.'

Kettelmann's eyes glinted dangerously for a moment, then he shrugged his shoulders.

'Why should I lie about an unimportant boy? We took him because I expected your men at the inn to bring the military about our ears before we could get clear. He was to be a hostage. I should have dropped him over the side weeks ago, if my—brother captain on *La Reine Noble* had not asked to have him.'

Lawson's eyes bored into him but the German met him calmly.

'Very well,' said the Captain. 'Release my men and I will leave you. Mind you,' he added, 'I give you no promise of an unmolested passage once I have taken your companion. If you have not got clear away I will be after you.'

Kettelmann scowled at Lawson. When he had first weighed the prospects of coming to terms, the idea he had had of Lawson had been the one formed in the market-place at Gibraltar when the captain seemed to lack the strength of character to drive off a crowd of urchins. This impression had been reinforced after the old Spaniard had bettered him. Now he found a man who was prepared to sacrifice one of his officers and a quarter of his crew.

The sighing of the restarted pumps and the hammering from below helped him to reach a decision. It was obvious that the frigate was in trouble. It was unlikely that it would be able to conclude a successful action against *Le Reine Noble*. Whilst he was in pursuit, *Die Reichmacher* would perhaps be able to creep under the protection of the Algiers battery or escape to sea.

'*In ordnung*,' the German said. 'On these conditions, you may have your men.'

21

KETTELMANN had been as good as his word. Hawbrook and the men from the sunken barque were safely aboard the frigate and she was already in pursuit of *La Reine Noble*. *Die Reichmacher* lay in full view, well within gun shot to starboard, with two hundred men swarming like ants about her decks, hoisting new yards and reeving fresh stays to support the charred masts. Most of them cast anxious glances over their shoulders as they worked. The frigate's gun ports were still open and the gun crews could be seen clearly crouching over the sights. Lawson was taking no chances.

Not that he was anxious. *Die Reichmacher* was in no shape to attack. The frigate could have sailed around her and pounded her timbers to splinters with little danger to herself. In a few hours perhaps things would be different. If the strengthened masts were able to bear a full press of canvas, Kettelmann could easily give as good as he received, particularly if *Comus* were further damaged in the approaching action against *La Reine Noble*. Lawson abruptly turned his thoughts back to the pursuit.

'How far do you think they are ahead of us, Mr Chandler?' he asked suddenly.

'I should say three miles, sir.'

'Nearer four,' volunteered Barty.

'Thank you, Mr Barty, but I did not ask your opinion,' said Lawson with ill humour.

Barty retired hurriedly and Lawson began to pace the deck thoughtfully. It was going to be a long chase and one that might well be unsuccessful. They could already see land in a haze of mist and the pirates might well have help when they drew nearer to Algiers. If they did *Comus* would have to get away as quickly as a leaking hull would allow her and she might have to fight her way out at that. Lawson was well aware that he was placing his ship in considerable danger by approaching the pirate stronghold but it had to be done. He had to justify his leaving Kettelmann without destroying him and there was no argument more likely to satisfy their Lordships than another successful action.

Aloft every sail was drawing but the breeze was light. Providing *La Reine Noble* was getting no more than the same light airs, the frigate should overhaul her rapidly because the pirates had no mizzen canvas and without its steadying influence they would tend to swing away from the wind and a great deal of rudder would have to be used to compensate. The resulting drag would be considerable.

'Send the men to breakfast,' ordered the captain when *Die Reichmacher* was far enough astern to offer no more danger.

Evans immediately appeared on deck, smiling broadly.

'Breakfast, sir?'

Lawson nodded. He was not interested in food but he had not eaten for twelve hours, and if he were to refuse there would be comments passed. It would not do for the entire ship's company to sense his agitation. Evans was still waiting.

'Shall I bring the table here, sir?'

Lawson noted that Chandler and Barty were hanging on to his reply. To eat on deck so early in the morning, when the sun had not warmed the air, would suggest either a lack of confidence in his officers or a consuming anxiety. It would not do to give the impression of either.

'In my cabin, of course,' he answered testily. 'Then you may set out my razor.'

'Yes, sir.'

The captain paused to scan the horizon, still obscured by grey mist, and take in once more the set of the sails before going to breakfast.

Some thirty minutes later the carpenter appeared on deck,

his clothes clinging wetly to him. Shading his eyes from the bright morning sun, he looked around for the captain.

'What is it, Mr Clark?' Chandler asked, noting with interest the water dripping from him.

'We've patched up, sir, but I shouldn't like to be responsible, begging your pardon, sir, if we find ourselves in any kind of sea. The timbers just wouldn't stand up to it.'

Chandler looked puzzled. This was the first he had heard of trouble below.

Patiently Clark explained the damaged stem and the danger in thrusting their bows more forcibly through the sea.

'It's a case of pressure, sir,' he added in a fatherly manner. 'If we goes any faster, the bows'll mayhap cave in and that will be the end of us.'

Chandler cast startled eyes aloft. Already the wind was fresh-ening and *Comus* was carrying every stitch of canvas. He lifted his speaking trumpet to give the order to shorten sail and then thought better of it.

'Kindly report to the captain,' he ordered Barty. 'You go along as well, Mr Clark.'

The men at the wheel had overheard. Rumour was already rife on the lower deck and they knew about Clark's experience on the ill-fated *Valiant*. Now, as Barty and the carpenter left the deck, they burst into excited discussion. Chandler stopped his pacing in astonishment.

'Quiet there,' he ordered.

The men lapsed into sullen mutterings and finally into silent scowls as the young lieutenant glared at them. Chandler watched them for a moment longer and then resumed his walk. Two minutes later Barty and Clark reappeared.

The carpenter looked worried as he hurried forward. Barty, as cheerful as ever, reported to the officer of the watch.

'Yes?'

Barty grinned.

'He said, "Very well, Mr Barty!"'

Chandler's jaw dropped.

'Nothing more?'

'No, sir.'

Chandler pursed his lips and turned away but an outburst from one of the men at the wheel made him swing back on his heels.

'What the devil is wrong with you? I'll have the next man who speaks, up for punishment.'

A burly seaman approached him and touched his forelock.

'If you please, sir, we don't like this at all. We've got wives and children and the way things is going on we'll likely be at the bottom of the sea afore long.'

'Master-at-arms!' shouted Chandler.

The man stood with his great hands on his hips, his lower lip thrust out sullenly but when the master-at-arms and a marine corporal came running aft to seize him, he suddenly went berserk.

'You're not putting me in irons in a sinking ship,' he shouted, and lashed out with a ham-like fist.

The redcoated marine went down but recovering quickly he grabbed at the man's legs. He was kicked in the face. The master-at-arms struck the seaman over the head with his baton but it appeared to have no effect and a moment later he was sprawling in the scuppers with his nose streaming blood, whilst his intended prisoner had sprung for the mizzen mast shrouds.

'Stand where you are,' roared the unmistakable voice of Captain Lawson.

The seaman paused in his mad scramble and then lowered himself until his feet were on the bulwarks. The wildness in his eyes had now given way to anxiety.

'Come here!'

At Lawson's curt, cold command, the man eased himself to the deck fearfully. All the bluster had left him. Slowly he walked across the planking and stopped with downcast eyes in front of the captain. Lawson thrust out a chin still soaped and lathered and streaked with blood where the razor had caught him.

'You silly fool,' he said witheringly. 'Where do you think you'd have gone after you'd reached the masthead?'

The man remained with his eyes lowered. Lawson swung around to take in those on the deck who were openly listening and obviously in sympathy with the views of the seaman.

'Is there anybody else who thinks we ought to let a prize slip out of our hands?' he demanded. He glared around. No one spoke.

'That ship is probably full of loot. We are going to take her and then we are going back to capture that other bloody pirate. When we return to England, which should not be long now, we are going to have some money in our pockets, and no bit of a hole in our bows is going to stop us.'

The men remained silent and, for the most part, avoided his eye.

'I'll chance owt for a bit o'brass,' an unmistakable Yorkshire voice said in the background.

The tension broke and the ship resounded with cheers, Lawson, turning away, felt no elation. The men's fears were justified. Nothing could save them if the bows collapsed. His speech had sent them back to their work with a will but it had placed the captain in a position from which he could not retreat. He was now committed to the chase and any reduction of sail would be looked upon both as a weakness and an admission that he was wrong. He glowered at the seaman in front of him.

'You'll be called upon to answer for your crimes. Meanwhile see to it that you are twice the sailor you were and maybe you'll have less than the three dozen strokes you deserve. Get back to your duties.'

'Aye aye, sir.' The man knuckled his forelock and rejoined the men at the wheel.

'Carry on, Mr Chandler.'

Duvalier-Winter and Hawbrook, who had rushed on deck a few seconds after the captain, stood by expectantly for orders but Lawson said nothing to them. He paused at the head of the companionway to glance once more at the spread of canvas above him. Then he went below.

The sun was high in the sky and the North African coast was visible when the captain next came on deck. He wore a newly pressed coat and fresh linen, and the silver buckles of his shoes gleamed against polished black leather. Had it not been for the cutlass which swung at his side instead of the ceremonial sword, and the brace of pistols half concealed beneath his coat, one might have thought he was about to attend a social function.

The stolid Hawbrook, who now had the watch, allowed no surprise to show on his face.

'We are close enough to try a shot with the bow chasers, sir,' he volunteered.

Lawson nodded. They might be responsible for his nephew's death but it was a risk that had to be taken.

'Do so, Mr Hawbrook,' he said gloomily.

He walked over to the windward side and examined the coastline while Hawbrook was giving his orders. He was desperately tired. For two and a half of the three hours that he had been absent from the deck he had been forward with Clark and his mates, trying to solve the problem of the weakened timbers. He had not been needed but it had helped to take his mind off the worries ahead. He had laboured physically, helping to wedge beams in such a manner that they would strengthen the bows. Then they had piled heavy timber about the damaged stem in the hope that the sheer weight would stop it from working. The result had not satisfied Clark that there would be no damage if the wind rose but he grudgingly admitted that they would be able to maintain their present speed—and perhaps a little more if necessary.

The roar of one of the two long guns, mounted forward, brought all the officers hurrying on deck. Duvalier-Winter took up his place near the captain and waited for orders.

'No need to rouse the men,' said Lawson, anticipating the

first lieutenant's question. 'The guns are still run out and there is nothing that they can do at the moment.'

The long gun on the starboard side of the bows fired at maximum elevation and those on deck became quiet as they waited for the fall of the shot.

'Damned close,' said Duvalier-Winter enthusiastically. 'Short, but dead in line.'

The captain nodded. The range would improve as the guns warmed and in any case they must be overhauling the pirate fairly quickly. Soon they would be hitting, if the gunlayers knew their business.

'They're firing at us, sir,' warned Duvalier-Winter.

'Yes,' replied Lawson in exactly the same tone he would have used if the first lieutenant had announced that visitors were coming alongside. Inwardly he was praying that none of their shot would smash through the weakened bows.

A spout of water appeared just ahead and directly in line with the frigate. It was followed by a cheer from the men grouped around the bow guns. *Comus* had scored a hit.

'Ploughed along their deck, sir,' Duvalier-Winter said, scrutinising the target through his telescope. 'Another hit!' he exclaimed with rising excitement. 'If we carry on like this we'll have the other two masts off her.'

Lawson made no comment and turned away. The nearest land was less than three miles off and Algiers must be within four leagues. Unless *Comus* could increase her speed, or slow down *La Reine Noble*, they would lose her. At any moment help could be sent out from the pirate stronghold and the closer the frigate approached the more precarious would be her position.

A plume of water to starboard, followed immediately by a crash somewhere forward, indicated that Yussaiff Ahmed had found the range. From now on it would be a test of gunnery until the gap closed and the main armament could be brought to hear. Then, and only then, could *Comus* demonstrate its superior broadside.

'Sail ho!' came a cry from the masthead, indicating that the man on lookout was doing more than watch the battle. 'Two sails on the starboard beam.'

Lawson looked around him until his eyes rested on Barty. The midshipman had already demonstrated that he had exceptionally keen sight.

'Please go aloft, Mr Barty,' he said.

Barty scrambled up the ratlines and Lawson turned his attention once more to the fight in progress. These were the waters of the Barbary Pirates, jealously guarded by the Dey of Algiers. The ships that had been sighted would probably be a part of his fleet but *Comus* still had a job to do. The pirate ship they were pursuing had to be captured or destroyed before it could reach the safety of the guns at Algiers. Yussaiff Ahmed had to be taken and Jim Saunders must be set free. If that could be achieved they would happily take their chance against odds of two to one in their escape.

'Two ships, sir,' came Barty's shouted confirmation. 'Can't say what they are. There's a mist.'

Lawson remained by the wheel. There was nothing he could do. To join Barty at the masthead would reveal his anxiety and could serve no useful purpose.

'The target seems to be on fire again, sir,' said Duvalier-Winter in some astonishment. 'Can't think how it could have happened unless they've had an accident.'

Lawson levelled his glass. There was certainly more smoke than would have been produced from the guns. As he watched, the smoke grew thicker until it was obscuring most of the deck. Then the ship, which had been racing in the direction of Algiers, suddenly changed course and ran her bows at the nearest land.

'They're going to drive her ashore,' Lawson exclaimed. 'Now what the devil——'

A sudden fear gripped him. Heward would not abandon his ship without good reason. The fire on board *La Reine Noble* must be in the vicinity of the magazine. The ship was in danger of blowing apart at any moment and young Saunders would go with it. It seemed unlikely that any of the pirates would risk their lives by going below to release a prisoner.

Every man, except those toiling at the guns in the bows, was breathlessly watching the drama. Few things move a sailor more than fire at sea and most would realise the significance of this sudden change of course. Perhaps they would see an explosion like the one when the magazine in the bay had gone up. A few cast uneasy glances at their captain standing aloof by the wheel.

He had a decision to make. He could either take *Comus* in and make an attempt to save Saunders or he could stand off at a safe distance and rake the fleeing pirates with grapeshot and ball. Suddenly Barty, from the masthead, brought the ship's company back to the other problem that was facing them.

'Four sail, four sail to starboard,' he shouted.

Lawson swung his glass around. The haze was thinning and he was able to make out topsails at about seven miles distance. Almost immediately another shout, this time filled with urgency, reached the deck.

'Two sail astern!'

'Damn me!' exclaimed Duvalier-Winter. 'We're in the middle of them.' He had spoken lightly but there was anxiety in his voice.

Lawson felt everyone's eyes upon him but still he hesitated before giving the orders that would seal Jim's fate. There was no doubt where his duty lay. The lowliest seaman could have told him. If the approaching ships were hostile, as might be expected so close to Algiers, *Comus* was in danger of being cut off from the sea. Clearly he must get away from the shore to gain space to manoeuvre.

'Make ready to go about,' he ordered abruptly, striving to keep the emotion out of his voice.

He strode purposefully to the ratlines glass in hand, to ascertain the danger for himself. Their Lordships would express their displeasure in no uncertain terms if they learned that the action had been discontinued on the report of a midshipman. He had barely reached the bulwarks when there was a sickening crunch and the deck beneath his feet lurched drunkenly, hurling him full length across the boards.

'We've struck!' someone shouted.

The ship trembled to the accompaniment of tearing timbers as her speed carried her over some obstruction. Lawson scrambled to his feet and hung out over the side. The water was in turmoil from the rolling hulk of a completely submerged, but partly buoyant wreck. One end now thrust itself out of the water, held for a moment and then slid back beneath the surface, spewing forth great bubbles of long-trapped air, laden with the foul stink of decay. The victim of some long-forgotten storm, or action, had been sent to its final rest.

One of the carpenter's mates was already running along the deck. He jerked to a stop in front of the captain.

'Sir, sir!'

'I know,' Lawson said savagely. 'Tell Mr Clark to keep her afloat for fifteen minutes.'

'Fift—fifteen minutes! Aye aye, sir.' He knuckled his forehead automatically but his face was grey when he ran back.

'Get the wounded and prisoners out, Mr Duvalier-Winter. Lie the wounded in the boats and detail crews to put them ashore. Reliable men you'll need and see that they are armed.'

Barty was already scrambling down from the masthead and Hawbrook was waiting for orders.

'Run her aground, Mr Hawbrook.'

Hawbrook turned away to the quartermaster and the Captain glared impatiently aloft.

'Mr Barty! Look alive, man.'

Barty leapt the last ten feet to the deck.

'Sir.'

'Join Mr Chandler on the gun deck. Ask him to bring his battery to bear upon any concentrations of men over there as soon as he is able but he is to make sure that Mr Saunders is not among them before he opens fire.' He indicated three boats being lowered from the side of the burning ship. Each one was packed with armed men. 'If he can sink any of those boats, so much the better.'

Meanwhile, deep down in the bows, Clark was having to shout his orders above the roar of the incoming torrent. The stem had broken completely and its lower half had been thrust back, leaving a space a foot wide and six feet long between the curved timbers. The gap was just below the waterline and the sea was arching through under pressure. The men were standing on the ribs above the level of the rising flood pressing their bodies against the walls of the frigate. A few were edging towards the ladder.

'Keep her afloat for fifteen minutes?' the carpenter said incredulously when the captain's reply reached him. 'Fifteen minutes! The Archangel Gabriel couldn't keep her afloat that long'—'All right, my lads,' he shouted suddenly. 'Don't think you're going anywhere. Carry on with those bales. Pass them along like I told you. O'Brien will get those shoulders of his under one of them and heave it on to the gap. You will help him, Jones. You're big enough. Handsomely now, handsomely—clumsy men!'

The first bale had toppled two of them from their perch. They disappeared briefly under the swirling water.

A second large bale of seamen's clothing was being manoeuvred along the rib. This time the carpenter, who was up to his shoulders, was helping to support it from underneath with a plank. Slowly they worked it along to O'Brien and Jones, who had positioned themselves above the fracture. They seized it together and jammed it onto the gap. A half of the flow was stopped. Now another bale was being eased along the rib on the opposite bow and one of the two men, who had fallen into the water, had been given the job of supporting it with the plank. O'Brien and Jones climbed around the stem and sealed off the other half of the split. Now the sea intake had been reduced to no more than a steady flow from the split seams below the main fracture. It was more than the pumps could possibly cope with but by comparison with the flood they had halted it seemed trivial. The men grinned their relief.

'Don't stand about doing nothing,' the carpenter shouted impatiently. 'How long do you think those bales are going to stay there? They'll fall apart directly. Pass more along. Look alive now.'

The crew of *La Reine Noble* were no longer concerned with beaching her. Indeed there seemed to be no discipline left on board. Men were leaping over the side into the water. Others were fighting for places in the overloaded boats.

As Lawson watched a desperate plan began to form in his mind. To take his men ashore was to place them at the mercy of the pirates and the Moors on shore. It would mean imprisonment against the payment of a ransom, slavery or death. The burning ship was their only hope.

The risk was tremendous. They could be blown to bits, but there was just a chance that the disciplined naval men, well used to regulation fire drill, would bring the blaze under control. He turned decisively to the acting quartermaster.

'Put me alongside her,' he ordered.

The man's eyes widened in alarm but he spun the wheel nevertheless.

Suddenly Lawson noticed that three men, half obscured by the swirling smoke on the pirate ship, were dragging a heavy object across the deck to a dinghy suspended by a hoist over the stern. He tensed with excitement. It was a wooden chest. He ran forward to the gunners in the bows.

'You see those men clustering in the stern?'

'Yes, sir,' the gun captain replied.

'They'll have a king's ransom in their hands at this moment, more than likely. Put a blast of grape into them before they can get that chest over the side.'

The man crouched eagerly over his gun. Lawson turned to face those on the upper deck and blew a long blast on his whistle.

'We're going to board that ship,' he shouted, after he had halted their activities. 'I want volunteers. Those of you who want to make for the shore can do so but there's a deal of treasure over the water and maybe we can put the fire out. Who is coming with me?'

There was no answering shout. The men looked at each other in silence until a grizzled old gunner straightened himself from the piece he had been attending and stepped forward. At the same time, the big man, who had earned Chandler's displeasure, raised his hand. A chorus of ayes immediately followed and Lawson nodded in approval. They had all volunteered.

Comus was now separated from the pirate ship by less than three hundred yards of water but the land was still half a mile distant and she was becoming sluggish from the sea she had taken. It was as well that he had decided against running her ashore. The chances were that they would sink before they reached the burning ship but they had to be ready.

'Mr Hawbrook, lay out whatever hose we have available and then make ready to grapple and lash us alongside. We'll go to windward of her, so you can prepare your tackle along the port side.'

There was, as yet, no sign of flame on the deck of the smoking vessel but at any moment it could burst through to consume *Comus* and those aboard her if they made the mistake of grappling to leeward. Lawson made a quick but comprehensive survey of the deck.

Most of the wounded had been brought out and were lying on rough litters on the bare planking. The two prisoners were shuffling out from below, blinking in the bright sunshine and rubbing at wrists which still bore the marks of the fetters. Duvalier-Winter was supervising a party heaving the ship's launch over wooden rollers from its place behind the main mast to the waiting party at the hoists on the starboard side. Doctor Fairweather was on deck adjusting a splint. A big man, deadly pale and clad in a blue coat stiff with dried blood, was directing the efforts of the seamen who were still carrying the wounded from below. It was Thompson. Lawson grinned a welcome and would have spoken but another was claiming his attention.

'Target destroyed, sir,' the captain of the long guns reported.

'Well done!'

During the excitement of the last few minutes he had not noticed the firing going on forward. Now he could see the three men sprawled around the chest that they had been carrying and the small dinghy with a great hole in its side. No one would be able to get the chest away now. In fact, as far as could be seen, the ship had been completely abandoned.

Captain Lawson stepped over the fire hoses which were being laid out and connected to pumps that were already sucking at the rising flood in the bowels of the ship. They would have plenty of water to fight the fire on *La Reine Noble*. He had already decided that *Comus* would act as a fire tender until she sank and the men labouring at the pumps would continue until the last possible moment.

'Starboard a point,' he warned the quartermaster when he had reached the wheel.

The frigate came around sluggishly and lurched towards the ship. Only fifty yards separated them. If the smoke-filled craft blew up now, *Comus* would be laid on her side and would sink like a stone and every man would go with her.

Comus crept alongside with a tormenting slowness. One minute they were engulfed in billowing clouds of black smoke, and then they were in the clear as the burning ship slewed round under the pull of the grapples.

'Pitch,' said Lawson as the sharp smell filled his nostrils.

A boarding party, led by the captain, leapt over the stern of *La Reine Noble* as the two ships grated together. Two of the men who had been shot down by the carronade sprawled lifelessly against the chest they had tried to save. The third man, bleeding freely from several wounds, had propped himself into a sitting position against a capstan. He wore the tattered remnants of what could have been a British military tunic.

Lawson would have hurried on but the man raised a hand to detain him.

'The fire—alongside the magazine. Forty tons of powder. Get your men off before——'

A spasm of pain crossed his face and he gripped his stomach. Lawson saw the blood oozing between his fingers and turned away to direct operations on the deck.

Hawbrook was already securing the frigate fore and aft with heavy cables and the two vessels were swinging slowly away from the wind. Chandler and his fire party were scrambling over from *Comus*, heaving live, writhing hoses in their wake; hoses which spurted tiny jets of water in all directions despite the numerous bindings and patchings along their length.

They had made their choice. Life and death hung in the balance.

22

THE fire party hurried down to the main gun deck, dragging their hoses after them. It was difficult to breathe there and they had to go on hands and knees to get below the hanging pall of thick black smoke.

'That's where it's coming from, sir,' Chandler said, pointing to a damaged hatch amidships.

They crawled towards the hatch. The deck boards were not hot and the pitch in the seams showed no signs of melting. It could mean that the fire was deep down, below the orlop deck, Lawson thought, or, on the other hand it was possible that there was more smoke than fire. There seemed to be only one way of finding out.

'Get that hatch off!'

The seamen tore at the thick lashings with axes. Chandler ordered his fire party to bring their hoses nearer.

'Leave it.'

The command cut through the noises of the ship causing the sweating men around the hatch to stop instantly, such had been its urgency and authority. Lawson swung around angrily.

'What the devil——?'

His exclamation ended abruptly. Yussaiff Ahmed, with scorched robes and smoke-blackened face, was within a few yards of him. Two seamen gripped his arms and another had a cutlass at his back but the renegade's head was held high and the glint in his eyes was that of a commander rather than a prisoner.

'Leave the hatch where it is,' Heward said.

'Who the hell do you think——'

Lawson's hot reply died on his lips. Midshipman Saunders

had emerged from the smoke and, apart from looking as singed as Heward, he appeared to be none the worse for his captivity. The captain's face lightened briefly in a smile of relief. There was no smile for Heward.

'You said, leave the hatch. Why?'

'Because there's more smoke than fire at the moment. Open that hatch and it will be a different story, for there's the devil of a hole in the ship's side from the action last night, and it needs only a through draught to start a blaze that will blow us off the face of the sea. I'm carrying a cargo of gunpowder.'

'What's burning?'

'It's four barrels of pitch, sir,' Saunders said. 'Oh, and a few scraps of tarpaulin which I pushed in the barrels.'

'Did you start the fire?'

'Yes, sir.'

'This hole in the ship's side. Is it big enough to push the barrels through?'

'There are three shot holes together, sir,' Saunders said. 'A few minutes' work with axes would perhaps link the holes and we should be able to knock out a section of timber.'

The captain turned decisively to Chandler.

'Have one of the boats taken around immediately. There'll be no time to transfer the wounded from it. Tell the crew to hook on to the shot holes.'

He cast a quick glance over the men around the hatch. O'Brien was there and Clark, the carpenter. The brawn and the brain together.

'Mr Clark. Take O'Brien with you into the boat that will be coming alongside. Make shift to breach the timbers at the point where the damage is. Look lively now.'

As they went he gripped Saunders by the shoulder and smiled; his eyes streaming from the smoke.

'Let's get out of this, lad,' he said.

They climbed to the open deck to find that one of the boats, with its load of wounded, had already been secured close to the shot holes and O'Brien was lowering himself into it. Now he had a great axe in his hands. With legs braced against the rock of the boat and two men steadying him, he was dealing the planking powerful, telling blows. Clark helped by levering with a crow bar and soon a length of timber fell away. Immediately they attacked another section.

The captain grinned at Saunders.

'Won't be long now, lad, before we have these barrels of yours in the sea. You took a great risk when you started your fire. There's a cargo of forty tons of gunpowder. One spark amongst that lot!'

'That's what the crew thought, sir, but it's all sand.'

'What?'

'The powder kegs are full of sand, sir. Your shot ploughed through them last night.'

Lawson strode across the deck to Heward, who had been brought out of the smoke-filled main deck by the two seamen and was being held, in the absence of further orders, near the mainmast.

'Saunders tells me that your powder has turned out to be sand.'

Heward's eyes blazed and his body tensed. The seamen gripped him more firmly but the anger had died. He shrugged and smiled bitterly.

'So my men ran away from a cargo of sand. Well, well! What a story for the courts! There are some good men of business in His Majesty's Service, it seems. On this occasion, Harry Doolan has been cleverer than usual. Forty tons of sand, eh?'

'Do you mean that these kegs are from government stores?'

'Where else? Since the British Navy has effectively cut off all other supplies, I was obliged to apply to the guardians of the King's arsenal at Gibraltar.'

He laughed mockingly at Lawson's expression.

'You should pay the Comptroller's staff a little more.'

'Well, I'll be damned!'

Lawson turned away and strode back to the bulwarks, his face set and angry. Whilst the ships of Britain had been suffering the privations of their constant blockade, Sir Harry Doolan, ex-slaver and keeper of the arsenal, had been making the most of the situation. He would have some awkward questions to answer, if they ever reached the Rock again to ask them. Lawson felt a sudden need for activity.

'Lower me down into the boat,' he growled at the nearest seaman.

They passed a rope around his waist and he climbed over the side. For a moment he swung helplessly. Then the men in the boat caught him and pulled him aboard.

There were three shot holes within six feet of each other and forming a rough triangle. The men had already joined the two jagged holes at the base of the triangle. There remained a formidable beam of twelve-inch oak above but there was a split from the shot hole on the right, through to the apex. Clark had inserted his crowbar in the split and was skilfully working it deeper whilst O'Brien was attacking the other side with powerful strokes of his axe. Lawson noted that the older man was tiring.

'Let me take over, Mr Clark,' he said.

The carpenter gave the bar a final twist, burying it still deeper, and stepped back gratefully. Lawson addressed the boat crew lying idly on their oars.

'Two of you help me,' he ordered.

The coxswain and another seized the bar with him whilst the wounded in the bottom of the boat watched listlessly. The wedge of timber moved under the weight of the combined heave. O'Brien plied himself vigorously with his axe at the point of resistance. Then Lawson and his helpers heaved again. The planks gave suddenly, throwing them all off their balance. The two men fell against the captain and before anybody could reach out a hand to save him, he lurched against the side of the ship and slipped into the sea.

He sank with the water singing in his ears and a nagging voice within him calling him a fool for not being able to swim. A hand caught him roughly by the hair and pulled him towards the boat. He clutched at the rudder and gulped in air. From there he was pulled back into the boat and lay retching and vomiting sea water. By the time he had recovered, O'Brien was already heaving himself through the enlarged hole.

'Wait!' shouted Lawson.

O'Brien paused expectantly whilst his captain went into a fit of coughing.

'A rope around your waist and wet rags over your face. We don't want—' He clawed for the side of the boat and retched violently.

One of the seamen snatched off his own shirt, thrust it under the water and then tossed it to O'Brien who, grinning self-consciously, tied it over his nose and mouth. The elderly carpenter was also busying himself with a rope. Lawson made an effort to control his stomach.

'Not you, Mr Clark,' he gasped. 'Send in two of these men.'

Groping about in a smoke-filled hold was not work for an old man. O'Brien was strong enough but even he might find himself in difficulties.

'I want you to direct the barrels through the hole when they bring them forward,' he added by way of lessening the blow to Clark's self esteem.

Suddenly O'Brien was back, his eyes streaming but with an expression of triumph on his face. Lawson waited for his report.

'I got one here, sir,' he said. 'Do you stand off whilst I heaves it out.'

'Well done!'

The boat was pushed away from the side of the ship and O'Brien returned to the smoke-filled hold. Soon a barrel, foaming black smoke appeared. It teetered on the edge of the exposed deck and fell, spewing burning pitch into the sea. O'Brien's blackened face appeared at the opening, strained but still cheerful. They drew the boat up to the ship's side and the other two men scrambled through the hole to join him.

In five minutes it was all over. Four barrels of burning pitch had been pushed into the sea and the ship was no longer in danger, as far as fire was concerned, but there was still the problem of the approaching ships, Lawson remembered with a shock. He grabbed the rope still hanging from the deck and shouting to those above to pull, he heaved himself out of the boat and, leaning well out, walked around the bulge of the hull to the main deck while three men hauled away at the line. Hawbrook, with face lined and anxious, met him as he dropped from the bulwarks.

'What are we to do with *Comus*, sir? I doubt if we can hold her much longer.'

There was a thirty-degree list to starboard caused by the weight of the sinking frigate. The supporting hawsers were stretched from ship to ship with the rigidity of iron bars and several men were ready with axes to cut *Comus* free should she become a danger to the prize. It was a situation calling for an immediate decision, one of the most difficult of the captain's career. It involved the destruction of his command.

He estimated the stretch of water separating the two ships from the shore. The shallows could be barely five hundred yards away and there was a possibility that they could beach *Comus* before she sank. It would mean risking the lives of Duvalier-Winter and the men who had been left aboard but it would be a justifiable risk. If that were the only consideration no captain could hesitate but the approaching ships must also be taken into account. Should they prove to be hostile, as seemed most likely, Lawson could not leave even a shattered frigate for them. The guns would be stripped from her to arm other pirates or to strengthen the fortifications at Algiers. If *Comus* were to be beached then a party would have to be left aboard to blow her to bits, should the unidentified vessels prove to be a part of the Dey's fleet. Decisively he walked over to the starboard side and shouted to his first lieutenant.

'Bring your men off, Mr Duvalier-Winter. We can do nothing more for her.'

As the pump party scrambled eagerly up the side of the prize, Lawson scowled gloomily down upon the deck of the frigate. It was bad enough to lose one's command; to lose it under such circumstances was heartrending. He tore his eyes away and nodded briefly to Hawbrook.

'Cut her free.'

The four cables, each as thick as a man's thigh, must have been very near bursting point. Hawbrook had positioned his men so that they would be safe from any backlash when their axes bit into the fibres. At his signal they poised in readiness.

'Now!' he shouted.

The axes slashed down together. The two forward cables parted with loud reports and the prize, partly released, jerked violently. The men at the remaining cables struggled for their balance and struck again. *La Reine Noble* lurched drunkenly away from the frigate and heaved so far over on her side that the sea foamed in through her lower ports. All those not holding on were thrown to the decks. There was a concerted rush to the side to see the last of *Comus*.

Lining the bulwarks they stared in awed silence. A dying ship is a compelling sight even when it is a stranger. When that ship has been one's home, with all its secrets and peculiarities a part of life, and when, in addition, all the belongings of the observers are on board, its passing becomes a personal tragedy which each man feels he must watch to the bitter end.

The frigate had already reached the point where her main deck was awash. She was sinking on an even keel, still held by the air trapped beneath her decks. Now it began to escape in mighty belches, rocking her gently, and with each vomit, loose materials, barrels, broken planks and personal belongings spewed out. She settled lower in the water.

Lawson tore himself away from the fascinating sight. Whilst they were standing in idleness they were being cut off from the sea by the unidentified ships.

'Stand by to wear ship,' he roared. 'Mr Duvalier-Winter! Have the boats hauled aboard.'

The men began to shuffle half-heartedly away from the side but there were orders in plenty now from officers and section

222

commanders, and the boatswain was among the laggards with his cane. Topmen sprang into the shrouds and climbed aloft, hazarding their necks by casting lingering eyes at the last struggles of their ship. A deck party began to clear away the derrick equipment to haul the boats in board and Hawbrook was driving a crowd of waisters on to the braces ready to swing the yards around as soon as the boats, with their loads of wounded, were clear of the water. Lawson turned from his survey of the activity about him to see the end.

She sank as gracefully as she had settled, with the water welling up from within her rather than pouring over the side. Now her hull had gone and only her masts remained : tall masts that described lazy circles as they slipped slowly beneath the surface. Lawson's eyes smarted and he savagely fought back the tears. There was no time for grief.

He glared around the upper deck but there was no one idle; no opportunity to relieve his feelings. All were working furiously or tensed, ready to do their part when the time came. Only Heward and his captors were not actively engaged in the preparations for sailing. There was a mocking smile, or so it seemed, on the prisoner's face. Lawson walked across to him.

'Don't look so sad, Captain,' Heward said. 'You'll find that *La Reine Noble* is fair compensation. She'll bring a good sum in the prize courts. There's also a fortune in that chest—if your men don't help themselves to it first.'

Lawson started. In the activity of the last half hour he had forgotten the chest and the three men who had been shot whilst trying to get it away. He looked along the deck and saw that some of the seamen lining the starboard braces had slid the chest over to the bulwarks and they were surreptitiously trying to prize off the lid.

'I'll have the skin off any man who touches that chest,' he shouted angrily. 'Mr Saunders! Have it secured and post a guard over it.'

Saunders ran aft. The captain watched until the chest had

been pushed back to the middle of the deck then turned again to Heward.

'Report back to your section,' he ordered the guards.

'Well, well,' Heward said after the men had gone. 'Who would have expected the correct Captain Lawson to take such a chance?'

'My pistol will bring you down before you have gone ten yards,' Lawson replied dryly.

He examined Heward contemplatively. He looked as proud as ever and Lawson knew instinctively that he would go that way to the gallows.

'You will be interested to learn that your sister would have paid the ransom you demanded.'

'Ransom?'

'Your friend, Kettelmann, delivered a note demanding twenty thousand pounds for your release from captivity.

'Kettelmann did that! Are you sure?'

'I think there is no doubt that he had it sent to Cecilia, but I thought you were involved. What a wonderful bunch of comrades you corsairs are! Now I can better understand your leaving Kettelmann to his fate on board *Die Reichmacher*.'

Heward's eyes hardened.

'I did not desert *Die Reichmacher*. I'd have had my men aboard you over the starboard side within minutes of quitting your deck last night, had not one of your parting shots brought a heap of wreckage about my head. I came to my senses to find you in pursuit, and *Die Reichmacher* out of sight.'

'So your men will not fight without a leader?' Lawson asked. This would be useful information for the Lords of Admiralty.

Heward smiled bitterly.

'The men you killed in the bay would have fought you to a standstill. The crew of this ship were too craven-hearted to fight and I had to drive them. Even after shooting two of them, I was unable to bring the rest to fight the fire that young Saunders started.'

'Deck there! Sir, sir! British frigates.'

The seaman who had been left, forgotten by everyone, atop the mainmast of *Comus* and who had transferred himself, at the last moment, to that of *La Reine Noble* by the simple expedient of running across the yards whilst they had been close together, shouted the warning in a voice crackling with excitement. Men craned back their heads to stare in fascination at the tiny figure on the mainmast. All work had stopped and the only sounds to be heard were the creaking of the yards, protesting against being held hove-to, and the wash of the sea against the rounded hull. Lawson cupped his hands and bellowed through them, back into the maze of ropes and spars.

'Give your report as you have been instructed.'

There was a pause whilst the man took hurried bearings.

'Four British frigates, west sou' west at five miles and on a course east by nor', sir.'

There was a tremendous cheer from the entire ship's company, a cheer which grew in volume until Lawson stopped it with a blast on his whistle.

'Mr Duvalier-Winter,' he said when silence had been restored. 'Are you ready to wear ship?'

'Yes, sir.'

'Very well. Bring her away.'

The foretopsails were hauled around and immediately the men lining the yards on the fore and main courses slipped the gaskets allowing the two great sails to fall into place and fill with the breeze. The ship heeled to leeward, dipped her bows, recovered, and surged around on a starboard tack, thrusting the land from before her to the starboard quarter in a sickening dizzy whirl.

Lawson scanned the spinning sand dunes with growing satisfaction. Not many of the pirate crew had escaped destruction and those who had done so had received enough punishment from the guns to give them a hearty respect for the forces of law and order. The loss of *Comus* was hard to bear, but she had fully justified her existence.

Heward eased away from the captain's side but his movement was noticed. Lawson looked at him sharply.

'Goodbye,' Heward said softly.

Lawson's hand fell to the butt of the pistol in his belt.

'You're my prisoner.'

Heward slipped between two of the men at the braces making it impossible for the captain to risk a shot.

'Stop him!' Lawson shouted.

Heward sidestepped the grasping arms of one of the seamen, thrust aside the bayonet of a marine and reached the bulwarks. Half a dozen men led by Duvalier-Winter rushed at him but they were too late. He had leapt over the side.

'Try to bring her around,' Lawson ordered.

The helmsman spun the wheel obediently but the ship had not enough way on her to respond and the uneven pressure on her depleted canvas prevented her bows from meeting the wind. This was what Heward had bargained on. *La Reine Noble* would have to gain steerage by running away before she could come back over her tracks.

'There he is!'

Immediately there was a rush for the starboard quarter but he had submerged again. The marines elbowed themselves through the crowding seamen and lined the side with their muskets at the ready. At the same time two men, under the direction of Hawbrook, crouched over the small carronade mounted on the poop deck.

Lawson suddenly found himself on the side of the fugitive. He watched the line of marines with loathing in his heart for their cold-blooded efficiency. Each man stood with his musket cocked, his face tensed with eagerness as he searched the contours of the water. There were few white tops to conceal the escaping man. As soon as he appeared, and appear he must, twenty musket-balls and the contents of the carronade would tear at him.

'There!'

The officer of marines pointed imperatively at the tiny dot

226

of Heward's head. The line of muskets swung around. There was a ragged volley followed by a roar of the carronade.

'That's the last of him,' Duvalier-Winter said enthusiastically. 'He must have been hit a dozen times.'

Lawson scowled at him. They had just caused the death of a brave man. Heward had gone below to save Saunders while his men were abandoning ship, and he must have expected the ship to blow apart whilst he was fighting his way through the smoke.

'Set a course to join the squadron,' he growled.

Five minutes later, Hawbrook approached the captain with Barty at his heels. The lieutenant looked angry. Barty's face suggested that he had just been told off.

'Sir, Mr Barty has just informed me that he is of the opinion that this fellow we fired upon has reached the shore. I have reprimanded him for not reporting earlier but——'

'What's this?' Lawson demanded.

'I'm not sure, sir,' Barty said defensively. 'I thought I caught a glimpse of him after the carronade had fired but every one seemed so certain he had been killed. Later I saw someone crawling from the sea and I informed Mr Hawbrook.'

23

THE British Squadron, which had gone about as soon as *La Reine Noble* had explained herself and stated that she needed no assistance, led Lawson in sight of Algiers Harbour, where a Naval fleet of considerable size for peacetime, lay hove-to about one mile from the city. Barty first reported the number of twenty-four but there were others concealed behind the massive walls of the men-of-war. They were not all British. Five of them were Dutch, Lawson heard with a thrill of excitement. Since Holland was at war with Algiers it seemed likely that the long promised punishment of the Pirate State was about to become reality.

'*Impregnable* is there, sir,' Hawbrook reported when they had approached within a league of the town. 'She's flying the Rear-Admiral's pennant.'

Lawson nodded. Rear-Admiral Robert Dullant, with his base at Gibraltar would certainly be present but he could hardly be in command of such a large force. Barty again reported from the tops.

'*Impregnable—Superb—Queen Charlotte—Minden——*'

'Can you make out who is commanding?' Lawson interrupted.

The midshipman scrutinised the broad flag flying fitfully from one of the masts of *Queen Charlotte*.

'The Commander-in-Chief, Lord Exmouth, sir.'

Lawson's eyes gleamed. He had served under Lord Exmouth in 1793 when as Captain Pellew, he had commanded a frigate and it was from him that Lawson had learned most of his seamanship. Neither the passing years nor his elevation to the peerage had changed Pellew from the hard-headed seaman that he had always been. He would not have concentrated so much force unless he expected to put it to good use.

'Mr Duvalier-Winter! Stand by to fire a salute.'

'There are four Algerian frigates and a score of small craft —gun boats and the like, lying in the bay,' the first lieutenant reported as they drew nearer. 'They won't have much to say for themselves against this force.'

Lawson grunted sceptically and swept his glass over the harbour defences. He had read that upwards of one thousand heavy guns lay concealed behind the massive stone walls of the forts.

In the city itself preparations were at fever pitch. Men poured through the narrow streets in jostling excited crowds, each man with a scimitar swinging at his side and a musket slung across his shoulders. All were moving in the direction of the batteries. The city was about to be attacked, but this had happened so many times that the citizens had grown confident in its impregnability. Happily they went to their posts. There was the North Battery with its eighty guns, and protecting shoals, the Mole Battery, which mounted two hundred and twenty guns, and the Fishmarket Battery, which formed the centre of the inner defences. The smaller emplacements filled up with the teeming Moors but still they came in their thousands to cluster along the quayside clutching their weapons and hurling abuse at the stationary fleet at the entrance of their harbour.

Duvalier-Winter turned in exasperation to Hawbrook.

'Why the devil doesn't Exmouth attack? He seems to be deliberately waiting for them to complete their defences.'

Lawson pointed to a launch bearing a white flag of truce. It had just left the quayside and was pulling across the bay towards *Queen Charlotte*. The lieutenant, sitting bolt upright in the stern, would be an envoy from Lord Exmouth, sent ashore with demands. Judging by the speed of the launch as it surged up to the flagship, the demands had either been refused or ignored. Probably the Dey deliberately kept them waiting for his answer. It was time *La Reine Noble* prepared herself.

'Clear for action,' Lawson ordered.

The men were weary after fourteen hours of exacting labour. Now they were called upon to join battle in an unfamiliar ship with a gaping hole that would admit tons of water if they were forced onto a starboard tack. They should have been sulky : yet they ran the guns out and manned the yards with the eagerness of fresh young seamen training off Spithead. Lawson's policy was bearing fruit.

'A fine body of men, eh, Mr Duvalier-Winter?'

'Excellent, sir!' the first lieutenant exclaimed with enthusiasm. 'As fine a company as—one will find.' His voice trailed away and he coloured violently.

Lawson grinned. There was no need to remind his second in command that he had regarded them as unwashed rabble only a few weeks ago. Duvalier-Winter was learning. He turned away to find Saunders at his elbows with a signal slate in his hand.

'Message from the flagship, sir.'

The boy's face was gloomy. Lawson snatched the slate from his hands, scanned it briefly and thrust it back.

'Acknowledge.'

Saunders ran back to the signal halyards. Duvalier-Winter waited expectantly.

'We are to stay out of it,' Lawson growled and walked away.

It was obvious to Captain Lawson why Lord Exmouth had excluded them. He had already given his orders and an extra ship insinuating itself into the ordered line of battle would only cause confusion. There were five large enemy corvettes, as well as the frigates and numerous gun and mortar boats seen earlier. It would be difficult to distinguish friend from foe when the light failed and *La Reine Noble* would be in danger of coming under fire from her own ships.

The fleet was already under way, sailing slowly into the bay. *Queen Charlotte* with her one hundred guns was in the van, with the heavy ships, *Impregnable, Albion, Minden* and *Superb* in line behind. Obviously their task was to destroy the Mole

Battery. The entire ship's company on board *La Reine Noble* watched in fascination as the flagship coolly dropped anchors within fifty yards of the Mole head and blasted her first broadside at the fortifications. The other men-of-war followed her example and splinters of rock began to fly. A slab of masonry crashed down carrying doll-like figures with it but tongues of flame were leaping from tiers of black squares on the fort.

Meanwhile the Dutch frigates, *Melampus*, *Frederica* and *Diana* had sailed through the entrance of the harbour and were making for the south batteries with *Leander*, *Severn* and *Glasgow* in line behind but already changing course for the Fishmarket Battery. Soon the whole fleet was in action with the vessels of forty guns and more hammering away from anchored positions opposite the batteries, while the lighter craft surged back and forth across the middle of the bay firing guns, rockets and mortars at the Algerian ships and the teeming quayside.

Lawson took *La Reine Noble* within a cable's length of the harbour entrance and dropped anchor. There was nothing more for him to do but watch the battle.

'*Impregnable* is in trouble, sir,' Chandler reported some thirty minutes later.

Lawson raised his glass to the ninety-eight gun man-of-war. She appeared to be drawing more than her fair share of the bombardment from the Mole Battery. Heavy balls were ripping into her all along her length, hurling showers of splinters into the packed ranks of her gunners. Already her upper deck was a mass of wreckage and as they watched, one of her anchor cables was shot away allowing her stern to swing towards the shore. If they did not act quickly her guns would soon be unable to bear and she would have no reply to the barrage that was crashing into her.

'Admiral Dullant is standing on the deck as calmly as if the guns were firing a salute for him,' Duvalier-Winter said in wonder.

'Nothing else for him to do,' Hawbrook grunted. 'Captain Hopton has the responsibility of getting his ship back into line.

231

It was the same at Trafalgar with Nelson. *Victory* was locked yard arm to yard arm and he strolled along the deck as though——'

'He's been hit!' someone shouted.

All the officers on *La Reine Noble* concentrated their telescopes onto the quarterdeck of *Impregnable*. A large gap had appeared in the bulwarks and huge sections of it, together with a smashed gun, lay strewn across the place where the rear-admiral had stood.

Seamen could be seen pulling at the debris. They lifted a limp bundle from the deck and placed it on a stretcher. An arm escaped the carrying party. It swung grotesquely. There was something final about that arm. Lawson lowered his glass and found his officers standing about in awed silence.

'*Impregnable* is signalling for assistance, sir,' Barty shouted excitedly.

A thrill passed through the group and the scene they had just witnessed was thrust into the background. The chances were that they would be in the midst of that terrible bombardment themselves before they were much older. Lawson closed his glass with a snap.

'Make ready to slip our cables,' he ordered.

The signal was for Lord Exmouth on the flagship and he would now be deciding which ship to detach from its assigned duty to go to *Impregnable*'s aid. Since *La Reine Noble* was disengaged, it seemed likely that he would call upon her. Anxiously they watched the tiny balls ascending the mizzen-mast on *Queen Charlotte*. They burst open and fluttered in the dying breeze.

'He's called up *Glasgow*, sir,' Barty reported.

'Damn!' Lawson exploded.

He swung away from his officers and began to pace the deck furiously. The Commander-in-Chief evidently intended to keep them completely out of the battle. Already the shadows were lengthening. Soon it would be dark and then *La Reine Noble* would be left outside the bay until morning. No matter what happened in the night Lawson had definite orders to keep his

232

ship clear of the fleet. He watched the fading scene with a resentment that was not in any way lessened by the knowledge that Lord Exmouth was behaving exactly as he himself would have done in the circumstances.

The wind was dropping away and the frigate *Glasgow* was having difficulties in reaching her new station alongside *Impregnable*. Shot reached out for her and raked her from stem to stern. Barrage after barrage smashed into her sides. The defenders seemed to be more interested in this part of their front than in any other. They were determined to make a kill and if they could prevent help from reaching *Impregnable* they could shatter her. Evidently they considered that the sight of the giant lying broken on the shoals would be a greater blow to the morale of the attackers than if they were to disperse the damage over all the smaller ships.

Lawson followed the fortunes of *Glasgow* and *Impregnable* for a while before turning his attention to the battery. The stone fort was situated at the end of the long strip of land which formed the mole and its sole purpose was to protect the harbour entrance. Its guns, he estimated, could cover an arc of perhaps two hundred and sixty degrees which was more than adequate since the shallows on the seaward side ruled out the possibility of a large force being landed behind the defences. A rutted road, stretching along the crest of the land strip, linked the battery with the town and four heavily laden carts were jolting along it. He watched them thoughtfully. A fifth cart lay tilted drunkenly in the ditch.

'Mr Barty!'

'Sir?'

'What are those carts carrying?'

Barty levelled his telescope.

'I think they're powder kegs, sir.'

'Now the one at the side of the road—can you make out what has happened?'

'I'm almost certain the wheel has come off, sir. Two men are unloading the kegs.'

'Watch the carts carefully, Mr Barty. I want to know which building they are using as a magazine. Fix the position of the broken cart in your mind and familiarise yourself with the road. —You may be walking along it within the hour.'

'Aye aye, sir,' Barty replied with enthusiasm.

The broken cart had given Lawson the germ of an idea. Now a plan of action began to take shape. Here was an opportunity for his men to take a useful part in the battle, a part which, if successful, would relieve the pressure on *Impregnable* and *Glasgow*. Lord Exmouth's orders had applied to *La Reine Noble*. He had not ordered her men to keep out of action.

'Mr Chandler!'

'Sir?'

'Detail a landing-party. Twenty marines and a dozen seamen.'

There was a stir of interest among the officers.

'Mr Duvalier-Winter, have you ever taken part in a landing operation of any kind?'

'No, I regret that I have not had the pleasure.' He adjusted his cravat. 'I don't believe it would be beyond my powers though.'

Lawson glowered. His first officer had replied in the same drawling manner he had found so infuriating at their first meeting. He felt his temper rising.

'Possibly you are right,' he replied bitingly, 'but it is a chance that I cannot afford to take. I will take charge of the landing-party. You will remain aboard and assume command of the ship in my absence. . . . Mr Hawbrook!'

'Sir?'

'You and Mr Barty will accompany me ashore. I will want half a keg of powder with a coiled fuse inside. There will be enough fuse to burn for four minutes, no more, no less. Can you do it?'

'Yes, sir.'

'Very well. Prepare it. Our lives may depend upon your accuracy.'

As Hawbrook hurried away, Duvalier-Winter moved closer to the captain.

'Surely the command of such a party should be my right, sir,' he said quietly.

Lawson turned upon him in some exasperation.

'In this Mr Duvalier-Winter, you have no rights. My orders to you are to take over the command of this ship.'

As the single boat, with its load of marines and seamen, skimmed away into the darkness, Lawson began to regret his bad temper. Duvalier-Winter should have been given the opportunity to distinguish himself, he realised. His nonchalance was probably assumed to cover his embarrassment at having to admit that he had never taken part in a landing operation. Probably he would have been a far better officer for the experience. He shrugged the thought away. It was too late to change over now.

He turned his mind to the task in hand. Its success depended upon their not being seen. Quietly he ordered the helmsman to steer a wide course, away from the reflected glow from the few burning buildings in the bay. The point of landing would be where the mole joined the mainland to the east, where there was shoal water enough to protect the Moors from attack. Lawson anticipated manhandling the boat over the shallows and then wading perhaps half a mile before they reached dry land. It would be a hazardous approach and one from which it would be difficult to retreat if they were discovered, but it was the only part that was not covered by the guns and it communicated with the tremendously strong Mole Battery.

'Shelving fast, sir,' Hawbrook whispered.

A few seconds later they ran aground, burying their sharp bows in the soft sand. Silently every man slid over the gunwales and lowered himself into the water. Then they began to push the boat towards the shore. Suddenly they were out of their depths again and those who could not swim clung to the sides until the water shallowed. They continued in this manner until they reached the rocks and the boat could go no farther.

'That's far enough, lads,' Lawson said quickly. 'Have the boat secured, Mr Hawbrook, and leave a picket. Two men should be enough.'

Cautiously, sometimes chest deep in water, and holding their muskets and powder above their heads, they waded towards the land. There were slippery rocks and deep pools. More than once a clash of steel against stone, followed by a splash, announced that one of the party had come to grief. Then all would freeze into stillness, breathlessly awaiting the expected challenge, or more likely, a hail of shot from the shore.

At last they reached the beach. To the right of them, at a distance of a mile, the bombardment continued unabated, casting flashes at the gathering clouds and hanging smoke to be reflected far over the water. Before them was the dark outline of the mainland where it bulged to form the base of the mole. Somewhere near lay the broken cart. If it had not been moved it would be within a few hundred yards. Quietly Lawson, Barty and five seamen stole forward, leaving Hawbrook in charge of the rear-guard.

Barty brought them unerringly to the place where he had seen the cart. It was still there with its useless wheel propped against a shaft. There was no sign of the carters, nor of the horse, but a dozen powder kegs were standing at the side of the road. They waited. At length the rumbling of wheels warned them that one cart at least was approaching from the direction of the fort. Lawson felt the seaman on his right stir excitedly and reached out a restraining hand. Success or failure depended upon surprise. Silently the party of seven crouched behind the kegs.

To an accompaniment of shouts from the shadowy figure pulling viciously at the lead rein, a high-sided cart jolted across the rough road, swung around, halted, and then began to lurch drunkenly backwards, onto the load of kegs. Two men assisted the near frantic horse by pushing at the wheels and Lawson noted, with some satisfaction, that though they were armed, they carried their muskets slung across their shoulders in the style of horsemen. A musket carried in such a manner, could not be quickly unslung and it was of vital importance that no shot should be fired. The tailboard of the cart bumped against the foremost kegs and Lawson rose to his feet.

'Take 'em, my lads!' Lawson shouted and was immediately knocked aside by the over-eager seaman who had been on his right. He sprawled across a keg and landed with his face in the gravel.

The carters who had been heaving at the wheels went down beneath the weight of four seamen. The man at the reins dodged under the belly of the horse as Barty sprang at him. Before the midshipman could follow, the terrified animal bolted, dragging the heavy cart across his path.

'Stop the horse!' Lawson shouted as he scrambled to his feet. Then he was gone into the darkness in pursuit of the fleeing carter.

The man had made a few yards start and Lawson could see his dark outline dodging from right to left as though he feared a shot. Soon he had merged into the darkness with only the sound of his feet scuffling the road as evidence of his progress. Lawson ran on doggedly, cursing the heavy coat which hampered his movements and the stones, some as big as a man's head, strewn along the path. Then he caught a glimpse of his quarry outlined against the flashes from the batteries. He snatched a pistol from his belt and hurled it with all his strength. It could have struck him or he may have stumbled. Certainly he measured his length on the ground and before he could recover, Lawson was at his throat.

A short time later a high-sided cart rolled up to the land-ward side of the Mole Battery attended by two robed men, whose faces, tanned as dark as any Arab from the North African Coast, contrasted most remarkably with their white feet revealed through the open work of their sandals. This curious difference in colour must surely have excited comment under normal circumstances but the fort with its unguarded gate and the frenzied activity of its cobbled yard could hardly be described as normal. Half-naked men hurried to and fro carrying powder and shot. Litter bearers staggered down from the battlements with wounded and every other man seemed to be screaming orders which were lost amid the roar of the guns and the crash of masonry.

The larger of the two carters looked around him for a moment and then concentrated his attention on an arched doorway, to the left of the yard, lit by a solitary lamp. The keg carriers seemed to emerge from this building and an empty cart, similar to the one they tended, stood neglected at the entrance. He leaned closer to his smaller companion.

'That's where we want to be,' he grunted, 'but not until I've fired the fuse.'

It had just occurred to him that if they were to place the cart at the entrance of the building, the men who were carrying powder to the guns would naturally take the kegs from the cart rather than from the magazine. If they were to do that they might discover the fused one or, more likely they would take most of the powder away and the success of the plan depended upon there being sufficient left on the cart to blast down the thick walls of the magazine. The alternative was to light the fuse immediately and hope that it was not faulty and that Hawbrook had cut enough to burn for four minutes.

They had arranged the barrels in the cart so that they completely surrounded the fused powder keg they had brought with them from *La Reine Noble*. Once Lawson had climbed over them it was the work of a few seconds to prize open the lid and to pull clear the end of the leather hose fuse. There remained only the lighting. He scraped his dirk over the flint. Then Barty called to him.

'Somebody's shouting at us, sir.'

Lawson cursed him for a fool and applied himself once again to the stiff fuse that had twisted in his fingers like a live thing, spilling some of its powder. Now he would have to cut off a few inches and it mattered not a damn if ten thousand Moors were shouting at them. They could do nothing about it. He gripped the elusive leather between his knees and applied the steel to the flint. It sparked and began to splutter, giving off a grey smoke. Quickly he tamped the cork home, thrust the end of the shortened coil back into the keg and hammered the lid into place with the butt of his pistol. Then he heaved another barrel on top of the fused powder and looked out.

Two men had approached. One of them, tall and dishevelled, had remained in the background. The other, fat and prosperous-looking, and armed with a brace of pistols prominently displayed in his waist band, had stormed up to Barty, shouting furiously. The midshipman had been unable to reply and was being cuffed about the head for his silence. Lawson slid his dirk from its sheath as he dropped from the tailboard but the sight of the tall man sent him dodging around the other side of the cart. There was no need to use the dirk anyway. The fat man's gestures were clear enough. He wanted them to get the cart to the magazine. The captain snatched the reins from Barty's hands and jerked the trembling horse forward.

'Sir!' hissed Barty when they had gained a few yards. 'The tall fellow is still watching us, and I think it's—Yussaiff Ahmed.'

Lawson nodded grimly. A flash of gunfire had revealed Heward to him in the moment that he had jumped down from the cart but he had been unable to believe the evidence of his senses. Now that Barty had confirmed it, the renegade's presence did not seem to be so incredible. It was eight hours since he had escaped. He would have had plenty of time to cover the twelve miles along the coast, and Algiers would be the natural place for him to go.

'He's shouting something, sir.—Now they're both coming after us.'

'Have your pistol ready,' Lawson ordered. 'Hold them off while I get this cart in position.'

The twin doors of the magazine were wide open, revealing a dozen stone steps leading down into a cellar. At the foot of these, under a suspended lantern, stood an enormous Moor whose naked, rolling paunch gleamed with sweat. The arrival of the cart brought him halfway up the steps, shouting instructions to Lawson and, over his shoulder, to unseen helpers below. Lawson swung the cart around and thrust the horse back against its traces. The rear of the cart smashed against the doorposts of the cellar with a force that jolted some of the barrels, forming the top layer, over the tailboard and on down the steps. He had a momentary glimpse of the magazine keeper and two others being toppled over before he concentrated on the important task of freeing the horse.

No humane motive prompted him in this; the animal's eyes were rolling in terror and it seemed certain that it would bolt with the cart behind it as soon as he left its head. He had slashed through the last trace when a sickening blow behind his left shoulder sent him reeling against the horse.

He swung around, thrusting instinctively with his dirk but there was no one in close proximity. He had been struck by a pistol ball. The man who had fired the shot was levelling his second pistol for another attempt and rushing in from the left was Heward with his sword poised for a thrust.

Lawson jerked his body to one side and felt the edge of Heward's blade slicing across his chest, cutting him to the ribs. He gripped the hilt desperately under his left arm and gasped in agony from the excruciating pain in his damaged shoulder when Heward wrenched the sword from his grip. He backed away towards the cart, groping inside his voluminous robes for his pistol, knowing that he would not reach it in time. Heward's next thrust must be the last and even if some miracle saved him from the sword, there was the Moor trying to get a clear field of fire.

'I saved your life,' Heward said bitterly, as he manoeuvred for a final stab. 'You repaid me with a farewell volley from your damned marines. Now you are going to die.'

'So are you,' Lawson replied, playing for time and tensing himself for a spring. 'If your friend with the pistol doesn't shoot you by accident, then we'll all die together in about thirty seconds. This cart's going to blow up.'

Suddenly the Moor gave a wild cry and fell to his knees. Barty, sprawling in the filth of the fort yard after an exchange of shots with Heward, had managed to reload and fire his pistol.

Heward reacted with no more than a flicker of the eyes but it had to be enough for a desperate man. Lawson hurled himself sideways to the ground and kicked simultaneously with a full-bodied swing. The sword swept down instinctively but Lawson's foot was already underneath it, and although the sharp edge slit the flesh of his calf, it did nothing to lessen the blow. Heward cursed and sagged. Lawson grabbed at his legs and toppled him off balance. Then they were rolling in the dirt, each struggling to get on top.

The captain had postponed death for a moment. His left shoulder was streaming blood and Heward must overpower him, unless he could get his pistol free. But it was no longer a battle for life. It had become a personal matter: a trial of strength between two strong men, and the satisfaction of the winner would last as long as it took the fire to splutter through the last few inches of the leather-hose fuse.

Now Heward had his knife out. Lawson seized at the hand which held it, brought up his knee with a force that drove a gasp out of Heward, and heaved himself into a sitting position on top. The blade of Heward's sword was within inches of his left hand. The hilt lay out of reach. Heedless of the razor edge he gripped it. A jerk would send the point between his opponent's ribs. Suddenly the renegade twisted, with the skill of a trained wrestler, and threw Lawson off. Even as he was falling, Lawson saw Heward's head jerk back as from a violent blow. There was no hearing a pistol shot in that bedlam of gunfire but one had been fired at them and the bullet had smashed into Heward's cheekbone.

Lawson swung around, expecting to find Barty close by.

Instead he saw the Moor with horror on his face and a pistol drooping from his hand.

'Mr Barty! Where are you?' the captain shouted as he scrambled to his feet.

The wounded Moor was still within hitting distance and Lawson now had both Heward's sword and his own pistol in his hands but he took no notice of the man. His one thought was to get on the other side of the fort wall with his midshipman. They were already living on extra time. Either Hawbrook had over-estimated the length of fuse needed for four minutes or there had been a gap in the coil of black powder. They would know soon.

'Mr Barty!'

'Here, sir,' a thin voice answered.

Lawson hurried towards the cart and found Barty trying to pull himself to his feet by the spokes of the wheel.

'Are you badly hurt?'

'I'll be all right, sir.'

He pulled Barty's arm around his neck and half ran him, half carried him towards the gate.

They were within twenty yards of comparative safety and struggling to keep going when the pursuit began. The magazine keeper and his two helpers had squeezed out from the stairway to find Heward trying to climb aboard the cart. They had chosen to run after the captain rather than help find the fused barrel. Now they were bearing down with scimitars drawn. There was no chance of Lawson getting Barty clear without a fight.

'Keep going, Mr Barty,' Lawson said, releasing him. 'If you can't manage to walk, then crawl, and don't stop until you reach Mr Hawbrook's party.'

'I'll stay with you, sir.'

'Do as you are ordered,' Lawson roared.

He swung around to face his attackers, with the sword in his right hand and the pistol held close to his body in his left. Immediately the three men were upon him.

He fired the pistol and almost shrieked from the shock to his left shoulder. The ball had missed but the shot had caused his pursuers to hesitate. He followed up his advantage with the sword, splitting open the fat stomach of the magazine keeper and turning the dripping blade to fend off the man to his left.

They were both afraid of him, he realised with fierce joy, but there could be no staying to fight and his retreat towards the open gate rallied them. Now others were running to cut him off. Amid the din of the guns and the shouts of the men closing in on him, he heard the scream of a horse and the pounding of hooves over cobbles. Then he was in the gateway fighting desperately and wondering vaguely if he would be cut down before they were all blown to bits. A blade cut into his side. He sank to his knees. Suddenly he was hurled to the ground with a violent shock under a heap of men. The freed horse, charging around in panic, had crashed into the crowd at the gate.

He clawed instinctively at the trailing harness and felt himself being dragged clear of the mass of arms and legs, through the gate and across the road onto the sparse grass beyond. Then night became day in a mighty sheet of flame and the earth shook. Lawson's last recollection, before he lost consciousness, was of a heavy jet of hot thick liquid striking his face and filling his mouth and nostrils. As he fought against suffocation, his failing mind struggled for the cause. It was the life blood of the wretched horse.

24

THE two months that followed would always remain vague in Lawson's mind. It was a period of great pain and sickness, of nightmares and ravings, of battles and storms, of arguments with colleagues long dead and of terrifying struggles against rose tendrils clawing for his eyes. There were half wakenings to the groans of ship's timbers, the visits from Cecilia, who sometimes changed into Yussaiff Ahmed, and throughout, ever imperturbable, always firm and capable of driving away most of the illusions, was Doctor Fairweather.

Then with the refreshing brightness of the morning sun, after a night of storm, Lawson awoke to find his mind clear. He lay, taking in his strange surroundings : the gilded deckboard above him, the spacious cabin, the luxurious cot upon which he lay and the two leather straps binding him to it. They were at anchor, his seaman's mind told him instantly. Lying in some bay or harbour with a gale plucking ineffectively at the topmost spars. He rang the small bell above his head and an orderly appeared.

'Where are we?'

'Lisbon Harbour, sir. Sheltering from the storm. I'll fetch the surgeon.'

Lawson stopped him with a gesture.

'This isn't *La Reine Noble*?'

'No, sir. She went down. This is *Queen Charlotte*.'

'*La Reine Noble*—sunk?'

'Excuse me, sir. My orders were to call the surgeon.'

The man bobbed his head in apology and left the cabin. Lawson closed his eyes and tried to think. Could there have been yet another action that he could not remember? Had

Lord Exmouth called *La Reine Noble* into the harbour after the landing party had left the ship? The effort of concentration proved to be too much for him. He awoke several hours later to find Doctor Fairweather at his bedside.

'So, the frigate doctor is now surgeon to the flagship,' he said with a tired smile. 'Promotion indeed.'

'Wrong,' Fairweather replied. 'Captain Lawson's private, unpaid physician, working his way back to England. And it looks as if I've earned my passage. You're on the mend.'

Suddenly Lawson remembered about *La Reine Noble*.

'How did the ship go down?' he demanded.

'Later, Captain. You must rest.'

'You'll tell me immediately, or I'll make shift to leave this bed to find out for myself.'

Fairweather sighed.

'Very well. I don't suppose you will have any peace of mind until you hear the full story. You'll take some sustenance while I'm telling you.'

The orderly approached the bed with a bowl of gruel and a funnel. Fairweather took the funnel from him and placed it between Lawson's lips.

'Mr Hawbrook brought you back,' he said as he carefully tipped a spoonful of the unappetising mess into the wide end of the funnel, 'though he'd have saved himself the trouble if he'd had a ha'porth of medical knowledge. I don't know to this day how you survived your wounds.'

'What about Barty?' Lawson asked, speaking around the end of the tube as one would with a pipe stem.

'I took a musket-ball out of his hip. He'll limp a bit on wet days, when he's an old man. As for the ship, you'll remember that you left a very unhappy lieutenant in command.'

'Duvalier-Winter.'

'He paced the deck from the moment you left until Algiers surrendered the following morning. Then the Commander-in-Chief sent a signal for *La Reine Noble* to collect dispatches from the flagship for delivery in Gibraltar. Chandler went off for them. No sooner had he left than Hawbrook identified a ship that we had been watching since dawn hugging the coastline, as none other than *Die Reichmacher*.'

Lawson's eyes gleamed with interest and he turned impatiently away from the feeding tube.

'Coming home for repairs with no idea that Algiers had undergone a change since he was last there, and—having seen *La Reine Noble* at the entrance of the harbour, he'd think that she'd escaped from *Comus*.'

Fairweather nodded and smiled.

'Duvalier-Winter weighed anchor, without so much as by your leave to Lord Exmouth, and sailed out to meet him. He hoisted Yussaiff Ahmed's colours. Kettelmann must have expected a helping hand from a colleague anxious to make amends for his desertion. Instead he received a broadside to add to his troubles.'

'And then?'

'There followed a battle of battles, under the eyes of the fleet, and not one ship able to come to our aid since the wind had dropped away to nothing.'

'I wish I'd been there.'

'My dear captain, you were there: strapped to a stretcher below and fighting the Lord knows what past action. Whilst we were pounding each other to bits we had drifted close to the shore. Finally *Die Reichmacher* grounded and he abandoned ship. Duvalier-Winter took a party and boarded her.'

'And she blew up,' Lawson said in a flat voice.

Fairweather looked at him in surprise.

'Aye, she blew up. It was a pity we did not have the benefit of your experience, for we lost a good officer and a score of men. *La Reine Noble* was laid over on her side and we were in trouble. One of the Dutch frigates managed to reach us thirty minutes before we went down.'

'What happened to young Saunders? Is he . . .?'

'He and Mr Hawbrook are outside this cabin demanding admission but I think we'll make them wait for a few days.'

'They can visit for half an hour, surely?'

'Not even a few minutes.'

He placed the funnel between Lawson's lips and carried on with the feeding.

During the afternoon of the fourth day after his recovery, the gale, which had been roaring in from the Atlantic, moderated and the restless fore and aft snatching at the anchor reduced to a gentle somniferous rocking movement. Lawson drowsed while the reflected, rippling sunlight swept to and fro across the cabin.

He had no responsibilities to weigh upon him, and the shock he had received when Hawbrook had told him of the heavy casualties on board *La Reine Noble* was already receding. He heard the deck officer hail an approaching boat and a few minutes later there were the unmistakable sounds of a number of people coming on board. Two voices were feminine. His thoughts flashed to Cecilia.

Hawbrook had confirmed that Rear-Admiral Dullant was dead but he had said nothing about Cecilia and Lawson had not cared to ask directly about her. Had she gone back to England? It didn't matter where she was, he told himself scornfully. Their paths would never cross again. Henceforth they would move in very different circles.

In the distance the ship's bell rang: four beats announcing the end of the second dog watch. He began to slip away into a deep sleep.

'May I come in?'

A woman's voice penetrated his semi-conscious mind. He stirred and struggled into wakefulness. She was standing at his side: the paleness of her face accentuated by the black dress she wore. It was Cecilia.

'I suppose you are real,' he said doubtfully.

She smiled and smoothed his pillow. He took her hand suddenly. There was a breathless moment of silence as they looked at each other. Her eyes were coolly appraising, Lawson thought. She was indifferent to the love that she must know he had for her. He released her. She took a chair and sat at the foot of the bed.

'I'm sorry to have neglected you for a few days,' she said, 'I went into Lisbon with Mrs Hopton and her son. We had such a frightening passage across the harbour that she would not enter the launch again until the weather improved. She's taken her husband's death so badly that I felt I must stay with her.'

Lawson nodded. Hawbrook had told him that Captain Hopton had been killed. He wondered how Cecilia was reacting to her widowhood. She sensed his question.

'My married life was a farce, as you probably know. I cannot pretend to feel any sense of loss.'

'And now?'

'Now I need time to think.'

She visited him every morning; usually in company with Mrs Hopton, much to Lawson's annoyance. Then, as the ship thrashed around the Bay of Biscay, and heavy seas foamed over the decks, Mrs Hopton took to her bed and Cecilia had two patients to attend. Never would she allow any discussion on the subject that most interested Lawson and daily he grew more morose.

Doctor Fairweather was quick to notice the change and shrewd enough to guess the reason. Since he could do nothing about it, he gave Lawson something else to think about by allowing him to leave his bed.

He stipulated that the periods should be short but the captain was in no mood for caution. Assisted by the ever-willing Hawbrook he shuffled around the cabin on his wasted legs until he was exhausted. Then after a brief rest, he would heave himself to his feet again and demand more exercise.

On the last day, when the Isle of Wight was slipping by on the port side, and Spithead lay before them, Cecilia came to bid him goodbye. She found him alone, staring pensively at the passing coastline. He smiled a welcome: the brief twisted smile of a man struggling to hide the heavy gloom that lay over him, and heaved himself to his feet. He swayed precariously.

She hurried forward and eased him back into his chair. Her hand lingered on his shoulder.

'My legs are like jelly,' he rumbled. 'I suppose I'll have to take a shore berth for a time before I make the journey north.'

She smiled.

'Is there any hurry?'

He sighed and shook his head.

'There's all the time in the world. Look out there.'

He pointed to a score or more ships lying at anchor between them and the shore. All were stripped of topmasts and yards, and wore the familiar canvas tenting of vessels laid up.

'Every one of those means a captain out of work.'

He gazed in silence over the water, his mind dwelling on his prospects. She watched him with a sad smile. He turned suddenly and caught her with tears in her eyes.

'Cecilia,' he whispered.

She came to him, placed her hands around his neck and kissed him tenderly. Then she held him possessively to her breast and stroked his hair.

There was a rumble of a cable and the splash of an anchor. The great ship jerked once and began to swing away from the breeze. Portsmouth Harbour, in all its glory, was now to be seen through the stern window, but they had eyes only for each other.